Bridges, Books, and Bones

WILLOW FALLS SERIES

PAT NICHOLS

Bridges, Books, and Bones by Pat Nichols

Published by Pat Nichols

ISBN: 979-8-9860519-0-1

Cover Design by Elaina Lee

Edited by Sherri Stewart

Available in print from your local bookstore or online.

For more information on this book or the author visit:

https://patnicholsauthor.blog

Printed in the United States of America

Bridges, Books, and Bones is a work of fiction. Names, characters, and incidents are all products of the author's imagination or are used for fictional purposes. Any mentioned brand names, places, and trademarks remain the property of their respective owners, bear no association with the author or publisher, and are used for fictional purposes only.

Library of Congress Cataloging-in
Publication Data

Nichols, Pat.

Bridges, Books, and Bones / Pat
Nichols

Books by

Pat Nichols

Contemporary Romance

Jenny's Grace

Women's Fiction

Willow Falls series

The Secret of Willow Inn
Trouble in Willow Falls
Star Struck in Willow Falls
Bridges, Books, and Bones

Butler Family Legacy series (2023)

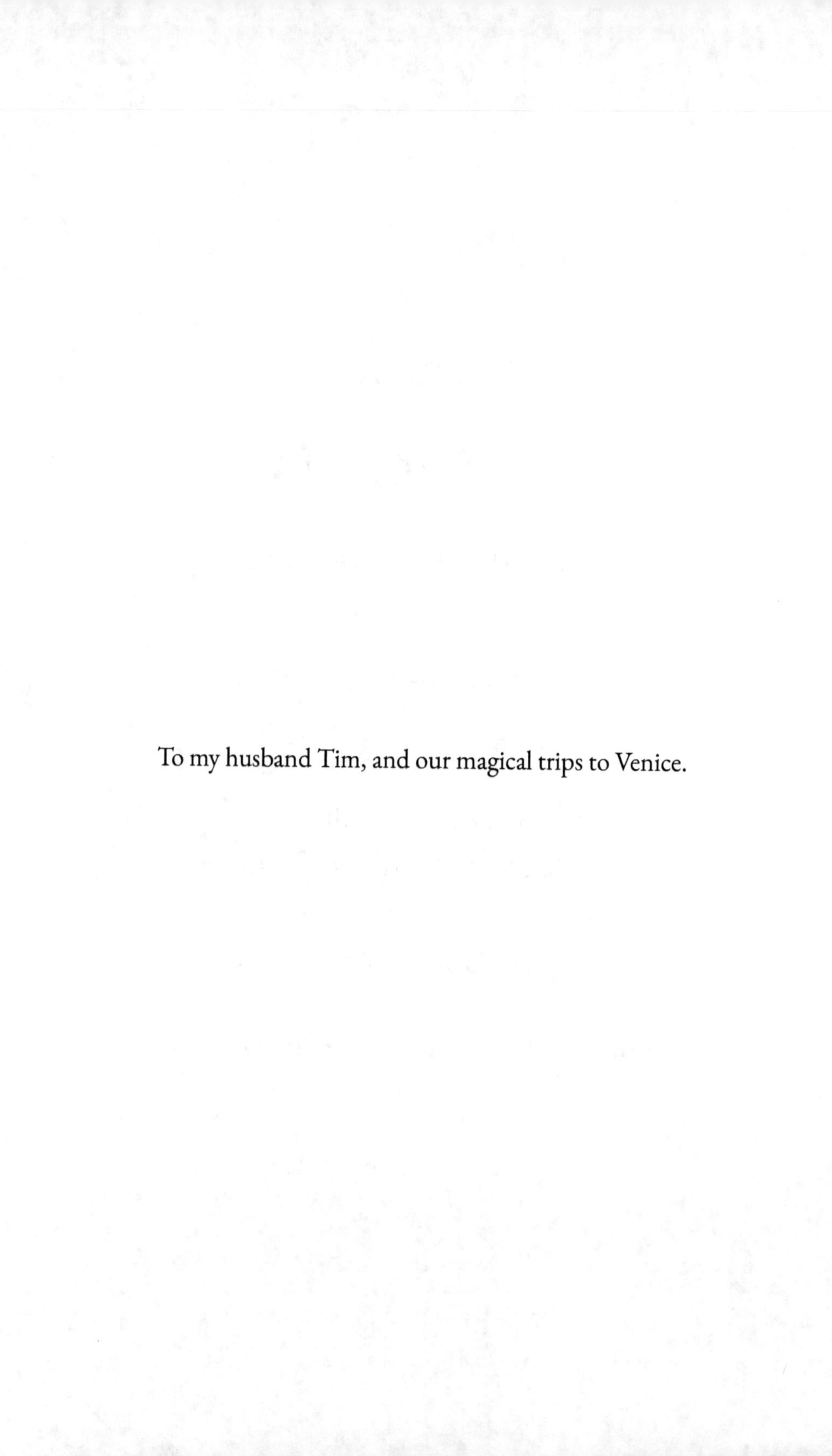

To my husband Tim, and our magical trips to Venice.

Chapter 1

Rachel Streetman Bricker gripped her husband's arm and peeked out the business-class window at the dense fog obscuring the terminal and shrouding the runway. "I can't believe we're taking off in this pea soup."

Charlie brushed a stray curl from her cheek. "People claim air travel is safer than driving."

Her pulse pounded in her ears. "Well, cars can't fall from the sky and crash in a giant ball of fire."

"I remember that grip of yours doggone near cut off my circulation when we rode up to the Sun Dial Restaurant during our first date."

"In a glass tube hugging the outside of a seventy-plus story building, thank you very much. At least that elevator was attached with some sort of cable. It's not logical that a multi-ton plane loaded with fuel, people, and a belly full of luggage can leave the ground, much less fly."

"It's all about lift and aerodynamics."

"What if the baggage handlers overloaded the cargo area?" She tightened her seatbelt. "Maybe too many heavy passengers boarded or a gang of thieves smuggled gold bars in their luggage."

Charlie chuckled. "Either you've picked up your sister's writer imagination or that dose of antibiotics you took a few weeks ago muddled your brain."

"Emily is my identical twin, and those pills cured my sinus infection." Rachel squeezed her eyes shut as the plane accelerated down the runway and abandoned solid ground. Turbulence shaking the aircraft conjured images of planes spiraling out of control. She dug her fingers into Charlie's arm. Worse takeoff so far."

He winced. "What do you do when you fly alone?"

"Pretend I'm still on the ground."

"How does that work?"

"Not so great. I have no idea how I'll survive flying for hours over an ocean full of sharks."

Charlie peeled her fingers off his arm. "You can relax. We're through the rough part."

Rachel forced her eyes open and peered out at blue sky above the low-hanging clouds blanketing New York City. As the plane banked south toward Georgia, she breathed deeply to slow her racing pulse. "If Dad hadn't been too busy building his business to take me on a plane when I was a kid, maybe flying wouldn't turn me into an irrational basket case."

The fasten-seat belt sign flashed off signaling the flight attendant to push a beverage cart into the aisle. After serving the first-row passengers, she stopped beside their seats. "I attended last night's *Joanie's Trial* premiere. What a wonderful movie, and I must say you delivered a top-notch performance, Ms. Streetman. Right up there with famous actors."

"Thank you." Rachel noted Charlie's not-so-subtle headshake. Maybe she should have ignored her agent's insistence she keep Streetman as her professional identity, even though the name had more commercial appeal than Bricker.

"Your hair is gorgeous. Love the curls." The attendant leaned close. "I'm guessing strawberry blonde is your natural color."

"Did my freckles give you a clue?"

"And your eyes. It's hard to believe that movie was your acting debut."

"Actually my career began on the stage. *Joanie's Trial* was my first film. Are you a big movie fan?"

"More like a fanatic. Anyway, I'd be happy to serve you coffee, juice, or something stronger."

"Coffee's fine. With vanilla creamer and honey if you have any?"

"We do. What would you prefer, Mr. Bricker?"

"Same as my wife but with sugar."

"My pleasure." She poured two cups before returning to the galley.

Charlie stirred sugar into his coffee. "At least she didn't call me Mr. Streetman, like those reporters last night."

"You handled it like a champ, honey." Rachel kissed his cheek. "The best part of the trip was sleeping in a fancy hotel suite with the sexiest guy at the premier."

He winked. "Definitely the trip's highlight."

Their attendant returned with honey and vanilla creamer. "Are you two newlyweds?"

Rachel nodded. "For a few more weeks."

"We treat honeymooners extra special, so let me know if you need anything else." She pushed her cart to the next row.

Rachel added honey to her coffee while listening to the attendant lavish praise on world-renowned Maggie Warren for her performance in *Joanie's Trial*. "She's definitely a serious fan. But then who doesn't love Maggie."

"In a few weeks, you'll have millions of fans. Especially with all the personal appearances your agent booked."

A mental image of her photo and tagline in the morning review popped into Rachel's head—*Fiery Redhead with Intoxicating Green Eyes Delivers First-rate Debut Performance*. "You know publicity is important to my career."

"Doesn't keep me from missing you like crazy every time you're gone."

"At least we have a few days before I leave for Venice."

"For six long weeks." He set his cup on the table. "With Justin Brooks as your costar."

"No need to worry about him. The gorgeous blonde hanging on his arm last night is his latest girlfriend. Besides, never in a million years could he snare this happily-married lady."

"I'm not worried about you. Can't say the same about Justin or what his agent might cook up. Like some crazy publicity stunt involving you."

"Trust me. I'll never let that happen."

Their attendant stepped back to their row. "I apologize for interrupting. The gentleman in the seat beside Ms. Warren asked for your autograph." She handed Rachel a postcard.

"My friend must have given him an earful."

"According to her you're on a fast track to stardom, Ms. Streetman."

"Maggie's a sweetheart and a mentor." Rachel signed her name along with a plug for *Joanie's Trial*. "Tell the gentleman thank you."

"I hear you're going to Venice to star in a movie. That is my all-time favorite Italian city. It's so romantic."

The moment she moved away, Rachel snuggled close to Charlie. "She's right about Venice. Which makes it the perfect place to celebrate our one-year anniversary."

"You know I can't leave town during our winery's first harvest. Besides, catching time with you in between scenes isn't my idea of romance."

"I understand." Confident Charlie would change his mind after she'd been gone a few weeks, Rachel lowered her window shade. She closed her eyes and drifted to sleep while imagining them kissing on every bridge in Venice.

A nudge startled her awake. She blinked. "Where are we?"

"On the ground in Atlanta."

"Are you serious?" She raised the window shade.

"The pilot managed to touch down without a bounce despite a few over-fed passengers. By the way, your purse pinged."

"You're hilarious."

"One of my most endearing traits."

Rachel retrieved her purse from under the seat and pulled out her phone. "A text from Emily. Seems residents planned some sort of welcome-home reception."

"A couple hours before the town's big movie premiere?"

"I suppose it's a bit much, even though small-town residents starring in a movie is something to celebrate." She released a sigh. "Unfortunately some folks will be disappointed to discover their scenes were cut."

"More like hopping mad and swearing to boycott Hollywood."

Rachel dropped her phone in her purse. "One thing about the locals, they're a passionate bunch."

When the plane pulled up to the gate, Charlie opened the overhead bin and handed Maggie her wide-brimmed, floppy hat. "Your camouflage."

"Along with these." She donned oversized sunglasses. "One day your wife will need a disguise to maneuver through crowds undetected."

"Unless she likes hordes of adoring fans."

Rachel's gaze shifted from Charlie to the silver-haired actress who had aged gracefully and could still turn heads. Was Maggie right about her longing for anonymity or would she crave attention like Justin? At least she lived in a small town where people treated her like regular folks. She held onto Charlie's arm as they exited the jetway, descended the escalator, and squeezed into the packed underground train.

After retrieving their luggage and exiting baggage claim, Charlie loaded their bags in the back of his truck and opened the passenger side-doors. "Your chauffeured ride home to north Georgia begins now, ladies."

"Best comment I've heard all weekend." Maggie sat on the back seat, removed her hat, and brushed her fingers through her stylish haircut. "One more premiere before my retirement officially begins in my new hometown."

Rachel slid onto the front seat. "Who'd have guessed Willow Falls' first movie in nineteen years would feature more than a handful of locals?"

"Thanks to the new theater your dad built." Maggie buckled her seat belt. "Greer has mellowed since I first met him at his Atlanta mansion. That day if someone had told me he'd end up buying a condo in Willow Falls, I'd have called them crazy."

"It took a heart attack to slow him down."

"He didn't slow down much." Charlie buckled up, tuned the radio to a country station, and backed out of the parking space.

"At least he's dividing his time between Atlanta and Willow Falls." After Charlie exited the parking garage and merged onto the highway, Rachel leaned back hoping they wouldn't run into too much traffic. At least she was riding on solid ground. When the Atlanta skyline came into view, she spotted the high-rise office building that housed Streetman Enterprise. She'd worked for seven long years in her dad's real estate development firm before pursuing her lifelong dream to act. Rachel studied Charlie's profile, his fingers tapping the steering wheel to the beat of the music. Somehow she'd struck a healthy balance between the career she loved and the personal life that filled her with more joy than she ever imagined possible. Could life get any better?

Chapter 2

Emily Hayes sliced through packing tape and lifted the flaps on the box from her publisher. Warmth radiated through her as she removed her second novel and traced the title with her finger. *Saving Willow Falls.* Other than her husband and twin, only Pepper Cushman, Redding Arms executive chef and owner of Pepper's Café, had read the story about the town's rise from the brink of failure.

Her husband, Scott, wandered in from the back yard with Jane and Clair—their three-year- old identical twins—and Cody, their golden retriever. Scott moved behind Emily and wrapped his arms around her waist. "Cover looks great."

She clutched the book to her chest. "What if the entire town considers the story too personal?"

"You didn't use real names."

"Everyone will know who's who. Like Pepper said, some folks will claim I got the characters all wrong, and others will accuse me of favoritism because they aren't included." She released a heavy sigh. "I should have changed the name of the town."

"Wouldn't have made a difference."

Emily dropped onto a chair. "Maybe I should hire an attorney."

"To defend you against gossip and grumbles?"

"Accusations of libel."

"You've obviously watched too many old *Law and Order* episodes."

"Those shows are about murder and mayhem, not civil suits."

"Good point."

The front doorbell echoed through the house.

"Maybe the FBI has come to arrest Georgia's notorious author." Scott chuckled while disappearing around the corner. He returned escorting Patsy Peacock. "Willow Falls new book store owner is paying us a visit."

"Your novels arrived an hour ago." Patsy set a white cake box from Patsy's Pastries and Pretties on the table. She adjusted the feathers on one of her many peacock-plumed hats. "I brought your favorite."

"Lemon with buttercream frosting?"

"None other." She lifted the cake from the box.

Clair tugged on Patsy's sleeve. "Is today's Mommy's birthday?"

Jane climbed onto her booster seat. "Where's the candles?"

Patsy grinned. "We're celebrating your mommy's new book."

Clair's eyes widened. "Does books have birthdays?"

"Sort of, but not like people." Patsy brushed a stray strawberry blonde curl away from Clair's cheek.

She climbed onto the seat beside her sister. "Mommy's book doesn't have pictures."

"The words your mommy writes create pictures in grown-ups' minds."

"That's silly." Jane giggled.

Patsy patted her cheek. "Maybe you and your sister will grow up and write books like your mommy."

"With lots of pictures."

After Emily set plates and forks on the table Patsy pointed to the box of books. "How many?"

"Two dozen."

"That makes 524 for the Book Nook's grand opening."

Emily stared at her. "You ordered 500?"

"Believe me, free cookies and a novel about our town will draw a gigantic crowd."

Scott removed a gallon of milk from the fridge. "You're one smart businesswoman, Patsy."

"I've learned a thing or two in my seventy-plus years." She served the cake while sharing plans to make her new bookstore as successful as her gift and pastry shop. When everyone finished indulging, she wiped her fingers with a napkin. "Time to head downtown for the big event."

Clair climbed out of her booster seat. "What's downtown, Mommy?"

"A big reception to welcome Aunt Rachel and Uncle Charlie back home."

"Where'd they go?"

"To New York City, a big town a long way from here."

"Bigger than Willow Falls?"

"Way bigger."

Jane licked icing off her fingers. "Can we go there, Daddy."

"Someday, sweet girl." Scott scooped her into his arms. "But not before we take a ride downtown in Mommy's car." He blew a raspberry on her neck triggering a nose scrunch and giggles.

After loading plates into the dishwasher, Scott and Emily carried the twins to the car and drove the short distance to town. They parked behind the family's historic Hayes General Store, moved the twins to their stroller, and pushed them up the alley.

When they reached the front sidewalk, Emily nodded toward a young couple walking out of the store. "Two more satisfied customers. I'm proud of everything you've done to turn our family's business into a successful tourist magnet, honey."

"Thank goodness I finally generate enough profit to afford a decent-size staff and can spend more time with my girls."

"That's the best part." Emily nodded toward the crowd lined up on both sides of Main Street. "Looks like more than half the residents showed up."

"Typical for our little corner of Georgia."

"With all the new business around here, our town isn't so little anymore." Emily's gaze shifted from the lakeside park to the picturesque façades of century-old storefronts sporting new awnings. Pepper's Café along with Patsy's Pastries and Pretties and Old-Fashioned Christmas Shoppe held center stage on Main Street. Wooden boxes adorned with plants and miniature American flags lined the sidewalks. Flower baskets hanging from streetlights alternated with colorful flags, welcoming visitors to Willow Falls.

Scott pushed the stroller to the park and maneuvered between the onlookers clogging the sidewalk, veering around two political signs—*Mirabelle for Mayor* and *Vote for Brick*. Last names weren't needed in a town where everyone knew everyone. "Good thing the election's tomorrow."

Emily brushed a curl behind her ear. "Do you suppose any other town charter dictates a council seat for the runner-up?"

"I don't have a clue. What I do know is Willow Falls' most outspoken citizen and Charlie's dad are guaranteed to lock horns over the latest controversy. One fact is certain. The winner will fill the board with like-minded residents."

"What will you do if Brick wins and asks you to stay on the council?"

"Turn him down and let someone else shoulder the responsibility."

They continued strolling through the park and found a space at the curb between the Redding Arms Hotel and Willow Inn, the home converted to an elegant bed and breakfast.

Clair pointed to a white vinyl sign stretched between two lampposts across Main Street. "What's that say, Mommy?"

"Willow Falls, birthplace of *Joanie's Trial* and home to Maggie Warren and Rachel Streetman."

"What's *Joanie's Trial*?"

"A movie filmed last year right here in Willow Falls. Aunt Rachel is one of the stars."

"Like Cinderella?"

"Exactly."

Jane climbed out of the stroller and sat on the curb. "Is Uncle Charlie a prince?"

Emily smiled. "He is to Aunt Rachel."

A woman standing beside Scott pointed to a truck turning onto Main Street "Here they come."

The crowd's cheers intensified as Charlie's truck approached. When he passed Falls Street, residents spilled off the sidewalk and rushed toward the vehicle. The second Rachel and Maggie stepped out of the truck, a sea of fans engulfed them.

"Looks like the natives are still seriously starstruck." Scott leaned close to Emily. "In my opinion it takes more talent to write a novel than to repeat lines from a script."

Doggone right. The unexpected thought gripped Emily's gut. Had envy crept into her psyche? Impossible. And yet, the sign stretched across Main Street didn't tout Willow Falls as the birthplace of her books, which unlike *Joanie's Trial*, didn't require the town's name to change to Floral Springs. "Guess I'd have to make a top-seller list to merit that much attention."

"Sorry, honey, I couldn't hear you for all the shouting."

Heat crept up her neck and attacked her cheeks. Had she said that out loud? "It's not important. Will you watch our girls while I capture some images for this week's paper?"

"Go get the latest scoop, Ms. Editor-in-Chief."

"I won't be gone long." Watching residents pose for selfies with her twin conjured up a comment Rachel's dad had made a year earlier. That rubbing shoulders with Hollywood types would take the little town in a whole new direction. The swarm of residents exhibiting serious cases of star obsession proved his prediction had merit.

Mirabelle Paine, the town's number-one mail carrier and mayoral candidate, emerged from the crowd sporting her new look. Thanks to last year's Hollywood makeup artist's instruction, she had transformed from plain to attractive. "We've scheduled eight showtimes to accommodate everyone for the premiere." She planted her hands on her ample hips. "Can you believe some folks accused us of rigging the drawings for each show?"

"Hard to imagine."

"At least all of us who starred in the movie have tickets for the first showing." Mirabelle lowered her hands to her side. "I bought a fancy dress for tonight. You're planning to take pictures for the paper, right?"

"And write a review."

"Here's an exclusive about tomorrow's election." Mirabelle glanced around then leaned close. "According to the poll—"

"What poll?"

"The one I'm taking. Anyway, I'm favored to win."

"Tomorrow we'll find out how accurate you are as a pollster."

"Prepare to be amazed." Mirabelle huffed and marched away.

Emily snapped photos and recorded comments of the crowd trailing behind Maggie as she headed to the corner and the condo Greer had created above the stores between Hayes General Store and the church.

Rachel moved to her twin's side. "Do you suppose they'll follow her all the way to her front door?"

"Probably. In case you haven't noticed, you're taking her place as Willow Falls' new Cinderella."

"Where'd that name come from?"

"Clair." Emily shot a photo of the banner stretched across Main Street. "Did you enjoy New York?"

"We stayed plenty busy."

"What about Charlie? How's he taking all this attention?"

"As long as no one calls him Mr. Streetman, he's hanging in there." Rachel glanced around. "Looks like the crowd has cleared enough for a getaway. I'll see you at six."

As Emily watched her sister return to Charlie's truck, the twinge of envy returned, then vanished. No way she'd leave Scott and her girls for one week, much less six. Grateful her writing kept her close to home and everyone she loved, she rushed back to Scott and her daughters.

Chapter 3

Emily slung her camera over her shoulder and kissed Clair and Jane before leaving them with Grandpa Brick and Mama Sadie—the name she and Rachel called their birth mom to distinguish her from their adoptive mothers. She held on to Scott's arm as they walked down Main under the glow of streetlights filtering through the row of willow oak trees. Cars parked on both sides of the street blocked driveways. "My guess is every downtown parking space is full."

Scott motioned toward the corner where Sheriff Mitch Cushman and a deputy stood guard to keep traffic from turning onto Falls Street. "Or blocked off."

"Brings back memories from a year ago when celebrities and trucks filled with equipment invaded our peaceful little town."

As they passed the palatial, white-columned home serving as the town's hospital, Emily gawked at the crowd spilling halfway across the street around the corner in front of the new movie theater. "Talk about star crazy."

"I still can't believe Mirabelle roped me into running the video camera. What is she planning to do with my handiwork?"

"Sell copies to locals and create a loop for the town's museum."

"No kidding. Who'd have guessed she has a marketing streak?"

They passed the municipal building housing the sheriff's office and a small courtroom—one of the sets in *Joanie's Trial*—and stepped around the crowd. Hundreds of locals and tourists stood behind ropes stretched along both sides of a red carpet extending from the theater down the sidewalk into the street.

"Time to go to work and record this for posterity." Scott headed to the tripod and camera set up to the right of the entrance.

Emily made her way to J.T. Brown, the town's adored tour guide who held a microphone. She winked at Scott, who stood across from him, then turned to J.T. "You're as handsome in a tux as you are in your dress blues."

"First time since your sister's wedding I've worn this getup. Can't wait to get back into shorts. My artificial leg attracts as much attention as the town's tourist sites." He nodded toward the street. "Our first arrival."

Emily spun and eyed the 1933 Rolls-Royce Phantom Two, donated to serve as one of the town's two taxis. "Are all the local celebrities arriving in style?"

"Only those with speaking roles."

"Good, otherwise we'd be out here all night." She scooted across the carpet and stood beside Scott.

A seventeen-year-old high-school senior dressed in his band uniform stood at the carpet's edge. He opened the Rolls' passenger door and extended his hand. Naomi Jasper, dressed in white slacks and a colorful, sequined tunic, stepped onto the red carpet. Jack Parker followed the famous artist. The crowd cheered as he escorted the tall woman with stylish white hair up the carpet to J.T.

"You look lovely, Ms. Naomi. Tell the folks about your outfit and your role in the movie." He held out the microphone

Scott nudged Emily. "How did our tough-as-nails army veteran turn all-Hollywood."

"He watched old movie premieres."

Naomi's animated gestures jangled her array of bracelets as she responded to J.T.'s questions. After she and Jack entered the theater, the town's second taxi, a red fifties Cadillac convertible, pulled to the curb. Gertie and Patsy stepped onto the carpet. During their walk of fame, Gertie blew kisses to the crowd.

"I can hear my soda-fountain celebrity now," Scott whispered. "She'll entertain our customers with stories about her famous stroll up the red carpet."

"She is our store's superstar."

"And one smart business cookie. Who else could have convinced me to sell sodas and homemade fudge?"

"Are you complaining, honey?"

"Heck no. Her suggestions drop a lot of dough onto our bottom line."

Emily snapped photos of Gertie snatching the microphone from J.T. when he asked about their outfits. She faced the crowd and launched into a story about Patsy's and her trip to Atlanta to purchase their gowns.

A woman standing across from Emily scowled, making it clear she would have a few words with the ladies who had dissed the local clothing store to purchase highfalutin city outfits. "Uh-oh, Gertie and Patsy have fallen out of favor with at least two residents."

Scott glanced at her. "What are you talking about?"

"I'll explain later."

After they waved to the crowd and moved into the theater heads turned toward the returning Rolls. Two stars in the town's signature play emerged. Missy Gibson, the pretty, blue-eyed, ex-con, and Dennis, the handsome young veteran Rachel had rescued from Atlanta's streets.

"Hey, Dennis," shouted a woman. "When are you gonna propose to your costar?"

Missy's cheeks pinkened. She clung to his arm. He placed his hand over hers while seemingly ignoring the question.

Good for Dennis. Emily snapped photos of the young couple who served as rich fodder for the town's overactive rumor mill. Everyone counted on another big wedding, which prompted unrelenting prodding for a proposal.

When J.T.'s interview with the young couple ended, Emily turned the camera toward the curb to capture the next arrival, Mirabelle, wearing a bright red gown, escorted by her husband Frank. "She actually looks like a movie star."

Scott chortled. "You mean a character actor."

Mirabelle sashayed up the carpet and spoke to admirers amid applause. After flashing smiles at the crowd and hyping her role in the film as the jury forewoman, she bragged about buying her dress at one of the local stores and her shoes at the other. "I always say it's smart to support our town's businesses. By the way, tomorrow's an important day for Willow Falls. Be sure to come out and vote."

Emily noted the store owner's grin. "Looks like she's captured one solid vote."

Mirabelle stepped over to Emily and Scott. Her overpowering perfume hinted of a compromised sense of smell. "Wait 'til you see who's escorting Maggie. I'm telling you there's something going on between those two."

Emily rolled her eyes. "Maggie and Rachel's dad are good friends, nothing more."

"Then why did he buy the condo next to hers?"

Mirabelle's husband placed his hand on her back. "Come along, dear, and leave these folks be." He escorted her into the theater.

"That man has the patience of Job." Scott aimed the video camera toward the street as Maggie and Greer stepped from the Rolls and began their stroll.

A woman leaned over the rope. "Love you, Maggie. Is tonight really your last big event before you retire?"

"Indeed, it is."

A man standing behind the woman pushed forward. "Hey, Greer, how much more land are you gonna buy? You darn near own half the town."

Greer, his posture ramrod straight and his white beard neatly trimmed, faced the man. "I made another good investment, sir."

The man dismissed the comment with a hand flick as Greer and Maggie made their way to J.T.

"Tell the folks about the New York premiere, Ms. Warren." J.T. held the microphone close to her.

"All I can say is this event is a lot more fun."

Deafening cheers erupted for the woman who a year earlier had never set eyes on Willow Falls and now called the town home. She held her hands up. The crowd quieted. "I want everyone to know that I am grateful beyond words for you welcoming me into your lovely community. Now I'm ready to enjoy life in peaceful obscurity with all my new friends."

"She's a charmer." Scott's voice rose above the applause.

"Yes, she is." Emily shot photos of Maggie and Greer before turning toward the street to capture the next and most important arrival.

Chapter 4

Rachel fingered an emerald earring as Charlie maneuvered into a reserved parking space adjacent to the mansion the town's founder built for his wife. "Are you sure Mirabelle wants us to stop here?"

"Positive." He pocketed his key. "A chauffeur is driving us over in the Caddy."

"New York has nothing on Willow Falls. Except a much bigger theater and more than four restaurants."

"Hey, two years ago, Pepper's Café was the only eatery in town."

"I'm not complaining. You know, I've come to adore this crazy little town." Rachel lowered the visor to check her lipstick. "In fact, I can't imagine living anywhere else."

"Does that mean you're finally ready to sell your Atlanta townhouse?"

"Like I've told you before, I'm waiting for the market to peak."

"Uh huh." Charlie glanced over his shoulder. "Our ride's here."

The driver dashed to their truck and opened the passenger door.

Rachel stepped out, lifting her gown's hem off the pavement.

"You look real pretty, Ms. Rachel."

"Thank you. How many people showed up?"

"Half the town." He escorted her to the Cadillac's back seat.

Charlie slid in beside her. "Sorry for bringing up a sore subject."

"The townhouse?"

"Yeah."

Rachel kissed his cheek and breathed in his musky scent. "You're forgiven."

"Are you nervous or excited about tonight?"

She wiped a smudge of lipstick off his face. "A little of both, I suppose."

Their driver backed up, drove onto Main Street, and turned toward downtown. At the corner, Sheriff Mitch moved the Falls Street barricade aside.

"Oh my." Rachel raised her brows. "Our hometown crowd is way bigger than the one in New York."

The young man glanced in his rearview mirror. "A movie premiere isn't an everyday event in Willow Falls." He eased the Caddie to the edge of the red carpet and cut the engine.

Charlie squeezed Rachel's hand. "Are you ready to wow your fans?"

"I'm not sure how much I'll impress anyone since around here I'm simply Rachel Bricker."

"Don't underestimate your status as a movie star."

The band-uniform-clad young man opened the passenger door.

Rachel stepped out amid cheers and applause. While she had become accustomed to audience accolades following her performances in *Percy's Legacy*, tonight the crowd's reaction seemed different. More intense. Would her friends and neighbors expect her to act differently, or would they let her just be Rachel Bricker? Charlie's wife. Emily's sister. Sadie's daughter.

The sight of her twin taking photos sent heat rushing to her cheeks. Emily, the hometown girl and author who had landed two publishing contracts, played second fiddle to her twin, the newcomer. The comparison didn't seem fair.

As Charlie stepped out of the Caddy and held his arm out, a woman leaned over the rope. "Hey, Rachel, what's it like being a famous movie star?"

Rachel slid her hand around Charlie's bicep and smiled. "The best part of my job is coming home to this wonderful town."

"Not as exciting as flying to Italy to star in a movie. Promise to post lots of pictures for all your fans back home."

"You mean my *friends*, and I will."

Charlie leaned close as they approached J.T. "They'll hold you to your promise."

"I know."

"Welcome back, Rachel. Tell us about your next movie." J.T. aimed the microphone at her.

"It's another fun, romantic comedy."

A teenage girl leaned over the rope. "Does your script include another hot love scene with Justin?"

Why did she ask that question? Rachel hadn't told Charlie about the bedroom scene. Although tasteful, she knew it would make him uncomfortable. "There's way more comedy than romance. What's most exciting is the location."

"A love story in Venice." The girl pressed her palms together. "How romantic. Are you jealous, Mr. Charlie?"

Rachel flashed a grin. "Why would he be jealous, sweetie? Everyone knows Justin can't hold a candle to my handsome, talented, muscular husband."

When cheers erupted, Rachel steered Charlie into the lobby. Her heels clicked on the gold and white checkerboard floor. "Thank you, for putting up with all the nonsense, honey."

"You poured it on a little thick out there."

She touched his cheek. "If we weren't married, every single woman in town would have their eyes set on you."

"Now you're overcompensating."

Emily swooped in and embraced Rachel. "Were you impressed with the red-carpet welcome?"

Rachel shrugged. "A bit over the top, if you ask me."

"Not for one of Willow Falls' famous movie stars."

"Around here I'd rather people know me as Rachel Bricker."

Scott followed Emily. "J.T is about to open the doors for ticket holders. We need to take our seats before the crowd rushes in and tramples us."

Inside the theater Rachel marveled at the deep red walls and royal blue ceiling before following Charlie into a row and settling beside her dad. "This isn't as big as the New York theater but way more intimate and inviting,"

He patted her arm. "I built this for you, Strawberry Girl. To make up for all those years I ignored your dreams."

She touched his hand. "I know, and I'm grateful."

"This seat is comfortable enough for a nap." Charlie reclined. "Wake me if I snore."

Rachel giggled and adjusted her seat to match his. As the movie began, she focused on the scenery. Despite the town's name change, views of Main Street and the park made it obvious the film had been shot in Willow Falls. She leaned close to Charlie. "The publicity should give tourism another big boost."

"Good news for our winery."

She relaxed and spotted subtleties she'd missed during the first viewing, until her love scene with Justin. Her back stiffened as she tried to imagine her reaction if she'd been forced to watch Charlie lip-locked with a beautiful actress. She reached for his hand hoping to ease his anxiety and quash her own reservations about the future love scene with the movie star known for hitting on his costars.

Chapter 5

Sunshine streaming into their bedroom nudged Rachel's eyes open. With a big yawn, she stretched then swung her legs over the side of the bed. Grateful to wake up at home, she picked her robe off the floor and moseyed to the kitchen. Rachel poured a cup of coffee, stirred in vanilla creamer and honey, and stepped out to the back deck where Charlie leaned against the railing. Their golden retriever bounded over. "Hey, Brownie. Are you keeping my favorite guy company?" She moved to the railing and nuzzled Charlie's neck.

"Morning, gorgeous." He slid his arm around her shoulders and pulled her close.

"Back at you, handsome." She gazed down at the winery's stone façade and steeply pitched, red-tiled roof. Her eyes drifted beyond the building with its charming old-world appearance to lush grapevines stretching across acres of rolling hills. "This view still takes my breath away." She sipped her coffee. "Are you hungry?"

"Starving. How about I treat Willow Falls' newest star to breakfast at Redding Arms."

"Oh my. A night of passionate love *and* breakfast at a fancy hotel."

"All for one of the two most beautiful women in Georgia."

"I assume the other woman is my twin."

A mischievous grin lit Charlie's eyes. "Think I'll keep you guessing."

"Maybe I need more romantic moments to keep you locked in my head while I'm traipsing around Venice."

"At your service." He winked. "After a hot shower."

"Hmm. I suggest we take one together." Her eyes drifted to his lips. "To conserve water, of course."

"Now you're talking." He lifted her into his arms, opened the French doors, and carried her into their bedroom.

Rachel and Charlie held hands while strolling into the town's one hotel. They headed to the dining room, passing the high-back, circular bench centered under the massive chandelier highlighting the gold veins in the marble floor.

The young hostess greeted them. "Nice to see you both this morning. I had tickets to last night's big event. It turned out even better than I expected."

Rachel smiled. "The movie or the event?"

"Both. But the movie was beyond awesome. Did you notice me in the park scene?"

"I did and you looked amazing."

"Thanks. Seeing my name in the credits gave me goosebumps. Oh, your mother and father-in-law ..." Her eyes shifted from Rachel to Charlie. "I mean your father and mother-in-law ... anyway, Ms. Sadie and Mr. Brick came in a few minutes ago. Do you want to join them?"

"We'd love to." As their hostess led them across the dining room, Rachel nudged Charlie. "My mother married to your father makes for interesting conversations."

"Indeed, it does."

Brick stood as they arrived at the table. A casual jacket clung on his wiry frame, his goatee neatly trimmed. "Our hometown star and her husband." His grin deepened the lines around his eyes and the creases in his cheeks.

"I declare." A smile lit Mama Sadie's face. "We've heard bits and pieces about last night's premiere. Now here you are to give us the real scoop."

Charlie pulled a chair out for Rachel. "I'll let my wife do the honors."

Rachel gazed into her mother's eyes, blue green like the eye on a peacock feather. "Love your new hairstyle."

"I kept the auburn shade. After all, fifty-one is way too young to give into a headful of gray. Now, about last night?"

"Willow Falls did itself proud." Rachel hung her purse on the back of her chair before entertaining them with details. "When are you two scheduled to see the movie?"

"Tomorrow night, as the new mayor and his wife."

"Or maybe a council member." Brick ran his fingers through his thinning white hair. "Mirabelle's a tough competitor."

"She is." Sadie patted his hand. "But you beat her hands down in the debate, honey."

"Not according to some folks."

The waitress arrived to pour coffee and take their orders. When she stepped away, Charlie reached for his cup. "Remind us why you're running for mayor, Dad?"

"I consider it my civic duty to help my adopted town deal with explosive growth." He fingered his goatee. "Besides, with you managing the winery, I have plenty of time."

"Sounds like a canned response. I'm guessing your decision is more about you needing a new challenge."

Brick grinned. "There is that."

Rachel eyed the deep garnet walls, white linen tablecloths, and filigree gold holders nesting artificial flicker-flame candles. "Three years ago when Charlie and I first drove into Willow Falls, this hotel was abandoned and unfinished. The town had one clothing store, a slew of empty retail spaces, and not a tourist in sight. Now every face in here is unfamiliar."

"Progress hasn't made everyone happy." Sadie stirred sugar into her coffee. "Some folks still complain about the traffic and having to lock their doors because strangers are roaming the streets."

"It's about time residents discover why doors come with locks." Rachel scoffed. "I can't believe the bank, the winery, and Scott's store are the only downtown businesses with security alarms."

Brick crossed his arms on the table. "Break-ins haven't happened yet, so folks don't see a need to spend the money."

Rachel reached for her coffee cup. "First time a crook robs one of them blind, they'll get with the program."

Charlie snickered. "My movie-star wife still thinks like a city slicker."

"Which is why ours is the one private home with an alarm, thank you very much."

"Our house and Naomi's also have alarm systems," added Brick.

"There you go." Rachel snapped her fingers. "You, Naomi, Charlie, and I lived most of our lives in a big city and know criminals lurk everywhere."

"Heavens to Betsy, honey, enough talk about alarms and crimes." Sadie leaned forward. "Ever since Sheriff Mitch arrested Winston Hamilton last year, we haven't had a bit of trouble."

"Willow Inn's most notorious guest." Rachel chuckled. "Maybe you should add his photo to your famous visitor display."

"I could start an infamous category. Except now Willow Falls is too popular with tourists to attract criminals looking to hide from the law."

"One more benefit of growth." Brick rapped his knuckles on his forehead. "Knock on wood."

Sadie laced her fingers. "Time to change the subject. I want to hear all about New York."

"Huge difference from Willow Falls." Charlie crossed his arms. "People and taxis everywhere."

"Unfortunately, between all the events, we didn't have time for sightseeing." A woman scurrying in their direction caught Rachel's eye. "Uh-oh, here comes trouble."

Lizzy, the town's most annoying stage mother, stopped at their table and glared at her. "That director filmed three scenes with my daughter, and only one of them made it in the movie. Good thing I didn't blink, or I'd have missed the whole ten seconds."

Charlie grinned. "And hello to you, too."

Lizzy waggled her finger at him. "Don't try to distract me. I want your wife to tell me why the prettiest girl in town got cheated."

Rachel steepled her fingers and tapped her thumbs. "I assume you read your daughter's contract."

"Of course, I did. I'm not a fool."

"Then you're aware it stated there were no guarantees the footage would make the final cut. Besides, your daughter looked spectacular in the scene that did survive. Like an honest-to-goodness movie star."

"Of course, she did." Lizzy sucked in air and blew out through pursed lips. "Which is why I'm hoping someone will discover her."

Rachel raised her brows. "Does she want to become an actress?"

"She says she wants to go to beauty school and maybe open her own place here in town."

"Good for her." Sadie spread her napkin on her lap. "You have to admire a girl with a mind of her own."

Lizzy shrugged. "I suppose it's time someone gave Pearl's Hair and Nail Salon some competition. Still, my girl has enough talent to make it as a famous movie star."

The waitress returned with their breakfast.

"I'll let you eat in peace." Lizzy paused, then eyed Brick. "I want you to know I voted for you."

"Thanks. I appreciate your support."

"Just remember what's best for Willow Falls when you go making important decisions. See y'all later." She walked away.

"What's best is rainbows and four-leaf clovers."

Her father-in-law's sense of humor about his superstitious nature made Rachel smile, then gave her pause. A lot would happen in the two months she'd be away. She pushed a piece of melon around her plate as images of life going on without her raced through her mind.

"Earth to Rachel." Charlie's voice broke through her musings.

"Sorry. What?"

"Your mom wants to know how long it takes to fly to Italy."

"I think around ten hours. Most of the time over a giant ocean." She stabbed the melon.

Charlie snickered. "My wife isn't wild about flying."

"The flying doesn't bother me. Falling out of the sky gives me the willies. Anyway, I'll miss you all and this crazy little town."

Sadie reached across the table and patted her hand. "The director will keep you so busy the weeks will pass before you know it."

Not busy enough to not miss Charlie. She glanced at him. He supported her career choice, even encouraged her, which meant he'd change his mind and fly to Venice to celebrate their anniversary. Wouldn't he? What if he continued to refuse? How many special occasions would her career force them to celebrate with nothing more than a phone call?

Chapter 6

Emily pushed her chair away from the worktable in the *Willow Post* headquarters and ambled to the window. Across the section of Main that turned north at the end of the park, the streetlight cast a warm glow on residents heading toward the church. Tomorrow, for the first time in a decade, someone other than Pastor Nathan would serve as mayor. One more change in a town that had maneuvered through more transformation in three years than the last six decades.

"Count is the same as last time." Sheriff Mitch's deep voice bellowed.

Emily spun away from the window. "Are we ready to declare a winner?"

He tapped a stack of paper ballots lying on the table. "With the vote this close, we'd best go through the process one more time."

Patsy adjusted her hat adorned with one peacock feather. "Mirabelle has already texted me three times asking if she won."

"One more reason we need to make sure we get this right." Mitch faced the five-member team. "If the new count matches the last two, we'll certify the election and deliver the news."

Emily returned to the table. "Who's making the announcement?"

"Our current mayor volunteered to take the heat." Mitch unclipped his phone from his belt and set it on the table. "I'll call him when we finish."

Emily dropped onto her seat, hoping the third round would make the results official. After counting the final ballot, she laced her fingers behind her neck and stretched her back muscles.

"Well, now." Patsy pressed her palms together and tapped her fingertips. "It seems we have ourselves a new leader."

Emily's phone pinged a text from Scott. "Thank goodness, because according to my husband, the crowd's patience is wearing thin."

"They won't have to wait any longer." Sheriff Mitch grabbed his phone and headed toward the door.

Emily slipped into her jean jacket and shouldered the newspaper's camera. She followed her fellow counters outside and across the street. The chilly night air added to her anxiety over residents' reactions and sent a shiver racing up her spine. She found Nathan Dixon pacing inside the church entrance.

"Good thing you're here." Nathan nodded toward the door. "Residents are restless as caged puppies."

Mitch clapped his hand on the pastor's shoulder. "You've served our town well, Nathan."

"It's time for someone else to wield the gavel."

While the sheriff escorted Nathan to the front, Emily scooted up the side aisle. She stopped beside the first row and snapped photos of residents filling half the seats. The crowd was small compared to a full-blown townhall meeting, but large enough for disgruntled residents to cause a ruckus.

The moment Mitch stepped up to the podium, the chatter stopped. At six-foot-four, he commanded attention. "I want to thank everyone for exercising their civic duty and coming out to vote." He detailed the count process, then massaged his neatly trimmed beard. "So, you can rest assured, the results are a hundred percent accurate. I'll let your pastor and outgoing mayor deliver the news."

"Thank you, Sheriff." Nathan removed the mike from its stand and stepped beside the podium. "Serving as your mayor for all these years has been a privilege and an honor. However, the time has come to turn the reins over." He paused. "I'd like to invite our candidates to join me."

Mirabelle and Brick joined him. Nathan stepped between them. "Ladies and gentlemen, these two candidates ran a noteworthy campaign. Now they will both serve on the council, under the leadership of our new mayor. By a vote of fifty-one to forty-nine percent, it is my privilege to announce—" He glanced from one to the other. "Reginald Bricker, better known as Brick, as Willow Falls' new mayor."

Emily aimed her camera at the audience. Half cheered. Some politely applauded. Others remained silent and stone-faced. At least no one initiated a shouting match. She turned her camera toward the two new council members.

Brick accepted the microphone from Nathan. "I'm honored you folks placed your trust in me, and I promise to serve to the best of my ability." He extended his hand to Mirabelle.

She squared her shoulders and accepted his hand. "Congratulations, Mr. Mayor."

"You were a formidable opponent, my friend. I look forward to working with you as we face the future together." He released her hand and faced the crowd.

The man who had confronted Greer outside the movie theater stood. "Hey, Mayor, when are you gonna deal with Streetman's insane idea?"

"And it begins," mumbled Emily as grumbles and protests erupted.

Brick emitted a shrill two-finger whistle.

The crowd fell silent.

"As my first order of business, I'm asking everyone to hold all comments about the project until the next townhall meeting right here, one week from tonight. At that time, I'll introduce your new council and address the proposal."

"Shirking responsibility already?"

"Just waiting for the right moment, sir. Thank y'all for coming out tonight. I hope to see you next week." Brick placed the microphone in the stand and headed for the aisle. He stopped at the first row and waited for Sadie to step out. She walked beside him while residents scrambled from their seats to congratulate and inundate him with homespun advice.

Scott made his way to Emily. "I'm surprised the vote came in that close."

"Mirabelle's poll didn't miss the mark by much." She snapped photos of the crowd surrounding Brick. "Maybe the results will keep her from turning council meetings into endless arguments."

"I talked to Brick before the announcement." Scott hesitated. "He wants you to serve on the council."

Emily lowered the camera to her side. "Are you serious?"

"Will you accept?"

"I'm already taking a huge risk with my new book release. Not to mention the heat I take as the paper's editor."

Charlie and Rachel joined them. "First time Dad runs for office, he wins. We might have unleashed a serious politician."

Scott guffawed. "One term as mayor in this town will sap any ambition right out of him."

"Not unless a herd of black cats crosses his path." Charlie chuckled. "For now, how about we head over for a victory toast in the hotel's new bar."

"What do you think, honey?" Scott reached for Emily's hand. "Can our sitter stay with our girls a while longer?"

"By now they're asleep and she's parked in front of the television, so yeah we have a little time."

"Well then, I'm up for a date with my wife."

They made their way outside, crossed the street, and stopped beside The Book Nook.

Scott pointed to a grand-opening poster featuring Emily posing with her new book. "Great picture."

Rachel nudged her. "My sister, the famous author."

"More like infamous when the locals read it."

"You can count on controversy to drive sales through the roof."

"Now you're a famous movie star and a marketing expert?" Surprised by her tone's sharp edge, Emily touched Rachel's arm. "Sorry, sis. I didn't intend to come across so snappy."

"Not to worry. I know you're a little uptight about the big reveal."

"More than a little."

They resumed their stroll. When they reached the corner, Emily pointed to the vintage, cast-iron mailbox. "Next year I'll bring our daughters here to mail letters to Santa, like Mom brought me." She eyed Rachel. "Long before I knew you and Mama Sadie existed."

"I wish I'd had a chance to meet your mom and dad."

"They would have adored being grandparents." Emily's voice faltered.

Scott squeezed her hand. "Their legacy lives on in Willow Falls."

At the corner of Falls and Main, Emily eyed the playhouse marquee displaying the town's signature play, *Percy's Legacy*. The weekly performance continued to draw a crowd a year after its premiere. "I've decided to say yes to Brick's request."

Scott stared at her. "To sit on the council?"

"I owe it to Mom and Dad to keep Willow Falls from losing its soul."

Chapter 7

A fist-sized knot blocked Rachel's throat at the sight of threatening clouds hovering over Atlanta's skyline. "According to my phone's weather app, the storm is due to hit right around the time my flight is scheduled for departure."

Charlie gripped the steering wheel as traffic slowed to a crawl. "The plane won't take off if the weather's too bad."

"What air-traffic control considers *too bad* is way different than my interpretation." She checked the app again. "New York's weather isn't much better, which means two dangerous takeoffs."

"Maybe you should order a stiff drink before the plane leaves the gate."

"That's not out of the question." She paused for a long moment and forced her mind to focus on more pleasant topics. "The past few days flew by way too fast."

Charlie reached across the truck's console and touched her knee. "I miss you already."

She squeezed his hand and blinked back tears. "We'll talk and blow kisses on Face Time every day."

"Thank goodness for modern technology." He lifted his hand. "The high-dollar hotel you're staying in faces the Grand Canal, which helps explain why it costs millions to make a movie."

"The price of doing business. Although as far as I know, Robert only booked five rooms at Hotel Danieli. One for him, most likely a fancy suite. The other three for me, the other female lead, and Justin Brooks.

"The fifth?"

Rachel shrugged. "Maybe for his personal assistant." As they maneuvered through the city, her emotions volleyed between angst and anticipation. By the time they pulled into the parking garage, her pounding pulse had unleashed a dizzy sensation. She gripped the dashboard.

Charlie leaned across the console. "Are you okay?"

She uncurled her fingers as tears spilled. "I wish you could come with me."

He tucked a stray curl behind her ear. "To hold your hand during takeoff?"

"By this time tomorrow, I'll be more than four thousand miles away. Surrounded by strangers. Preparing for my first lead in a Robert Nordstrom movie. What if I'm not good enough?"

"Are you kidding?" He turned her face toward him. "You're an amazing performer, loaded with talent. Any time you need to talk, day or night, I'm a phone call away."

"What would I do without you, Charlie?"

He wiped her tears. "We make a great team."

Thunder rumbling in the distance sent a shudder ripping through Rachel.

"Everything's gonna work out for the best, gorgeous. For now, you need to check in."

She filled her lungs and slowly released the air. "Okay, I'm ready."

Charlie dashed to the passenger side, removed her luggage from the back seat, and held her hand while they strolled to the terminal.

After checking her bags, Rachel shouldered her Italian leather computer bag—a gift from her father—and clung to Charlie's arm as he pulled her carry-on through the circular atrium. When they arrived at the security checkpoint, Rachel wrapped her arms around him and breathed in the alluring scent of his cologne. "I'm sorry we don't have more time."

"I'll count the days until you're back home in my arms."

"I love you with all my heart, sweetheart." Fearing his touch would compel her to abandon the trip and return to Willow Falls, she pulled away. "Promise you'll text me the results of the townhall meeting?"

"I promise." He stroked her cheek. "I love you."

She swallowed the lump rising in her throat and moved past the checkpoint. Five steps into the queue, she turned and caught one more glimpse of Charlie as he walked back toward the atrium.

Fat raindrops pelted the plane as Rachel moved from the jetway to the second row in business class. She stashed her carry-on overhead, then scooched close to the window and slid her leather bag under the seat in front of her.

"Good afternoon and welcome aboard, Mrs. Bricker." The attractive, middle-aged flight attendant flashed a smile. "May I bring you a beverage before takeoff?"

"Water, please." Rachel winced at a the sight of dark clouds. "Wait. Make that a glass of wine. Red."

The woman smiled. "Don't worry about the weather."

"Am I that obvious?"

"Twenty years of experience. I'll bring that wine." She stepped away. Moments later she returned carrying a glass. "This will help take the edge off."

"I'm counting on it." Rachel breathed in the wine's earthy scent, a habit she'd adopted from Charlie. She tasted. Not bad. What if lightening hit the plane? She took another sip. What if turbulence snapped a wing off?

A woman carrying a book sat in the seat beside her, nodded, and opened her book.

Good. Another passenger who preferred solitude. Rachel sipped more wine. Maybe the weather would clear by the time they landed in New York. Another sip. How long before movie goers recognized her from *Joanie's Trial*? Maybe she should buy a big hat and a pair of giant sunglasses before flying home. What if nobody recognized her? Another sip.

After the flight attendant collected glasses, Rachel tuned into the pre-flight instructions. She didn't want to miss anything in the event of an emergency landing. *If* she managed to survive a fiery crash. Stop already. Like Charlie said, flying is safer than driving.

As the plane pushed back from the gate, the wine's effect kicked in. Rachel lowered the window shade, tightened her seatbelt, and squeezed her eyes shut. They remained closed until the pilot announced the final approach to LaGuardia.

An hour after landing in New York, Rachel boarded the largest plane she had ever seen. How could such a behemoth make it off the ground? Lift and aerodynamics. Charlie's explanation failed to ease her anxiety as she entered first class and noted the aisle separating her from the pair of center seats. A welcome perk for a star in a major motion picture.

After she stowed her bag, a young flight attendant stopped beside her seat. "Welcome aboard, Ms. Bricker. We're in for a smooth flight all the way to Italy."

Had he heard about her insane reaction to flying? Impossible. "Good to know."

"May I bring you something to drink?"

"Water's fine. On second thought, make that a glass of Champagne." Responding to a ping, Rachel pulled her phone from her purse. A text from Charlie. *Miss you already. Townhall meeting about to begin.*

Looking forward to details. On board Venice flight. Hugs and kisses. She added a string of hearts and pressed send. After setting her watch ahead six hours, Rachel geared herself for the long flight across the shark-infested Atlantic.

Chapter 8

Emily walked up the side aisle to a table placed beside the pastor's podium. She sat at the end beside Pepper and glanced at the other council members. Patsy Peacock, attorney Harold Bishop, and Mirabelle chatted among themselves as residents continued to fill the pews. "Looks like standing room only."

Pepper nodded. "Willow Falls is an involved community."

"Sometimes to a fault."

At seven straight-up Brick walked to the podium and rapped his gavel. The crowd fell silent. "Welcome, ladies and gentlemen. Thank you for coming out tonight." After introducing each council member, he read a list of pending decisions. "Which brings us to the number-one issue. I've asked our part-time resident and owner of Streetman Enterprise to bring us up to speed."

Greer ambled to the podium and faced the crowd. "More than two years ago, Rachel approached me with a request to fund the Redding Arms' final refurbishment. I gave the project and this town less than a fifty-fifty chance to succeed. Because she's my daughter and I owed her and Emily, I said yes. Fortunately residents proved me wrong and transformed Willow Falls into one of Georgia's most popular tourist destinations. Which makes investing in the town's future good business."

Greer lifted the microphone from its stand and carried it to the railing. "The undeveloped land across from the Willow Oak Vineyard and Winery is the ideal setting for another development. My intention is to purchase it to develop a first-class golf course and build a conference center, a hotel, and luxury vacation homes."

An elderly woman in the second row stood. "That all sounds good, Greer. The problem is our town's already struggling with a traffic nightmare. We don't need more cars clogging our streets."

"Easy for you to say." A man wearing a plaid shirt popped up. "You don't own a downtown business."

The woman pointed her finger at him. "Is everything about money with you?"

"Darn right. For the first time in years, I'm making a decent living."

A teenage girl stepped into the aisle. "Mr. Brick and Mr. Charlie cleared a giant piece of land to plant their vineyard and build the winery. Now you want to cut down more trees and destroy the homes of all the animals living in that forest?"

"Yeah." A man dressed in overalls nodded. "And mess up the best deer-hunting site in the county."

The girl propped her hands on her hips. "Shame on you and all your friends for killing innocent animals."

"If it wasn't for us hunters, the deer population would outnumber residents ten to one. Probably already does."

Greer lifted the microphone. "There's no need for either of you to worry. We'll leave plenty of forest."

The town's most vocal curmudgeon lifted off his seat. "How much are each of those houses you want to build gonna cost?"

Greer stroked his beard. "In the neighborhood of a million."

Gasps abounded.

Curmudgeon crossed his arms. "Ain't nobody living 'round here can afford to buy 'em. Don't you know a bunch of northerners will swoop in and invade us like some foreign army?"

Plaid Shirt waggled his finger at Curmudgeon. "You think we've got some invisible fence to keep folks who aren't from around here from moving in?"

"Wait 'til one of 'em wants to marry your daughter and turn her into a Yankee."

Greer stepped closer to the front row. "Sir, a lot of southerners love golf and want to escape the city for weekend getaways."

A woman in the front row held up her hand. "Mr. Streetman, how many jobs will your project create?"

"Good question. First, the local construction company will need to expand its crew."

The woman's eyes widened. "Will Dennis Locke head it up so maybe he'll make enough money to propose to Missy?"

"Well, ma'am, that's up to Dennis." Greer paused. "To further answer the jobs question, we'll also need to hire staff for the hotel and golf course."

The town's realtor stood. "And a new agent to sell those million-dollar houses."

Greer nodded. "The fact is Willow Falls will benefit financially."

Curmudgeon crossed his arms. "Until the new hotel steals tourists from Redding Arms and Willow Inn and puts 'em both out of business."

"I appreciate your concern, sir." Greer's tone hinted of irritation. "But the conference hotel will attract an entirely different clientele."

"Yeah, a bunch of partying, liquored-up convention goers."

Gertie stood in the front row and turned to face Plaid Shirt. "For goodness sakes, you are one narrow-minded, irritating old goat."

"Says the woman who thinks milkshakes can cure everyone's problems."

"You should come to our store and try one. It might make you more tolerable."

Laughter erupted.

The man's daughter lifted her girth off the seat. "I don't know what people who go to conventions are like. What I do know is Pop, and some of us who've lived here all our lives are worried about Willow Falls losing its small-town charm and attracting some not-so-desirable businesses."

The owner of the local clothing store raised her hand. "We're doing fine with the way things are. Why risk everything on some fancy idea? Besides, who around here even plays golf?"

"No one," shouted a young man from the back. "Because we don't have a freaking golf course."

As the heated debate continued, Emily noted Brick's stoic expression. Which side of the fence beckoned him? Would the council end up embroiled in controversy? Why had she agreed to take this insane assignment?

Following another half hour of debate, Brick rapped his gavel and dismissed the audience. While residents grumbled and spilled into the aisle, he led his team to a small conference room adjacent to the pastor's office. "Despite the crazy comments, both sides presented valid arguments. My first question is how did the town end up owning all the property in question?"

Attorney Harold propped his arms on the table and laced his fingers. "Ten years ago, the original owner's wife died. He denounced his daughter after she abandoned him."

Mirabelle pointed her finger at Harold. "Because Buster Bishop was one miserable son-of-a-snake."

"Whatever the reason, he handwrote a will leaving the acreage to the town. After you purchased the land and planted the vineyard, the value moved from worthless to middling. Now, it's a potential windfall."

Emily leaned forward. "Greer's a smart businessman. He'll expect a fair price."

Brick nodded. "If we go along with his proposal, we'll negotiate a deal beneficial to both parties. Pepper, Patsy, you have personal stakes in downtown. What are your opinions?"

"First a question." Pepper leaned forward. "Did you ever attend an out-of-town convention?"

"Couple of times."

"In small towns?"

"Big cities."

"With airports. Why would anyone plan a conference in a town where the nearest airport is more than an hour away?"

"Greer plans to promote the center as an alternative to big-city venues." Brick opened a folder, removed a document, and flipped to a page. "Amenities will include shuttle services from Atlanta and Greenville."

"I don't know." Pepper tapped her fingers on the table. "It still seems like a risky venture."

"I've known Greer for years." Brick glanced around the table. "Believe me, he didn't create the largest real-estate firm in the country by making uncalculated decisions."

Patsy laced her fingers. "I agree with Brick. Besides, the property is a couple of miles from downtown. Far enough to keep from spoiling our century-old charm and close enough to boost business. Plus, the council can put the proceeds from the sale to good use, like expanding and repaving the parking lot at the end of Main Street."

Brick turned to Mirabelle. "You have your finger on the town's pulse. What's your opinion?"

"You'll get a lot of complaints from residents who don't like change, maybe even some protests. Folks around here need to be more open-minded, like me."

An unintended chortle escaped Emily followed by an over-exaggerated throat clearing as images of past Mirabelle-led demonstrations leapt from her memory.

Mirabelle's eyes narrowed at Emily. "What?"

"You never cease to amaze me."

"Okay, folks." Brick flipped to the document's first page. "Before we vote, I'll read Greer's proposal aloud to make sure we haven't overlooked anything."

As Emily listened to the details, she couldn't imagine anyone with an ounce of common sense rejecting the proposal.

Chapter 9

Coffee aroma wafting through the first-class cabin nudged Rachel's eyes open. Groggy from two hours of sleep, she yawned, removed her sleep mask, and repositioned her bed back to a seat.

"Good morning, Mrs. Bricker. We're two hours from our destination. Would you like a cup of coffee?"

"No thanks."

He lowered her tray table and set down a menu. "Let me know when you're ready to order breakfast."

Rachel stared at the menu. Her body ached for more sleep, not food. She removed her script from her leather bag and focused on the lines until images of her family sitting around Mama Sadie's and Brick's two nights earlier invaded her thoughts. The laughter. The love. She set the script on the tray, closed her eyes, and drifted into a deep sleep until the plane's final approach to the Marco Polo runway.

Rachel brushed her fingers through unruly curls while standing in the slow-moving customs queue. The young couple locked in an embrace in the line beside her unleashed an overwhelming desire to call Charlie. Until she remembered the time difference. The sun wouldn't show up in Willow Falls for another three hours. She pulled her phone from her purse and read his latest text. *Lively townhall meeting. Mixed response. Council voted yes on your dad's proposal. Love you.*

A twinge of envy erupted at the thought of friends and neighbors embroiled in heated controversy without her. A year ago if someone had told her she'd miss the small-town spectacle, she would have claimed they were barking up the wrong tree. The mental reference to one of Mama Sadie's favorite sayings sparked a giggle. She tapped her phone's keypad. *Landed safely. Wish you were here. Love and kisses.* She slipped the phone in her pocket, yawned, and waited as the line inched forward.

After clearing customs, Rachel followed the crowd, trusting they would lead her to baggage claim. When she arrived, a young man approached. "Ms. Streetman?"

The abrupt change from Bricker to her professional name startled her. "Yes."

"I'm Peter, Mr. Nordstrom's assistant. He sent me to escort you."

"Thank goodness, because I don't have a clue what to do next."

"Don't worry, I'll take care of you." After collecting her luggage, he led her to a dock and a sleek, wooden boat.

She breathed in the salty sea air as the driver helped her step into the immaculate thirty-foot water taxi. "Welcome to Venezia. Please, take a seat."

"Thanks." She ducked her head, stepped into a closed cabin, and settled on a plush leather seat facing front. Peter loaded the luggage and stood beside the driver as he moved the boat away from the dock and through the waterway. Once they entered open sea and sped through turquoise water, an exhilarating tingle shot through her. Until intense loneliness replaced the sensation. Charlie should be sitting here, holding her hand. She fought back tears and blamed her emotional state on a serious case of jetlag.

Somehow, she focused on the ride until the boat slowed to a crawl and eased into a canal. Rachel pulled her phone from her pocket and stepped out of the cabin. Her mouth stood agape at the multi-story, centuries-old buildings hugging the narrow body of water—each with a unique façade. "This is amazing."

The driver grinned while maneuvering around small anchored boats and under ornate bridges. "Nothing like it anywhere in the world."

"No kidding." Rachel snapped photos of narrow windows, layers of peeling paint, crumbled plaster exposing brick, and colorful flowers flowing over balcony railings. When they docked beside Hotel Daniele's private entrance, she slipped her phone into her purse.

"Welcome to your home for the next six weeks, Ms. Streetman." Peter handed her luggage to a bellman before escorting her to the honey-colored wooden concierge desk. "You're already checked in." The concierge lifted a clunky key attached to a red tasseled ring off a wall peg and handed it to Peter. "When you're away from your room, you can leave your key, here."

"You obviously arrived safe and sound."

Rachel turned at the sound of Justin's voice and noted his arm wrapped around a woman wearing a wide-brimmed hat, body-hugging pants, and an off-the shoulder white sweater. "Safe, yes. The sound part is up for debate."

"Jet lag's a pain in the rear, but you'll adjust in a day or two. Meet our costar, Bethany Taylor."

"My friends call me Beth." The stunning, blue-eyed brunette touched Rachel's arm. "We're on our way to Café Florian for breakfast. Won't you join us?"

"If you don't mind, I'll take a raincheck."

Two tourists stopped to gawk and ask for autographs from the stars who acted more like a couple than business associates. So much for the blonde who accompanied Justin to the New York premiere. Rachel turned and eyed the red-carpeted grand staircase leading to the multi-level foyer bathed in honey-toned marble. Her mouth fell open. "This is more elaborate than Percy's Mansion."

Pete glanced over his shoulder. "Pardon me?"

"The view reminds me of a tourist attraction back home in Willow Falls."

He pointed to massive columns supporting ornate arches, and beyond to an opulent lobby. "The bar's over there. It's always cocktail hour in Italy."

"Thanks, but I need time to unpack and adjust to the time change."

"Best to stay awake until nightfall."

"So I've heard." She followed him to the elevator and up to her third floor room.

Pete unlocked her door and handed her the key. "Your schedule is on the desk. Good news is you're free 'til morning."

"Thanks." Rachel closed the door and set her purse and computer bag on the king-size bed. She kicked off her shoes and let her feet sink into the thick carpet while eyeing the luxurious space awash in subtle shades of beige, blue, and white. Her home away from home.

She dropped her key on the desk, opened royal blue drapes flanking two tall windows, and gazed beyond the narrow balcony to the Grand Canal and Venice's version of heavy traffic. Sending Charlie pictures of the spectacular views would surely convince him to change his mind about flying over for their anniversary. She picked the schedule off the desk. At least she had time to acclimate to the new time zone before her first scene.

After the bellman delivered her luggage, she unpacked and placed two framed photos on the nightstand. One posing with Emily the night of the *Percy's Legacy's* premiere. The other of her and Charlie the night before their wedding, standing on their deck and gazing into each other's eyes with the sun setting behind them. Determined not to break down in tears, she grabbed her purse and headed to the elevator hoping a brisk walk would help her fight off mind-numbing fatigue and heart-wrenching loneliness.

Chapter 10

Emily switched on the bedside lamp and turned off her phone alarm. Scott rolled out of bed and padded to the bathroom while she read a text from Rachel and scrolled through photos. She imagined visiting Venice—strolling across centuries-old bridges, mingling with locals, sampling the cuisine. Cody's muffled bark disrupted her musings. "You ready to go out, fella?" She slipped the phone in her robe pocket and followed Cody to the kitchen. After opening the sliding-glass door she poured two cups of coffee and carried them to the table.

Scott ambled in, plopped across from her, and reached for his cup. "Did you hear from your sister?"

Emily nodded. "*Willow Post* readers are gonna love the pictures she sent."

"You're writing about her?"

"A new feature, "Rachel's Venice Adventure." Would you like to travel abroad sometime?"

"Can't say it's on my bucket list."

"Maybe this will convince you to think again." She slid her phone across the table.

He set his cup down and swiped his finger through the photos. "Must be fun living the high life on someone else's dollar."

Emily breathed in the rich blend of coffee, vanilla, and honey. "Except she's in an exotic, romantic setting thousands of miles away from Charlie."

"The price of fame and fortune." Scott returned her phone. "Maybe after the girls are grown."

"What?"

"We'll fly to Italy."

"Does that mean you've added travel to your bucket list?"

"Down toward the bottom." He drained his cup and headed for a refill. "Are you excited about today's big event?"

"I suppose. Unlike last year's book-signing, I won't end up being interrupted by an invading movie crew and truck caravan." She joined him at the counter. "Although we're still living in North Georgia's magnet for unexpected events."

"Sounds like your author imagination on overdrive again." Scott set his cup down and slipped his arm around her shoulders.

She faced him and laced her fingers behind his neck. "Are you complaining?"

"Never." He stroked her hair then kissed her until the patter of little feet struck the kitchen floor. "We have company."

"Daddy's kissing Mommy." Clair and Jane tugged on their parents' pajamas.

He scooped the twins into his arms and delighted them with kisses and raspberries. When their giggles subsided, he carried them to their booster seats. "Maybe we shouldn't wait 'til they're grown."

"Sounds like traveling abroad just moved up on your bucket list."

"A notch or two."

"Maybe I'll earn enough royalties to pay for a trip." Emily pulled a box of cereal from the cabinet. "That is, if the locals don't sue me."

"No way."

"The royalties or lawsuit?"

"The latter." Scott chuckled. "After all, you're the mirror image of the town's newest celebrity."

"Rescued by my sister—" Emily poured cereal into two bowls. "Again."

"If you're talking about the two of you collaborating to finish writing and casting *Percy's Legacy* play, I'd call the rescue mutual."

"We are a good team, and now we're both living our dreams. Although hers is far more successful." She added banana slices to the cereal and carried the bowls to the table. "At least mine keeps me home with my sweet babies and charming husband."

"Until you become famous and head off for a nationwide book tour."

"Now whose imagination has gone bananas?" She sat across from Scott. "Thanks for taking the day off to watch the girls."

"How about I take them to watch their talented mommy sign books?"

"I'd like that."

Emily parked in front of the Book Nook, stepped from her car, and stood on the sidewalk. Would enough people show up to buy all the copies Patsy ordered? If crowds did respond, would her hand survive hours of signing?

Patsy opened the door and motioned Emily inside. "Are you ready for our big day?"

"I'm getting there." She turned in a slow circle and eyed tall shelves filled with books hugging the side walls. Framed posters of well-known authors' latest works filled the space above. "Wow, this looks amazing." Her eyes drifted to a Naomi Jasper original painting hanging above a plush couch close to the front window. Two overstuffed easy chairs completed the reading section. "So cozy and inviting."

Patsy pressed her palms together. "You're my first celebrity author."

Emily moved to an opening along the back of the waist-high, four-sided counter ten feet from the entrance. A stack of her books lay on one side. The rich aroma of chocolate, brown sugar, and cinnamon wafted over a tray of oatmeal raisin and chocolate chip cookies set on the front section.

"Come with me. I want to show you my favorite section." Patsy led her past free-standing bookshelves separating the space into two aisles to an arched entrance.

Emily pressed her hand to her chest as she stepped into a room painted pale yellow, with a star-studded blue ceiling. Red bookshelves surrounded child-size tables and chairs along with free-standing cutouts of well-known fictional characters. The total effect created an enchanting setting for young readers. "This is magical."

Patsy plucked a book off a table. "I want to ignite the love of reading in our youngest residents."

Emily pointed to a Winnie the Pooh mural adorning the back wall. "Nathan's daughter's artwork?"

"How'd you know?"

"She painted the Cinderella castle in my girls' room." A sharp rap on the front window drew Emily's attention. "Is it time?"

Patsy glanced at her watch. "Not for twenty minutes."

As they headed toward the front, Emily spotted Mirabelle and the residents lined up behind her. "Looks like our runner-up mayor wants the first signed copy."

"What do you think? Should we open up early?"

Emily eyed the stack of books waiting for her signature. "If we wait much longer Mirabelle is likely to break the door down."

"Go ahead and take your place while I unlock the door."

Emily settled on a stool behind the counter.

Mirabelle swooped in, grabbed a book off the stack, and handed it to her.

"What do you want me to write?"

"Whatever you think is appropriate."

Emily penned a note she hoped would offset any negative reaction to her story.

The owner of the first signed book opened to the first page. "To Mirabelle, a town leader, my friend, and inspiration." A grin lit her face. "Can't wait to find out what you wrote about me."

Emily's stomach churned at the sight of the town's mail carrier grabbing two cookies and settling on the couch in the reading corner. After signing copies for other early arrivals, a glimpse of the mail truck told her everything she needed to know. Delivering the mail came in a distant second to reading another book about Willow Falls.

Two hours after Emily signed Mirabelle's copy, customers continued to pack the Book Nook. With more than half the books sold, she laid her pen on the counter and massaged her right hand.

Patsy motioned toward the reading corner. "Other than turning pages, Mirabelle hasn't moved a muscle."

"She's either fascinated or gearing for a nasty confrontation."

"Are your accurate depictions of real people?"

"With different names and tweaked physical descriptions. Although your character wears peacock feather-adorned hats."

"I suppose that makes me one of your most peculiar characters."

"More like charming and lovable."

"Can't wait to read it." Patsy stashed a book under the counter. "Don't let my copy get away."

The bell jangling over the front door announced another arrival. Gertie strolled in, plucked a cookie off the tray, and pointed it toward Emily. "Your husband won't tell me if I'm in your story."

Emily leaned on the counter. "How could I write about Willow Falls without including our famous soda-fountain specialist?"

"First I land a part in a movie and now I'm in a novel."

"With a different name."

Her brows raised. "How will people recognize me?"

"Let me think." Emily pinched her chin between her thumb and index finger. "We have a slew of soda fountains around here ... oh wait, we only have one."

"The best in Georgia." Gertie snapped her fingers. "Make that the entire South." She lifted a book off the counter and handed it to Emily. "What name did you give me?"

"You'll have to read the story to find out." She signed and returned the book.

Gertie opened to the first page. "To Gertie, Your wisdom and ingenuity inspire everyone who has the privilege to know you, especially me." Her eyes lit. "Thank you, honey. Your comment warms this old lady's heart more than you can know." She craned her neck. "Mirabelle looks like she ate a barrel of sour pickles. Do you think she'll mind if I join her before I head back to the store?"

Emily glanced over her shoulder. She must have read the chapter about her accusing Sadie's character of stealing her credit card. "I doubt she'll notice."

"Okay then." Gertie grabbed another cookie before settling on one of the easy chairs.

"I called that right. She has no idea Gertie sat across from her."

Patsy moved beside Emily. "If everyone becomes as engrossed in your story as Mirabelle, you'll have another successful novel."

Emily released a heavy sigh. "Or a town full of angry residents." She continued signing books, accepting compliments, and answering questions until she spotted Mirabelle standing in front of the cookie tray, her lips pressed tight and her brows pinched. Before Emily could say a word, she broke eye contact and dashed to the door as if she suddenly remembered abandoning a truckful of undelivered mail.

"Mirabelle's obviously in one of her snits." A middle-aged woman wearing a pink sweatshirt stepped up to the counter. "How long has she been here?"

"Since the store opened."

The woman shook her head. "There goes any chance for on-time mail delivery."

No kidding. "I hope you're not expecting anything important."

"My first *People* magazine. Now that we have two movie stars living in Willow Falls, I want to keep up with all the Hollywood goings-on."

The elderly woman next in line plucked a book off the dwindling stack. "One day soon you're bound to see a story about Rachel. When will you begin sharing pictures of your sister's trip, Emily?"

"Next week's *Willow Post*. Until then you can see photos on her social media pages."

"Guess I'd better ask my grandson to show me how to do that highfalutin stuff. By the way, you know my land is beside the property Greer Streetman bought."

Emily nodded. "Which means the value will increase big time."

"Not until all those bulldozers are gone. They started clearing today."

Pink Shirt scoffed. "I hope they don't hurt any wildlife."

"Don't worry about the animals. They'll move up the road or over to my backyard. Good thing Charlie and Brick have dogs to keep the critters out of their vineyard."

Moments after Emily signed the books, Scott arrived with Jane and Clair.

The elderly woman grinned. "My goodness, your daughters look more like you every day. When is Rachel planning to start a family? She's not getting any younger, you know."

Sweatshirt elbowed her. "This is the twenty-first century. Don't you know lots of women wait 'til they're well into their thirties to have a child?"

"All I have to say is she'd best not wait too long."

"Rachel and Charlie will decide when the time's right." Emily laid her pen on the counter. "If you ladies will excuse me, I want to show my girls the children's section."

"You go right ahead, sweetie." The elderly woman tucked her book under her arm and stooped to pat the twins' heads.

Clair lifted her chin. "Mommy's signing books for grown-ups. Did you buy one?"

"Yes, I did and I can't wait to read it."

Jane swirled a curl around her finger. "It doesn't have pictures. Daddy says we can buy a book."

The twins scampered to Emily as she stepped from behind the counter.

"Hey, sweet girls. Do you want to see a special place Miss Patsy created for you and all your friends?"

"Where is it?"

"You'll see." Emily held their hands as they made their way to the children's section.

An older child greeted the girls with a hug and led them to the bookshelves.

Scott stood beside Emily. "How's everything going?"

"Looks like we'll sell most of my books. Mirabelle spent half the day with her nose buried in her copy before she decided to deliver today's mail."

"Did she say anything before she walked out?"

"Not one word. Based on her expression, I'm guessing she's planning to boycott me and Patsy's store."

Scott shoved his hands in his pockets. "She'll cool off when she discovers her character is one of the town's heroes."

"If she reads that far before burning the book."

Clair rushed over with a book in hand. "Can I have this one, Mommy?"

"You picked a good one, sweet girl."

"Did you write it?"

Emily knelt and tucked a stray curl behind Clair's ear. "No. When you and Jane are older, maybe you can help me write a children's book about Willow Falls."

"And draw pictures?"

"As many as you want."

Clair's eyes widened as she looked over Emily's head. "Hi, Uncle Charlie. Are you gonna buy Mommy's book?"

"Maybe more than one."

Emily stood to greet her brother-in-law. "Thanks for coming by."

Charlie handed her his phone. "Rachel wants to say hello."

She smiled at her twin. "Hey, sis."

"I hear the grand opening is a smashing success."

"Way better than I expected."

"Sorry I had to miss it. Save a book for me."

"Will do. How's everything going in fabulous Venice?"

"We start filming tomorrow. Our costar is an interesting woman. I think she and Justin have a thing going."

Emily chuckled. "He already replaced the New York blonde?"

"You know what they say about out of sight. I miss everyone even more than I expected."

"After two days?"

"I know. Who'd have guessed? Anyway, hugs and kisses."

"Back at you." She returned the phone to Charlie.

He held it close and whispered before ending the call and clipping the phone to his belt. "Sorry I can't stay longer."

The sadness she noted in his eyes tugged on Emily's heartstrings. "Why don't you come to our house tomorrow after church for lunch and watch football with Scott."

"Can't. Jack and I are knee-deep in grapes, so to speak. Maybe another weekend."

"The invitation is open-ended, so anytime."

"Thanks. See you guys later."

Emily watched him maneuver through the crowds. Did Rachel have any inkling how much Charlie missed her?

Chapter 11

Rachel followed the hostess through the Terrazza Danieli restaurant to a table beside a railing fronting the awning-shaded terrace.

Director Robert Nordstrom stood and pulled a chair away from the table. "The view from here is spectacular."

"Thanks."

He sat beside her. "Adjusting to the time change is a bear."

"Nine straight hours of sleep helped." She gazed at boats navigating the Grand Canal and beyond at a small island anchored by a classical white structure and a tall brick tower. "What's the building across the water?"

"San Giorgio Maggiore Church. Built in the tenth century. The tower's new. Only a couple hundred years old. It matches the bell tower in Saint Mark Square."

Rachel pulled her phone from her purse and snapped a photo. "All this fascinating history and gorgeous scenery is overwhelming."

"The perfect venue for a romantic comedy." He nodded to the left. "The rest of our party is on the way over."

Rachel spotted Justin and Beth approaching, fueling her speculation they'd become romantically involved.

Justin flashed a grin as they settled across the table. "Looks like you got some rest."

"Enough."

"Good. After breakfast my publicist wants to photograph me, you, and Beth."

"You have 'til noon, Justin." Robert tapped the folder sitting on the table. "After that we need you for a shoot."

"Guess my schedule will leave you ladies to explore the city on your own."

"How fun." Beth pressed her palms together. "We'll visit those adorable stores in St. Mark Square."

Rachel spread her napkin across her lap. Traipsing around town with an ego-driven super star and his publicist, then spending the afternoon on a useless shopping spree didn't come close to making her top-fifty list. Maybe she could beg off. Claim she needed more rest. Except she'd already said she'd had enough sleep. Besides, it wouldn't hurt to learn more about Beth and find out what was going on between her and Justin. "Seems we have a plan."

After the waiter took their orders, Robert removed papers from the folder and handed each a set of pages. "A schedule adjustment due to the rain forecast later this week, plus a couple of script changes. You can read them later and call me with any questions."

For the next hour, they devoured a Venetian-style breakfast of coffee, croissants, and pastries amid conversation about the latest Hollywood movies, the last flood to engulf Venice, and news about the profits from *Joanie's Trial*. After Robert signed the bill, the threesome made their way down to the hotel lobby where they found Justin's publicist pacing.

He kissed the woman's cheek. "Sorry we're late. You know how it is when you're with the boss."

"I'm on a deadline with two magazines, which means I have to take photos and write copy by eight A.M. U.S. time."

"Ladies, meet Priscilla Benton, the sharpest and most demanding publicist in the business."

"From the man who believes flattery excuses all discretions." Priscilla flipped her silky, dark hair with her hand. "We'll start with canals and end in the square."

Justin glanced at his watch. "I'm available for three hours."

"Plenty of time if we get cracking." She shouldered her camera, led the trio to the front door, and staged a photo of Justin sandwiched between Rachel and Beth. Outside she dashed to the bridge closest to the hotel and shooed tourists out of the way with a promise of autographs. "Okay, ladies, one at a time." She pointed to Beth. "You first."

Following Priscilla's instructions, Beth gazed at Justin with dreamy-eyed admiration.

"Your turn, Rachel."

No way she'd fall for this nonsense. Her refusal to make eye contact with Justin elicited a snarl from his demanding publicist. After signing autographs and following the women to the next site, Rachel crossed her arms and leaned against a pillar. Again, she refused to follow Priscilla's instruction. By the third bridge she had enough.

"Next stop—"

"I'm sorry, Priscilla." Rachel feigned a yawn. "But I'm struggling with a serious case of jetlag. I need to bow out."

"Pity." Priscilla glared at Rachel. "You're forcing me to change my strategy."

"Here's an idea. Leave me out of the article. You have plenty of great footage with Beth and Justin."

The publicist lifted her camera and seemed to focus on the LCD screen. "Not a problem. I have what I need."

Beth pulled Rachel aside. "What about us shopping?"

"An hour of rest will do the trick. I'll meet you half past noon at the bell tower in St. Mark's Square."

"I'll see you there."

Rachel waited for them to scurry toward the next bridge before she strolled through narrow alleys and snapped pictures for her fans back home. After savoring a scoop of lemon gelato, she headed to the bell tower and scanned the square's massive piazza enclosed on all but one side by three-story buildings. At ground level, columns supported a series of ornate arches opening to a covered walkway fronting shops, cafés, and restaurants—some expanding into the open space.

"Isn't this delightful?" Beth's voice oozed enthusiasm.

"It looks bigger than two football fields."

"Filled with tourists and pigeons instead of hunky athletes. I'm glad we have the afternoon alone. Yesterday I couldn't convince Justin to walk into a single store."

"Is this your first trip to Venice?"

"Second. I honeymooned here with my first husband. That's another story."

"Are you married now?"

"To number three." Beth's eyes widened. "I'm surprised you haven't read about us."

"I live in a small town, so I don't follow Hollywood stories." A lame excuse even to her ears.

"Guess I'll have to fill you in while we support the local economy." Beth slipped her arm around Rachel's. "Starting with a darling clothing shop we simply must visit."

By their second stop, a jewelry store, Rachel had learned Beth's third husband, a famous rapper, had earned one platinum and two multiplatinum recordings. "He's as rich as Oprah." Beth pointed to a pair of emerald earrings in a glass case. "I'll take those."

The clerk grinned. "Excellent choice."

"Show my friend that diamond and emerald pair."

The woman placed the earrings on the counter in front of Rachel. "These are perfect for a redhead."

"They're beautiful." Maybe she should buy them. She resisted the urge, pushed them away, and turned toward Beth. "Do your busy careers allow you and your husband time to spend together?"

"Not much." Beth handed the female clerk her credit card. "He spends most of his time performing to sell-out crowds all over the world. Life in the fast lane. What about you?"

"Charlie and I married last year. Our first anniversary is in a few weeks."

"How fun. Is he flying over?"

Rachel looked away. "I hope."

"What do you mean 'you hope'?"

"It's our winery's first harvest, so he's busy."

"If he makes you celebrate alone, you'll definitely need to buy yourself an expensive piece of jewelry." Beth accepted a small gold bag from the clerk. "Did he give you that gorgeous bracelet?"

Rachel fingered her diamond and emerald tennis bracelet. "This was the last gift my dad and I gave Mom before she passed. That was a long time ago."

"So sad. But what a precious memory. Next stop, an adorable little artsy shop."

By mid-afternoon, Beth had shipped six expensive purchases to her home address and carried four small bags. "I'm starving. How about a bite to eat?"

"I'm ready to get off my feet."

They opted for an outdoor table in front of a fancy restaurant. After ordering, Beth dug a compact from her purse and checked her image. "When we finish lunch, I want to check out that toy store we passed by. My kids will expect gifts."

"You have children?"

"Two girls and a boy. One from each husband." She replaced her compact with her phone, pressed an icon, and pushed it across the table. "Thirteen, seven, and two."

Rachel stared at the children sitting on a couch beside a pleasant-looking woman with salt and pepper hair. "They're adorable. Is she their grandmother?"

"My nanny. I hired her a month before my oldest popped out." Beth's head tilted. "Do you have kids?"

"No."

"If you ever do, take my advice and hire a top-notch professional nanny. They're worth whatever salary they demand. Mine's bringing the kids over for a visit. I booked them a room."

A fan stopped at their table to request an autograph and to a snap a selfie with Beth.

Rachel waited for the woman walk away. "That's number eight."

"Far fewer than normal. Seems I'm not as well known outside the U.S. I hope this film changes that." Beth paused. "I've been dying to ask about your experience working with Justin."

"He's a talented actor—"

"That's obvious. What's he like personally?"

Didn't she know? "He's nice enough. Although in my opinion too self-centered."

Beth leaned forward and crossed her arms on the table. "Did you two have an affair?"

"What? No." She couldn't risk alienating her costar. "Charlie and I were engaged."

"Still in the romantic stage of your relationship." As Beth shared stories about actors she'd worked with, then switched to career goals, Rachel found it strange she didn't talk about her children.

Her mind shifted to Charlie. Although his fortieth birthday loomed closer and his desire to start a family remained strong, he agreed to postpone pregnancy so she could focus on her career. Or until her maternal instincts kicked in. Hopefully, not any time soon.

Chapter 12

"Are you kidding me?" Rachel laid her napkin on the table in the hotel restaurant and glared at a photo of her standing on a bridge to the left of Justin. Her arms crossed and her head turned away from the actor and Beth who gazed at each other as if they'd discovered their long-lost soulmates. Her nostrils flared as she read the caption. "*Is jealousy brewing over Hollywood's hottest male star*? This is insane."

Justin propped his arms on the table. "Why are you so ticked?"

Rachel slapped his phone on the table and glared at him. "Oh, I don't know." Glances from the couple at the next table forced her to lower her volume. "Maybe because this is a sham? You know good and well that I didn't pose for that picture. Obviously, Priscilla photo-shopped it. You have to stop her from using it, Justin."

"Too late. She already posted the piece on social media and scheduled it for an online publication."

"Is this how your publicist exacts revenge?" Rachel sent the phone skidding across the table.

Justin caught it seconds before it slid off the edge. "What'd you expect after walking out on us?"

"A little respect and honesty."

Beth set her coffee cup down. "You know publicity is always a plus in our business."

Rachel frowned at her. "No ... it's not. You don't understand. I live in a small town where everyone knows everyone's business. This will make Charlie and me the topic of all kinds of wild rumors."

Beth shrugged. "My husbands never seemed to mind—"

"Yeah? Well, maybe I want to keep my first." Rachel cringed the second the comment rolled off her tongue. "I'm sorry, Beth. I wasn't trying to insinuate anything."

"No big deal." Her sideways glance at Justin hinted she might have already entertained the notion of moving beyond to husband number four.

"I should never have agreed to go along with that photo shoot. Believe me, the next time anyone other than my agent wants to take pictures, I'll tell them to take a hike. That is, if I survive this fiasco." A mental image of Mirabelle cornering Charlie and firing questions at him triggered a wave of nausea. Beads of sweat popped out on Rachel's forehead and upper lip. She pressed her hand to her mouth.

"You look like you're about to toss your cookies." Beth giggled. "A line from my last movie. I never thought I'd have a chance to use it in real life."

"Aren't you fortunate I gave you the opportunity?" Rachel's tone came across as snarky. "Sorry again. Either Italian coffee is way too strong or my stomach is revolting over this photographic disaster. Whatever's going on, I need to head back to my room before I upchuck and create an unpleasant scene." She grabbed her purse off the back of her chair.

"What can I do to help?"

"Nothing, Beth. Hopefully, I'll see you in makeup in an hour." Rachel dashed from the restaurant, narrowly avoiding a collision with a waiter. By the time she rode the elevator to the first floor and retrieved her key from the concierge desk, a dull ache attacking her neck and shoulders had replaced the nausea. In no mood to talk to anyone, she headed straight to her room.

Inside her private sanctuary, she plucked a water bottle off the desk and stared out the window at a police boat racing up the Grand Canal. Its swells rocked a water bus loading and unloading passengers in front of the hotel.

Maggie had warned her about falling prey to unscrupulous publicity. Why hadn't she listened to her instincts and declined Justin's self-promotion jaunt? Maybe no one in Willow Falls would see the publicity. Fat chance. Too many residents had discovered the lure of Hollywood gossip. She had to give Charlie a heads-up.

She dug her phone from her purse and pressed his number. The call went straight to voicemail. "Get a grip, Rachel." She picked her script off the desk, dropped onto a wingback chair, and flipped to today's scene—scheduled for an outdoor shoot in a piazza with Beth. She stared at the page.

Maybe she should sue Justin's publicist. Make her pay big time. Mental images of headlines about her accusing Priscilla of libel zipped through Rachel's head, followed by captions touting her as a naïve newcomer to the world of stardom. Difficult to deal with. A director's nightmare. Unemployable.

She tossed the script aside and headed to the bathroom to find something to ease her mounting headache. A glance in the mirror revealed paler than normal skin, accentuating her freckles. She swallowed two aspirin, grabbed her purse, and strode out of her room. Maybe fresh air would calm her nerves and bring color back to her cheeks.

Outside, she donned sunglasses, turned left, and crossed a bridge. She wandered past outdoor dining spaces, dozens of free-standing kiosks, and hordes of tourists taking photos and buying souvenirs. She crossed two more bridges and stopped at the top of a third. Her eyes wandered to a narrow canal-side park with two rows of red benches facing each other. Three elderly women sitting across from a young woman holding a baby conjured images of Willow Falls' park and the foot-high retaining wall at the water's edge.

A young couple stopped beside her, holding hands, speaking French. Honeymooners? Would Charlie refuse to take a few days off and fly over for their anniversary? Perhaps she should heed Beth's suggestion and treat herself to an expensive piece of jewelry.

Rachel glanced at her watch. Fifty minutes before she was due in makeup. Time enough if she hurried. She maneuvered through the crowd to St. Mark's Square. When she arrived at the jewelry-store window, she stared at her reflection in the glass.

"Excuse me."

She turned toward the female's voice.

The middle-aged woman towered over her. "I don't mean to bother you, but I saw your picture in a magazine. You have a new movie coming out, right?"

"*Joanie's Trial*. Are you from the U.S?"

"Ohio. Do you mind if my husband takes a picture of us?"

"I'd be honored."

The woman slid her arm around Rachel's shoulders and smiled for the camera. "One more thing." She removed a small notebook from her purse. "I'd love to get your autograph."

"My pleasure. What's your name?"

"Gloria."

She signed, *To my new friend, Gloria. Rachel Streetman.*

"Thank you, Ms. Streetman, and count me as one of your fans."

As soon as the couple walked away, Rachel entered the store and pushed her sunglasses up. The female who'd sold the expensive bauble to Beth greeted her. "Welcome back. Are you looking for a gift?"

"Maybe some earrings, for me."

"The pair I showed you earlier?"

"Way too expensive."

"Perhaps some gold hoops?"

Buying jewelry for herself didn't make a lick of sense. "You know what? Maybe I'll think about it for a few days."

The clerk's smile morphed to irritation. "Come back any time."

She walked out, lowered her sunglasses, and made a mental note to contact her agent and find a way to counter Priscilla's deplorable publicity stunt.

Chapter 13

Emily carried a cup of coffee to the worktable in the newspaper office, set her phone down, and sat across from Mary Dixon—Pastor Nathan's wife, and her reporter. "Four days ago, Mirabelle began reading my book. I haven't heard a peep out of her."

"Maybe that's a good sign."

"When she walked out of the Book Nook, she looked like she could spit nails."

"You know what she's like when she's in one of her moods."

"Yeah. Unpredictable." Emily sighed. "Enough about her. How's the layout for *Rachel's Venice Adventure* coming along?"

"Today, your sister sent her best photos yet." Mary turned her computer toward Emily.

She peered at a picture of Robert and Justin. "Reminds me of a year ago. Somehow, we managed to survive two months of movie-making craziness."

"All the hubbub gave J.T. a lot of great stories to share with tourists."

"You have to love his enthusiasm."

The front door swung open emitting a blast of cool air as two sixty-something women darted in. Each carried a copy of Emily's new book.

Mary pushed away from the table. "Hi, ladies. What can we do for you?"

"We need to talk to Emily." The shorter woman slapped her copy on the table, turned to a bookmarked page, and pointed to a highlighted paragraph. "I've been trying to tell Myrtle this character is me."

"Not a chance." Myrtle glared at her friend. "You know good and well the description fits me to a tee, Ethel."

"In your dreams. Did you read what Emily says she's wearing? A blue dress like mine."

"You think you're the only woman in Willow Falls with a dress that color? Did you forget about the one I wore to church last week?"

"That dress is more purple than blue." Ethel huffed. "All you need to do is ask around. Everyone will agree I'm the one she's writing about."

Myrtle tapped the highlighted paragraph. "The character's hair is silver, like mine."

Ethel dismissed her comment with a hand flick. "You're salt and pepper. I'm silver. The only person who can set you straight is the author." She zeroed in on Emily. "Tell us which one of us is right and settle this debate once and for all."

"Well …" What kind of response would satisfy them both? "Actually, the character is both of you."

Ethel planted her hands on her hips. "If you ask me, that's a bunch of hooey."

"Are you going to let me explain?"

"Sorry. Go ahead."

"Thank you. Do you both read a lot of books?"

Myrtle nodded. "Fair amount."

"Same here."

"Good. Then you know that too many characters in a story are confusing to readers."

"You're right." Ethel tilted her head. "I read one story that had so many characters I had to start a journal to keep up. It's especially hard when the names are foreign or spelled funny."

"Which is why several important characters—including the one you're questioning—are blends of real people. Ladies, the character you're questioning is a composite of both of you. Which means you each have bragging rights."

Myrtle's eyes narrowed. "Are you sure you're not saying that to shush us?"

Ethel thumped Myrtle's arm. "You can't go accusing Emily of fudging the truth."

"Why not. She's a writer with a big imagination."

"Because she has too much integrity to blow us off." Ethel retrieved her book. "I suggest we go to lunch at Pepper's Café and tell everyone we're *both* a big part of the story."

"I suppose you're right. Today's my turn to treat."

"No way." Ethel thumped her friend's arm. "You treated last time."

"You're right. So, we'll go Dutch."

"In that case, I'm skipping dessert."

The moment the two women walked out, Mary burst out laughing. "Good move, Emily. So, did you give her an accurate explanation?"

"Most of the minor characters are composites."

"By the time those two spread the word, everyone in Willow Falls will claim they're one of your characters."

"Maybe I won't face a libel charge after all. Uh-oh, I spoke too soon." Emily pointed to the front window. "The mail truck just pulled up."

"If Mirabelle comes in, do you want me to send her away?"

"Not before I find out what's going on in her head."

Mirabelle climbed out of the truck, carrying a stack of mail. She stepped onto the sidewalk and stopped to face the window before walking past.

"She's definitely coming back." As the minutes ticked by, Emily's pulse quickened. "I'm not afraid of her. However, I'm painfully aware that when she's on your case, you'd best look out."

"After watching you handle Ethel and Myrtle, I'm not worried about you taking on our mail lady."

"We're about to find out. She just grabbed another stack of mail from her truck."

A man approached Mirabelle as she stepped onto the curb. She waggled her finger at his face.

Emily drummed her fingers on the table and watched the drama unfold. "Maybe we should lock the door and hide."

Seconds after the man stalked away, Mirabelle shoved the front door open. "That man's a menace." She scowled and tossed a stack of mail on the worktable.

This wasn't good. "Nice weather for delivering mail."

Mirabelle plopped onto a chair beside Emily. "I read the final chapters of your book last night."

"Let me explain—"

"I haven't finished. You included all the important people in town, and I can tell from your descriptions who's who."

"Like I told Ethel and Myrtle a few minutes ago, most of the characters represent more than one person." Keep talking. "Of course, I tried to represent everyone fairly. Take Gertie for instance—"

In one swift move, Mirabelle wrapped her arms around Emily.

A headline raced through Emily's head. *Mail Lady Squeezes Author to Death*.

"The more I read the better I understood." Mirabelle released her

"Understood what?"

"That you exaggerated my character to make her more interesting." Mirabelle's face beamed. "Best of all you made her one of the town's heroes. I'm gonna write lots of good reviews to let people know that I recognize talent when I see it. Right now, I've gotta get back to work. We don't want folks complaining about late mail." She popped up and headed toward the door while waving over her shoulder. "I'll see you ladies later."

Emily's jaw dropped. "Pinch me so I know I'm not dreaming."

Mary laughed. "Good thing she believes you exaggerated her character."

"Lucky for me Mirabelle isn't endowed with keen self-awareness."

"Which means you can relax."

"You mean celebrate." Emily grabbed her pinging phone. "A text from Sheriff Mitch. Something's going on at Greer's build site the paper needs to cover."

"Want me to go?"

"Let's take a break and go together. It'll give us a chance to dissect the strange twist in the Mirabelle saga."

"Do you honestly think we can figure her out?"

"No, but we'll have a lot of fun trying." She shouldered her purse while Mary grabbed the camera and followed her to her car. Emily circled the block, turned left onto Main Street, and drove past Willow Inn, Naomi

Jasper's museum, and Percy's mansion. "What do you suppose is going on at the construction site?" She turned onto County Road.

"I don't have a clue. One thing I do know, Mirabelle isn't involved." Mary paused. "Given what little I know about her upbringing, especially with an alcoholic mother, I understand why her self-awareness is skewed."

Thanks to Patsy, Emily knew far more about Mirabelle's past than she could reveal. "You're a smart woman, Mary Dixon."

"Being married to a pastor has given me insight I wouldn't otherwise have."

"I can only imagine." As Emily rounded a curve, blue lights flashing atop the sheriff's two new cruisers drew her attention.

"Maybe it's an accident."

"Why would Mitch call us to cover a car crash? Unless…" Emily's heart jumped to her throat as memories surfaced of a fatal accident three years earlier. The one that changed her life forever. As she neared the scene, she slowed and pulled off the road.

Mitch stood beside a pickup truck with a cell phone glued to his ear. He faced a bulldozer sitting idle ninety feet from the road at the end of a wide swath of cleared land. A man dressed in jeans, sweatshirt, and work boots leaned on the tread, smoking a cigarette.

"I don't see any mangled vehicles." Mary pushed the passenger door open.

"Thank goodness." Emily stepped out and spotted Charlie crossing the road from the winery driveway. "Any idea what's going on?"

"Maybe the crew dug up a trunk full of confederate money."

"That would make a good plot for a historical whodunit or a noteworthy editorial."

"Or a sequel to *Saving Willow Falls*." Charlie removed his cap and pointed to the deputy stepping out from the front of the dozer. "Something's going on down there."

Out of earshot, Mitch gestured wildly with his free hand.

"Something's not right." As the minutes passed, Emily's imagination kicked into high gear. "Maybe the woman who complained about destroying the forest chained herself to a tree. Or a mama bear defending her cubs attacked the bulldozer."

Charlie gestured toward the sheriff. "We're about to find out."

Mitch clipped his phone to his belt and motioned them to follow him down the red-clay path.

Emily breathed in the scent of fresh-cut pine and pictured rolling hills cleared to accommodate a golf course. At least Greer planned to leave as many trees as possible. As they closed in on the scene, the man wearing jeans flicked his cigarette butt on the ground and squashed it with his boot.

Mitch stopped in front of the bulldozer. "What you're about to see will impact Willow Falls far more than Robert Nordstrom's movie crew. I've contacted GBI."

Charlie's brow furrowed. "Georgia Bureau of Investigation?"

Mitch nodded. "Greer's on his way up from Atlanta."

Emily's heart pounded. "What are you trying to tell us, Mitch?"

"Follow me." He led them beyond the tread and stopped ten feet from the dozer's scoop suspended over a hole.

Emily stared at large clumps of clay. She moved closer and spotted a smooth round object with a hollowed orb. Her hand flew to her mouth as bile erupted in her throat. "Is that a human skull?"

"More than one." Mitch pointed to another round object. "It's possible we've uncovered a crime scene."

Mary gasped. "How is that possible?"

"The closest house is a half mile away. Perfect spot to dump bodies."

Emily recovered from the shock, slipped into reporter mode, and snapped photos of the remains. "Any idea how long they've been here?"

"No way to tell. GBI's sending investigative and forensic teams."

Charlie crossed his arms. "Most likely followed by news crews."

"And gawkers." Mitch gestured toward onlookers gathering beside his vehicle. "We need to secure the area stat." He sent his deputy for a roll of crime-scene tape. "Emily, will you and Mary stick around to cover this for the *Willow Post*?"

"Of course."

"Charlie, you come with me. I'll need your help with crowd control."

"Yes, sir." He yanked his phone from his belt hook. "Jack's working at the winery. I'll call him to join us."

Emily lowered her camera and approached the jean-clad man. "Are you the bulldozer operator?"

"Yes, ma'am. Name's Hank. I live over in Clayton."

"When did you discover you had uncovered human remains?"

"Soon as I seen that skull." He plucked a cigarette package from his shirt pocket. "Want a smoke?"

"No thanks."

"Mind if I light up? I'll stand downwind from you."

"Go ahead."

He leaned against the tread and struck a match. "First time I dug up human bones."

Mary turned away from the scoop. "Must have been a shock."

"Didn't expect to find anything like that around here. My wife's brother's a reporter with the Atlanta newspaper. He's coming up to check this out."

At the sound of Scott's ringtone, Emily stepped away and pressed the phone to her ear.

"I hear something's going on across from the winery."

She revealed the discovery.

"How many bodies?"

"Two for certain." Emily glanced at the mound of clay. "When word leaks out, reporters and curiosity seekers will show up in droves."

"While the rumor mill runs amok."

"Willow Falls has come a long way from an obscure little spot on the map." Emily sighed. "What do you think that Travel Titan who called the town a real snore would write about us now?"

"She for sure couldn't call us boring. I have a customer to take care of. Keep me posted."

"I will." Emily pocketed her phone and returned to Hank. "Any idea what will happen next?"

"All I know is the project is coming to a screeching halt till someone figures out what the devil went on here. Maybe one of them TV shows about unsolved murders will show up."

Mary swatted a fly away from her face. "Except we don't know for certain if this is a crime scene."

Hank stared at her. "You think some poor mountain family dug a hole and dumped their kinfolk in without putting them in boxes?"

Mary shrugged. "I suppose anything's possible. Although that scenario seems a bit far-fetched."

"You think?" Hank flicked ash from his cigarette.

Emily scrolled through the photos she'd snapped. "One fact is certain. We have a new front-page story for this week's paper and another drama to fuel the town's rumor mill."

Chapter 14

Following three hours of filming, Rachel dropped onto a chair at a table in the Ristorante's outdoor setting and accepted a bottle of water from a crew member. "Thank you."

Beth settled across from her, shaded by white umbrella. "Don't you love this cozy piazza?" She pointed to a tiny single-story brick building with autumn vines clinging to the front façade. "Especially that cute little gift shop. Did you notice the candles in the window? The owner invited us to come in. She probably wants our autographs. I found an adorable shoe store after you left me and Justin this morning. I bought four pairs. Genuine Italian leather. When we finish shooting, I can take you there."

Did Beth ever stop buying stuff? "Maybe another day."

"Whenever you're in the mood. How fun to live in one of these piazzas, steps away from all the action."

"And hordes of tourists." Rachel eyed rows of four-story structures, each painted a different earth tone. "Back in my hometown ..." the phrase rolling off her tongue with ease released a wave of melancholy. Five more weeks before she could stand on their deck with Charlie, watching the sun set over the vineyard. Or spend Sunday afternoon with her family in Emily's and Scott's or Mama Sadie's and Brick's dining room. Or hug her nieces.

"Hello." Beth waved. "Where'd you go?"

Rachel blinked. "Funny how things change. A little more than a year ago, I struggled with the idea of moving to a small town hours from Atlanta. Now I can't imagine living anywhere else."

"I'd shrivel up and die if I didn't live minutes from dozens of shops and high-end restaurants."

Rachel noted Beth's wide-eyed expression. Did her penchant to shop substitute for happiness, or had she fallen victim to the rich and famous lifestyle? "We each find what makes us happy."

"I suppose. Justin broke up with his girlfriend before he flew over."

So much for the New York blonde.

"All the up-and-coming actresses are dying to play opposite him. I admit I'm a little envious of you playing his girlfriend. His hotel room is next to mine. Hope you don't mind."

Had he pegged Beth as wife number three or simply his honey of the month? Remembering how Justin hit on her during a lakeside love scene while filming *Joanie's Trial* triggered a smirk. She'd shocked him with a resounding rejection.

"He knows how to make love scenes zing." Beth leaned forward. "If you get my drift."

"Believe me, whatever goes on between you two is none of my business." Rachel broke eye contact and focused on the film crew repositioning equipment. Intimate girl talk had never been on her list of fun activities. Especially with someone she'd only known for a few days. Somehow she had to play nice with a woman who treated her as a new best friend.

"Excuse me, ladies, Mr. Nordstrom's ready to resume filming."

Rachel finished the bottle of water while makeup artists scurried to their table.

Two more hours passed before Robert announced a final cut. "Beth, you're finished for today. Rachel, I need you and Justin for a night scene at the gondola dock across the Bridge of Sighs. Makeup and wardrobe at seven." He turned and walked away without waiting for an answer.

Beth donned a pair of sunglasses and nudged Rachel's arm. "I'm meeting Justin at five for dinner. You're welcome to join us."

"Thanks for the invitation, but I need to rest and talk to Charlie."

"Then breakfast tomorrow. Before you leave, we have to visit the gift shop." She reached for Rachel's hand. "We simply can't say no to a fan."

"A quick visit."

They walked across the piazza and stepped inside the tiny space. The owner welcomed them with a plate of biscotti while smothering them with accolades in a blend of Italian and English. After posing for pictures and signing autographs, Beth shopped.

Not wanting to appear ungrateful or cheap, Rachel purchased a hand-blown glass holder with a vanilla scented candle before bidding their host goodbye. Too tired to find her way through a maze of alleys and bridges, she headed to the nearest water taxi and rode back to the hotel. Eager for an hour alone, she headed straight to her room, kicked off her shoes, and dropped onto the bed. Visions of Willow Falls floated in her head until she drifted into oblivion.

A ringtone startled Rachel awake. She grabbed her phone. Her agent. "Thanks for returning my call, Brenda." She relayed the Priscilla-initiated publicity disaster.

"Don't you worry one little bit. We'll go on the offensive and make that woman sorry she ever messed with you."

Rachel sat up and swung her feet over the side of the bed. "As long as we don't create an even bigger problem."

"I'll let you know when I've countered her move."

"Thanks, I knew I could count on you."

Moments after Rachel ended the call, Charlie's ringtone sounded. She pressed Face Time. "Hey, handsome."

"Hey, gorgeous. How's everything going?"

"Filming's coming along okay. What's all that noise? Where are you?"

"Across the road from the winery, watching a mystery unfold. Here, I'll show you." He turned his phone away from his face. "Do you see all those people by the bulldozer?"

Rachel moved the phone closer. "Mitch. Your dad. Who are the other guys?"

"GBI personnel."

"What in the heck are they doing?"

Charlie turned the phone back toward him. "Counting body parts. Looks like Willow Falls' future golf course is a crime scene. The forensic pathologist plans to take the remains to Atlanta to identify the victims."

"Are you kidding me? Where's Emily?"

"Taking pictures and making notes for *Willow Post*'s newest section. The crime beat."

Rachel walked to the window and watched people on the sidewalk below. Some rushing. Others strolling or shopping at kiosks. "When word gets out, curiosity seekers will flock to town."

"One thing I've learned about Willow Falls' residents, they'll find a way to make hay out of the latest fiasco. Maybe I should put up a new sign. *Stop here for a taste of wine and the latest scoop about North Georgia's mysterious mayhem.* Or set up a road-side wine stand and make a killing."

Rachel laughed. "Good one, honey."

As Charlie revealed more details about the unfolding event, Rachel waffled over revealing the publicity photo. Wouldn't a snippet of Hollywood gossip pale in comparison to the discovery of dead bodies? Besides she couldn't keep Charlie in the dark and risk him finding out from someone else.

"... earth to Rachel."

"Sorry." Her eyes drifted to a couple standing close to the water, kissing. She turned away from the window and glanced at the clock on the bedside table. "Oh my gosh, it's five past seven. I'm late for makeup and wardrobe."

"You'd better get going"

"Hugs and kisses."

"I love you, gorgeous."

"Back at you, handsome."

Rachel set her phone on the nightstand and stared at the photo of her and Charlie. She'd tell him about the publicity tomorrow.

Chapter 15

Emily sat on a tree stump at the dig site and mentally sifted through details she had gleaned prior to writing her first novel about Willow Falls' early days. Nothing about locals mysteriously missing. Were the remains strangers dumped by an outsider? A shiver skittered up her spine as she stared at the skull half buried in the clay. How long had it lain hidden in the dirt? Months? Years? Decades? Maybe a resident with a dark secret buried the bodies. After all no one knew about Robert Liles' penchant for violent behavior before Sadie admitted why she pulled the trigger and shot him dead.

Mary picked a twig off the ground. "Feels like we're actors in a gruesome movie scene."

"If we discover our town is harboring a killer—"

"Are you suggesting a local is capable of murder?"

Emily scrolled through the photos she'd shot. "I'm saying anything's possible."

"We don't even know if the bulldozer unearthed a crime." Mary snapped the twig in half and let the pieces fall to the ground. "Or like Bulldozer Hank suggested, relatives buried by some dirt-poor farmer."

"That doesn't make sense. I mean who wouldn't take time to build a simple wooden box?"

"Someone who had little respect for the dead. At least that explanation is preferable to someone we know committing a horrendous crime."

"Whatever happened, it will provide new gossip for the locals." Emily's attention turned to Sheriff Mitch and Brick rushing past the bulldozer toward a television news truck pulling onto the shoulder. "Didn't take long for word to spread."

"Looks like we need to put our reporter hats back on."

"Big time." Emily fell in step behind the men. When they arrived at the scene, a member of the news crew hoisted a camera on his shoulder and aimed it toward Mitch. A reporter held his microphone close. "What can you tell us about the discovery, Sheriff?" The man thrust the mike in Mitch's face.

"During the process of clearing land to build a golf course and convention center, a heavy equipment operator uncovered human remains."

"How many bodies?"

"We don't have any more details."

"More than one?"

"My answer hasn't changed." Mitch moved away from the microphone and motioned residents to back away.

The reporter approached Brick. "Who are you, sir?"

"Reginald Bricker, Willow Falls' mayor."

"What can you tell us?"

"As you can see, we've cordoned the area for further investigation. GBI will transfer the remains to Atlanta for identification."

"Why not do it here?"

"We don't have a forensic pathologist."

"Then you're confirming the discovery is a crime scene."

"I'm not confirming anything. If you'll excuse me..." Brick ducked under the yellow crime-scene tape and headed back to the bulldozer.

The reporter approached Emily. "Are you with the sheriff's department?"

"The local paper."

"What can you tell us, ma'am?"

"Sorry. Nothing more than our sheriff and mayor already stated."

The reporter sighed heavily, then turned toward the camera. "Skeletal remains unearthed in a wooded area outside Willow Falls hint at the discovery of a horrific crime scene..."

As he speculated a list of possibilities, Emily shook her head. "Rumors will spread faster than a wildfire in a field of dried brush."

Mary nodded toward Mitch. "For now our sheriff is keeping those people away from the reporters."

"Next time they roll into town, if there is a next time, they'll interview everyone willing to talk. Until then, we have a story to write."

A black sedan pulled onto the winery driveway. A man wearing a suit stepped out, dashed across the road, and headed straight to the television reporter. "Who's in charge here?"

The television reporter thrust his thumb over his shoulder. "The local sheriff. You with the press?"

"*Atlanta Journal and Constitution.*"

"You won't get much out of him or the mayor. The redhead is a local reporter."

"Thanks." The man approached Emily. "My brother-in-law, Hank, is the heavy equipment operator who found the remains."

"If you're looking for a story, there isn't much to tell."

"When details surface, I'd appreciate a heads-up." He removed a business card from his jacket pocket and handed it to her. "Okay if we stay in touch?"

She read the card. "Clark Weston."

"At your service. Do you mind if I walk down and take pictures?"

"It's an active crime scene, so our sheriff isn't allowing access to anyone."

"I understand. How can I reach you?" He added her number to his contacts. "I'll be in touch." He loosened his tie and snapped photos beyond the crime scene tape before returning to his car.

After the news crew packed up, Emily tuned into the conversations around her.

"Is it true there's dead bodies down there?"

"If you ask me, Buster Bishop lost his mind and went on a killing spree after his wife died and his daughter up and left him."

"Are you nuts? True, everyone knew he was a miserable old coot. But, capable of murder? No way."

"Hey, Emily. You got a first-hand look. Tell us what you think's going on."

She shrugged. "All I know is a couple of skeletons—"

"What do you mean by a couple?"

"Two. Anyway, someone buried them who-knows-how long ago. Maybe centuries before Willow Falls ever existed."

"Not likely." The town's retired biology teacher stepped up. "Bones decay like flesh but slower."

A woman cradling a small dog nodded. "Seems impossible anyone's gonna figure out who they are."

The man standing beside her swatted at a fly. "If you ever watched any of those NCIS shows, you'd know there's techniques to identify anyone."

"This isn't television."

"You're right. It's way better."

As a debate about the accuracy of TV programs accelerated and the news truck drove off, Emily pulled Mary aside. "Are you ready to go back to the office?"

"More than ready."

"Do you mind if we stop by the store first? I want to bring Scott up to speed."

"Perfect timing. Nathan needs me at our store for a couple of hours."

"In that case, let's call it a day and work on the paper tomorrow."

"Great idea."

After climbing back into the car, Emily pulled a U-turn and headed toward Willow Falls. "It won't take long for everyone in town to concoct some kind of bizarre theory."

"Maybe one of those theories will pan out and give you material for another book."

"I'm counting on it." When Emily slowed and turned onto Main Street, she spotted Kat Williams walking up Sadie's and Brick's front walk. "Our hotel manager is paying Mama Sadie and Brick a visit. Hopefully it's social and not a Redding Arms' issue. We have enough drama to deal with without adding tourist troubles."

Memories surfaced of Brick purchasing the house two years earlier and moving up from Atlanta, early in his relationship with Mama Sadie. Now they were both respected members of the tight-knit community. While driving past the Victorian-style home painted pale teal with white trim, she made a mental note to call Mama Sadie and find out if everything was okay.

Chapter 16

S adie swung her front door open and embraced her ex-con friend. "Glory be, is this a social visit or are you looking for a scoop about the dead bodies?"

Kat's eyes widened. "What dead bodies?"

"How haven't you heard?"

"I've been dealing with a disgruntled guest for the past hour. What's going on?"

Sadie relayed the discovery while escorting Kat to the den. They sat on the sofa facing the slate fireplace, sandwiched between two matching sofas completing the U around a square coffee table.

Kat ran her fingers through her tight black curls. "Talk about trial by fire for our new mayor. I hope Brick isn't superstitious about dead bodies."

"Black cats and walking under ladders, yes. Skeletons, no. Is this a social or official visit?"

"Missy called a few minutes ago. She wants to talk to us."

"Is there a problem at the inn?"

"All I know is she sounded upset."

Sadie popped up. "Whatever's going on calls for cookies and lemonade."

"You're the consummate southern lady, Sadie Bricker."

"Born and bred in Georgia, honey child."

Kat followed her to the kitchen and sat on a stool at the island. "Training Missy to share your innkeeping duties serves you both well."

"She took to the job like a squirrel to an oak tree. The guests love her as much as everyone else in town does." Sadie removed a pitcher of lemonade from the fridge, filled three glasses, and set them on a tray.

"Missy's a different woman than she was the first day she showed up in prison."

"Thanks to you unofficially adopting her." Sadie removed the lid from a cookie jar, releasing chocolate and brown sugar scents.

"She landed in jail too naïve and scared to survive unscathed without protection." Kat rapped her knuckles on the island. "Calling prisons the department of correction facilities is ironic. It's a miracle anyone survives without going mad or turning into lifetime criminals."

"It takes a lot of prayer and a keen sense of awareness of everything going on." After arranging cookies on a platter, Sadie swept her arm in a wide arc. "Some mornings I wake up and for a split second think I'm dreaming. Then I see my Prince Charming lying beside me. and I know despite all those years I lived behind bars, God has blessed me beyond anything I ever imagined possible."

"You're an amazing woman." Kat reached across the counter and touched Sadie's hand. "And your Prince Charming is one lucky guy."

"I discovered fairy-tale endings are possible for people like me." The doorbell chimed. "We're fixing to find out what's going on with your unofficially adopted daughter." Sadie pushed the tray to Kat. "Take the cookies and lemonade to the den while I let her in." She rushed to the front door and found Missy with her blonde hair pulled into a ponytail, facing the street.

She turned. Her blue eyes were rimmed with red. "Is Kat here?"

"She's in the den, honey."

Kat greeted Missy with an embrace. "Looks like you're having a tough day. Did a guest give you a hard time?"

She shook her head.

Memories of Missy's transformation from a timid girl to a confident young woman played in Sadie's mind as she watched her pull away from Kat and drop onto the sofa.

Kat sat beside her.

Missy sniffled, her shoulders slumped. "After growing up in foster homes and getting arrested ... I didn't think I'd ever amount to anything. You and Ms. Sadie made me feel loved. Then we moved here and I met Dennis."

Kat held Missy's hand. "And now an entire town adores you."

"Everyone expects us to have a big wedding like Rachel's and Charlie's." She glanced at Sadie. "And yours and Brick's. We talked about getting married in the park where we met. Except ... everything's changed." Missy's eyes cast downward.

Sadie sat on the sofa facing the back window. Had the town's darlings broken up?

"I wore a big hat and sunglasses so no one would recognize me when I bought this." Missy withdrew a blue and white pen-like object from her jeans pocket. "It's positive." Missy's voice faltered.

Sadie drew in a deep breath as she stared at the pregnancy test. Her mind spun back thirty-four years to the day a friend drove her to another town for her own stealth purchase.

Kat wrapped her arm around Missy's shoulders. "How did Dennis respond?"

Missy bit her lower lip.

"You haven't told him, have you?"

She shook her head. "What will everyone think when they find out?"

"We're living in the twenty-first century, honey. People don't judge like they used to."

"They do in Willow Falls." Tears spilled down Missy's cheeks. "I don't know what to do."

"The decision isn't yours alone to make. You need to talk to Dennis."

"Kat's right." Sadie handed Missy a tissue box.

She dabbed her cheeks and blew her nose. "Is it okay if I invite him over here?"

"Of course."

Missy pulled her phone from her pocket and plodded out of the room.

Sadie sighed. "I didn't see that coming."

"We shouldn't be surprised. They're young and madly in love." Kat reached for a glass of lemonade. "What are the chances her disguise worked?"

"Three years ago I'd have said zero. Today, with all the tourists, maybe fifty-fifty." Sadie released a long sigh. "Old bones and new life all in the same day."

"Funny how things work out."

Missy returned. "Dennis is on his way over."

Kat stood. "You two need some private time. Text me when you've made a decision." She motioned Sadie to follow her to the back patio. "You know, residents put those two on a giant pedestal." She pulled out a chair and set her phone on the glass-top patio table. "It's not easy living up to unrealistic expectations."

"Maybe I should remind her why I spent thirty years in prison."

"She knows. Besides, it's their decision not ours."

Sadie set her phone beside Kat's and sat across the table from her. "Missy's right to worry about the town's reaction."

"Not everyone will judge."

"Some will."

"I suggest we change the subject."

"What do you want to talk about?"

"I don't know. Recipes? The *Joanie's Trial* premiere?" Kat snapped her fingers. "How about your grandbabies?"

"You mean the most adorable little twins in Georgia?" Sadie tapped her phone and pushed it across the table. "The latest pictures."

Kat laughed. "Typical grandmother."

"Wait 'til Missy has her baby. Unless … what if they can't cope with the small-town gossip. They might move away. Or worse."

"We have to trust they'll make the right decision."

"Right for who?" Tension tightened Sadie's neck as the minutes ticked by. A half hour turned into an hour. "What's taking them so long?"

"They have a lot to talk about."

"That's what scares me." Sadie eyed two squirrels playing tag on a low-hanging limb. "This is akin to waiting for a jury to return a verdict."

Twenty more minutes passed.

Kat's phone pinged a text. "They want to talk to us."

They returned to the den and found Missy sitting between Dennis and Naomi Jasper.

He held Missy's hand. "You three ladies are family, which is why we wanted you to understand what we've decided to do." He paused. "Willow Falls made it possible for both of us to leave our pasts behind and start fresh. At the same time, we understand the downside of living in a small town where there are no secrets."

"We considered starting over in another town." Missy fiddled with her earring. "Except we both love our jobs and our roles in the town's play."

Dennis nodded. "Plus people who live here came into our lives when we most needed them. Like Rachel, who found me begging on an Atlanta street and believed in me enough to invite me to spend July Fourth in Willow Falls. And Kat, you crossed racial barriers to take Missy under your wing and treat her like your daughter."

"The best decision I ever made."

"Missy and I talked a long time about what's best for us. For our future. Which is why before we invited y'all in, I drove home so I could do this properly."

Sadie's pulse pounded. What did he mean?

Dennis removed a small box from his pocket. He touched Missy's cheek. "The day I first met you in the park, I knew we both struggled with painful pasts. Maybe that's why we were attracted to each other. At first. Until we fell in love. I only have two family possessions. My dad's pocket knife—" He slid off the sofa, dropped to one knee, and opened the box. "And my grandmother's engagement ring. The day before she passed, she asked if I would one day give it to the woman who captured my heart. You are that woman, Missy. I want to live the rest of my life beside you, making you happy, and experiencing all the joys and challenges a family brings. Will you do me the honor of becoming my wife so together we can raise our child?"

"Yes. A thousand times yes."

Naomi's face beamed. "Do you know what this means, Kat?"

"That two women who never had children are months away from becoming honest-to-goodness grandmothers?"

"Exactly, which I call one glorious miracle."

Sadie pressed her palms together. "Before you two start buying baby clothes, we need to get these two married."

Dennis lifted off his knee. "We want a private ceremony with a few close friends."

"How about right here? This room is big enough."

Naomi scooted to the edge of the sofa. "Great idea, Sadie."

Missy's eyes widened. "What about Mr. Brick? Him being the new mayor and all?"

"He's a romantic at heart, honey. Besides, he already won the election, and I don't think the town would cotton to the idea of firing him."

"Well now." Kat grinned. "What do you say we begin planning this wedding?"

Sadie popped up and removed a pad of paper and a pen from a cabinet. "Starting with the guest list."

Chapter 17

The ancient wood floor in Hayes General Store creaked as Emily strolled past barrels, cabinets, and wooden shelves displaying old-fashion tools, housewares, and country-style accessories. The hundred-plus-year-old tin ceiling and exposed brick walls conjured mental images of days long past. She imagined ladies wearing fancy hats and dresses with long skirts, carrying parasols to protect their skin from the sun.

An elderly couple snuggled on the player piano bench in the corner by the window and hummed along to "I'll be Seeing You" while two older gentlemen hunched over a barrel table engrossed in a serious game of chess.

Emily stopped beside the stairs leading to the second-floor arts and craft consignment shop. Half the size of the main level, the space overflowed with an eclectic array of items created by residents eager to cash in on the tourist trade.

Scott appeared on the stairs, wearing a black frock coat to exemplify the store's history. He tucked a framed photo under his arm while escorting a customer down the stairs. "The photographer is our local dentist."

The woman smiled. "There were so many delightful items to choose from. Willow Falls is populated with talented folks."

"Yes, ma'am. Would you like to learn more about our little town?"

"Indeed, I would."

"May I suggest you visit the Book Nook and buy copies of *Percy's Legacy* and *Saving Willow Falls.*" Scott winked at Emily as he reached the bottom step. "They're novels about the town's history and its struggle to survive. Both written by a talented local author."

"Great idea. Thanks for the suggestion."

Emily settled on a stool at the soda fountain while Scott led the customer to the sales associate manning the cash register.

He moseyed over and sat beside her. "Any more bodies uncovered?"

"Not yet." She tilted her head. "I know you keep copies of my books under the counter."

"Uh huh."

"So, you're paying it forward?"

"More like paying back. The sweet young lady managing the Book Nook for Patsy sent three tourists here yesterday. They all bought stuff." He leaned close. "Besides, my customer paid top dollar for the photo. Which means I can afford to treat you to a milkshake, on the house."

"Hmm. I do have a couple of hours before I pick our girls up from nursery school."

The customer completed her purchase and tapped Scott's shoulder. "Thanks again for the book suggestion."

Emily swiveled and faced the woman. "If you bring them back within the hour, I'll sign them for you."

Her brows raised. "You're the author?"

"I am." She extended her hand. "Emily Hayes."

"Pleasure to meet you. I'm Bonnie Jones." Her eyes drifted to Scott's name badge. "You two are a couple, aren't you?"

"Have been as long as I can remember."

"I love when a husband supports his wife. I'll return in a jiffy with copies." She headed straight to the door.

"Looks like you have a new fan, honey." Emily patted Scott's cheek, then swiveled back toward the counter.

"You're the celebrity around here, not me." He motioned to his soda-fountain superstar. "How about two small milkshakes, Gertie? One chocolate. One vanilla."

She adjusted the collar on her nineteenth-century dress and leaned over the counter. "Have you seen Justin's newest post?" Her voice barely rose above a whisper.

Scott's brows lifted. "I thought you considered social media a colossal waste of time."

"I liken it to my first taste of wine—the sweet kind anyway—which turned out way better than I expected. You didn't answer my question."

Scott faced Emily. "Have you logged on today?"

She shook her head. "I've been tied up with newspaper duties."

"And I've been busy selling goods."

"You both need large milkshakes with extra whipped cream and two cherries."

"Why?" Scott chuckled. "Did you come across something scandalous?"

"See for yourself." She removed her iPad from beneath the counter, tapped the screen, then turned it toward them.

Emily stared at the caption over the photo of Rachel, Justin, and the brunette. "*Is jealousy brewing over Hollywood's hottest male star?* I can't believe my sister posed for this."

"If you ask me, the picture is fake." Gertie placed empty tall glasses on the counter. "Which is why I commented to let people know what's what."

"You responded?"

"I couldn't let anyone think poorly about your twin. I wrote, 'Rachel's married to Charlie who's more handsome than this overrated movie star. Besides, she gave Justin the boot in Willow Falls, so no way she's jealous.'"

Emily propped her forearms on the counter. "How'd you know about that?"

"Some of the movie-crew guys came in every day for milkshakes. Would you believe those people gossip almost as much as small-town folks?"

Scott laughed. "It seems we need to rebrand this space as Gertie's soda-fountain and news-flash venue."

"You'd be surprised what people tell me. I guess I'm like a bartender. Except my customers leave stone-cold sober." Gertie stashed the iPad under the counter. "Do you suppose Charlie's seen the photo?"

"He didn't mention it when he showed up at Greer's new development."

"I heard something was going on over there." Gertie leaned closer. "Did the crew dig up something like buried treasure? Or bodies?"

"The news is bound to leak out, but you have to promise to keep what I'm about to tell you under wraps until the paper hits the street."

"Cross my heart."

"Okay." Emily top-lined the discovery.

"Glory be." Gertie's eyes widened. "Everyone in town knows Buster Bishop was a loathsome old coot—you know he used to own that land. I wouldn't put it past him to shoot trespassers. His wife and I hung out a lot in high school. Why such a sweet lady married that man is beyond me, except pickings were slim back then. One good thing about old bones, they're more exciting than Hollywood gossip."

"We'll soon find out if you're right." Scott tapped his fingers on the counter. "How about those milkshakes?"

"Coming right up, boss."

Emily opened her phone's app, found Justin's page, and glared at the photo. "Rachel must be furious if she even knows about this. I have to call her." She pressed the number. The call went to voicemail. After Emily left a message, she called Charlie. No answer. "Do you think hometown folks will believe the photo's real?"

"Those who still consider Charlie and Rachel outsiders might."

"I need to get the real scoop." Emily pocketed her phone.

"Investigative reporting?"

"More like truth in journalism."

Gertie returned with the shakes and eyed Emily. "Have you talked to Rachel?"

"Not today."

"When you do, tell her not to worry. I'll keep on setting folks straight."

"I'm sure you will." The bell jangled over the front door.

Bonnie dashed to the counter and removed books from a Book Nook bag.

"Wow." Emily stared at six copies. "You bought three of each."

"Two for me plus gifts for my mom and sister. As far as I know, they never met an author face-to-face either. I've considered writing a book, but I never seem to find the time."

While Emily signed the copies, each with a personalized note, she listened to Bonnie rattle on about ideas for a romance novel between two old college pals. "You know, it's never too late to follow your dreams."

"Maybe one day." She placed the books in the bag. "Thanks for signing. How can I stay in touch?"

"I have all the information." Scott pulled Emily's business card from his pants pocket and handed it to Bonnie.

"Your husband is one of the good guys. Don't let him get away."

"I won't, and thanks again for buying my books."

"You're welcome. I'm on my way to meet my husband at the hotel." She shook her head as she headed toward the door. "That man would rather chew nails than go shopping with me."

Emily grinned, then turned to Scott. "Do you always have my business cards handy?"

He fished a handful from his pocket and set them on the counter. "Today's stash."

"Bonnie's right." She kissed his cheek. "You are a keeper."

Chapter 18

Rachel stood on the sidewalk at the top of steps leading to a gondola boarding site and stared at the water glistening under the overhead klieg lights. She surveyed the space between two narrow canals and giggled.

Justin adjusted the collar on his chest-hugging shirt. "What's got you tickled?"

"Hotel Cavalletto with those gorgeous wrought-iron balconies and red awnings are so Venice. As are most of the other old buildings surrounding us." She pointed to the left. "Then there's Hard Rock Café with its plate-glass front trying to look authentic with those tall columns."

"Proof this is a tourist city."

"When my dad built a new movie theater in Willow Falls, he designed it to match the town's original architecture and vibe."

"You spend a lot of time talking about that town. I spent two months stuck there. Believe me, there isn't that much to say."

"Hey, you're talking about a place I love. Besides, you didn't seem to mind when most of the female population treated you like royalty."

Justin shrugged. "The price of fame."

"Who do you think you're kidding? You loved every minute."

"Except your rejection." He leaned close. "We'd still make a great couple."

"Have you forgotten that I'm married?"

"So's Beth. Doesn't seem to hold her back."

"Sugar, you're a great actor, and as Mama Sadie would say, good looking as all get-out. However, if I was single and you were the last man on earth, I'd turn you down faster than I'd drop a hot burning coal."

He stared at her, then burst out laughing. "Guess I didn't learn my lesson the first time you snubbed me."

"I'm surprised you admit it."

"There's something about you that brings out my honesty." He winked. "Anyway, no one can say I didn't give it my best shot."

"Then it's settled. We're business associates, nothing more?"

"Make that friends, and we have a deal."

"Fair enough."

Robert handed a clipboard to his assistant and moved beside Justin and Rachel. "Are you two ready?"

Justin nodded. "Raring to go."

Robert touched Rachel's arm. "Stepping into a gondola is tricky. We'll try to limit the number of shots."

"Thanks, the last thing I want to do is fall into a canal."

He moved to his director's chair while a production assistant marked a slate and clicked the clapper.

Following five shots from varying angles, Rachel and Justin settled in the gondola for the next scene. An hour later, Robert directed his crew to set the final shots—the gondola approaching a bridge and appearing on the other side. When filming ended the gondolier returned to the steps where extras and onlookers lined up for autographs and selfies. When the crowd dispersed, Rachel massaged her aching neck muscles. "I'm ready to call it a night."

Justin touched her elbow. "Mind if I walk you to our hotel?"

"As my friend, right?"

"That's our deal." He escorted her through a pedestrian alley to St. Mark Square. They moved through the crowds unnoticed as music from two bands entertained late-night diners and tourists. When they arrived at the hotel, Justin nodded toward the lobby. "I'm meeting Beth in the bar. How about joining us for a nightcap?"

"I don't know. It's late and I'm exhausted."

"Not a problem. Our next scene isn't 'til noon tomorrow, so you can sleep late. Besides, you shouldn't reject your friends."

Rachel rolled her eyes. "You're not over it, are you?"

He looped his arm around hers. "I'll get there faster if you accept the invitation."

"You're an interesting man, Justin."

"Is that a yes?"

She sighed. "One drink."

They found Beth chatting with an elderly couple. She motioned them over. "Meet my new pals all the way from North Dakota."

The gentleman stood and extended his hand to Rachel, then Justin. "Pleasure to meet you both. It's way past our bedtime, so my lovely bride and I will leave you three to enjoy the evening." He helped his wife out of her chair and escorted her from the bar.

Beth crossed her leg over her knee. "I love when fans recognize me."

Justin sat on the sofa beside Beth while Rachel opted for an overstuffed chair facing them. After their tuxedoed waiter took drink orders, Beth stared at her. "Decaf coffee?"

"Wine this late will keep me awake."

"Too bad." She turned to Justin. "How'd the shoot go?"

"We attracted some new fans."

"Not as many as we added on social media. Pricilla's publicity photo generated hundreds of comments. One of the most interesting from Willow Falls."

Rachel's body froze. "The picture's out there already?"

"Big time."

Cold sweat erupted on her upper lip. Why hadn't she warned Charlie when she had the chance? "If you two will excuse me, I need to call home."

"What's the big rush?"

Rachel stared at Beth. Didn't she have a clue? Of course, she didn't. "I'll see you on the set tomorrow." She scurried out before Beth or Justin could inundate her with questions. After retrieving her key from the concierge desk, she dashed to the elevator and waited. Charlie didn't pay much attention to social media, so maybe she still had time. Unless someone told him. She tapped her foot. Was the elevator stuck on another floor?

A ping announced its arrival. Rachel's jaw tensed as she waited for three people to exit. By the time she reached her floor and entered her room, her pulse pounded in her ears. She grabbed her phone and checked the time. Six in the morning back home. Hoping Charlie was awake, she pressed his number. The call went to voicemail. "Sorry I missed you, honey. Call me. We need to talk."

She dropped onto the bed and called her twin.

"Hey, sis." Emily's cheery tone seemed out of place.

"Have you seen it?"

"If you're referring to the 'Is She Jealous' photo, yeah, I've seen it."

Rachel released a heavy sigh. "You know the picture isn't real."

"Of course, I do."

"How many people know about it?"

"Other than Scott and Gertie, I have no idea."

Probably half the town. "I tried to reach Charlie ... he didn't answer."

"Last time I saw him, he and Jack were standing guard at the dig site."

"He doesn't go anywhere without his phone."

"I suspect his hands are full. You know what happens around here when something out of the ordinary happens."

"Yeah, everyone goes a little crazy." After listening to Emily's update on the bone discovery, Rachel ended the call and set her phone on the nightstand. Her stomach grumbled, reminding her she'd skipped dinner. After calling room service, she sat by the window. What if Charlie didn't pick up her message? Maybe she should call him again. Best to wait.

She stared out at the dark sky and imagined the chaos unfolding back home. Residents speculating about why someone buried bodies in Willow Falls. She yawned and leaned her head against the back of the chair until Charlie's ringtone sounded. She grabbed her phone. "I hoped you'd call tonight."

"How's everything going?"

"Okay, I guess."

"Same here." He paused. "The town crier showed me the photo earlier today."

"Mirabelle?" Rachel dropped onto the bed.

"Why didn't you tell me about it?"

The hard edge in his voice sent a dull ache spreading through her skull. "You know the photo is fake."

"It looks real enough. How did it happen?"

"Justin's publicist convinced me to tag along for publicity shots."

"Why am I not surprised."

"I'm sorry I didn't tell you earlier."

"Did you think I wouldn't understand?"

"No ... I don't know what I thought."

A knock drew her attention. "Someone's at the door."

"If that crazy woman is looking for another publicity shot, kick her in the shins for me."

"Good idea, unless the local police arrest me for assault and battery."

"Justified self-defense. Besides I'd come over and bail you out."

"In that case, I'll find a reason to land in jail." Rachel opened the door and directed the waiter to set the tray on desk. She dug a tip from her purse, then returned to the chair. "Room service."

"Kind of late for dinner."

"Late-night shoot." She fixed her eyes on the dark sky and caught sight of a shooting star. "On a gondola. With Justin."

"More publicity footage?"

"No way." She paused. "If you fly over for our anniversary, we'd create our own sizzling publicity."

"Nice try, but the investigation going on across from the winery makes it even more impossible for me to get away."

Why was he being so stubborn?

"And I have to defend your reputation if any more crazy pictures of you and Justin show up on social media."

"I won't let that happen." Same promise she'd made before, so why would Charlie believe her. "Justin's publicist deserved far more than a kick in the shins." Moments after the call ended, an idea formed and took root. Rachel sat cross-legged on the bed and booted her computer. Forget waiting for her agent to take action. She'd make Priscilla regret ever messing with her.

Chapter 19

Emily propped her feet on the living room coffee table, set her computer on her lap, and scrolled through *Willow Post*'s emails. "Look at all those letters to the editor. Seems half the residents have theories about the town's newest mystery."

Clair climbed onto the couch and stood beside her. "What's a mystery, Mommy?"

"Something we don't understand, sweet girl." She read three emails while shaking her head at the wild assumptions. "No one can claim locals lack imagination."

Jane looked up from her coloring book. "What's 'magnation?"

"It's ideas we think in our heads."

"Do you have lots of 'maginations?"

"Yes, I do. Which is why I write books."

Clair faced the window framing the front yard. "Grandma's here."

"She is?" Emily glanced over her shoulder and spotted Mama Sadie walking up the sidewalk. "Our favorite visitor."

Jane and Clair scurried to open the door. Cody followed, his tail setting his backside in motion.

Sadie knelt and gathered her granddaughters in her arms. "My favorite little girls in the whole wide world."

"Will you read us a story, Grandma?"

"I promise. After I share some news with your mommy." She straightened and held the twins' hands while moving into the living room.

Emily set her laptop on the coffee table. "Let me guess, you have a scoop about the latest discovery."

"Not the one you're thinking about." Sadie sat beside her daughter. "It's about Missy and Dennis." She leaned close and shared the details.

"Wow, that is big news."

"Naomi and Kat are treating them to a honeymoon in Atlanta, at the Peachtree Plaza Hotel."

"I'm surprised Dennis agreed. According to Rachel, that's close to where he hung out as a homeless guy."

"He suggested it. Says he wants to show Missy how far he's come."

"They've both triumphed over a lot of heartache. I'm happy they found each other."

"They're two beautiful butterflies who emerged from suffocating cocoons."

"Great analogy. Who knew you had a poetic streak?"

"I have my moments. Anyway, they want you to interview them and publish their story while they're on their honeymoon."

"To give the town time to absorb the news." Emily plucked a crayon off the floor and set it on the coffee table. "Only one problem. How will they keep their wedding from leaking?"

"We're limiting the guest list to a select few who know how to keep a secret."

"Worked last year for your surprise-birthday party. I suppose there's a chance it will work again."

"We're counting on it. There's one unresolved issue. Do you think Rachel would mind lending Missy her wedding gown?"

"She'd be honored."

"Will you ask her?"

"I'll call her tomorrow after I interview Missy and Dennis."

Sadie patted her knee. "Thank you, honey."

Cody scampered from the room at the sound of the backdoor closing and footsteps striking the kitchen floor.

"Either Scott's home early or a neighbor's wandered into the wrong house."

"Daddy." Jane skipped to the foyer. Clair followed.

"There's my girls." He scooped them into his arms and nuzzled their necks.

"Grandma's here." Jane wriggled out of his arms. "They gonna have a wedding."

"They are?" He set Clair beside her sister and dropped onto the overstuffed chair facing the couch. "Who's getting married?"

"I'll give you the news later."

"Speaking of news, have either of you seen the latest Rachel-Justin drama?"

Emily scooted to the edge of the couch. "What are you talking about?"

"Check out Justin's social media page."

"Are you becoming a social media junkie, honey?"

"Not me. Gertie."

Emily found Justin's page, scrolled to Rachel's post, and stared at a picture of her twin nose to nose with Charlie, her fingers clasped behind his neck. "I remember taking this during their wedding reception."

"Read what she wrote."

"'Me jealous? In your dreams, Justin. The only man who sends tingles racing through my limbs is a handsome, small-town guy named Charlie. Every other man on the planet pales in comparison.'"

Scott propped his ankle on his knee. "Wait till you see Rachel's page."

Emily pulled up her sister's post—five shots of her and Charlie. "She says, 'these photos of the man who captured my heart are real, unlike the fake picture Justin Brook's over-zealous publicist posted. Don't believe everything you read on social media.'"

Sadie nudged Emily. "At least your sister's taking action."

"So's Gertie." Scott pointed to Emily's laptop. "Read her response."

Emily scrolled down. "Gertie says, 'Rachel is a nice, southern lady who loves Charlie. She didn't want to kiss Justin in that movie scene but had to because the director made her.'"

Sadie laughed. "Your soda-fountain star is full of spunk. If the locals follow her lead, they'll rally around Rachel and Charlie like mother bears protecting their cubs."

Clair picked a book from the corner basket and climbed onto the couch. "Can you read us a story now, Grandma?"

Sadie ruffled her hair. "Maybe even two."

Emily closed her laptop and motioned Scott to follow her to the kitchen. "I don't like the word battle Rachel unleashed."

"What's wrong with setting the record straight?"

"I know my sister. She acted out of anger. Sometimes it's best to let things die down on their own."

"You sang a different tune last year when our teenage-wannabe FBI agent circulated risqué pictures of Carrie Fleming."

"That was different." Emily set her laptop on the counter. "I understand about getting caught up in publicity, but you remember how Rachel's love scene with Justin in the park upset Charlie. And now she's thousands of miles away with the same skirt-chasing, ego-driven guy."

"Charlie understands."

"Does he? I mean how would you react if it was me instead of Rachel?"

"I'd trust you and ignore everything online. Although I'm glad you're an author and not an actress."

"See what I mean? You would mind."

"Rachel's and Charlie's marriage is strong enough to survive social-media nonsense." Scott wrapped his arms around her waist and pulled her close. "Same as ours."

Emily nuzzled his cheek with her nose. "Thank you for reminding me, honey."

"Any time. Now about that wedding."

Chapter 20

The hotel phone startled Rachel from a deep sleep. She switched on the bedside lamp and squinted until the clock came into focus. Six A.M. Fighting the urge to squeeze her eyes shut and bury her head under a pillow, she grabbed the receiver. "Hello?" Had she swallowed a frog?

"Sorry to wake you, Ms. Streetman."

Peter, Robert's assistant. Why was he calling at the crack of dawn? A script change? "What's going on?"

"Mr. Nordstrom wants you, Justin, and Beth to meet him in his suite in forty-five minutes."

She bolted upright "Why? I mean, yeah ... okay."

"He'll have breakfast available." He ended the call.

Rachel trudged to the bathroom and caught her image in the mirror. Dark shadows under her eyes confirmed she needed more sleep. She stepped into the shower, counting on hot water to ease her tense muscles and clear her mind.

Forty minutes later, with damp curls cascading over her shoulders, she knocked on the director's door.

Peter answered. "Come on in and fix yourself a plate."

She walked into the elegantly appointed salon and spotted Justin and Robert standing by the window, deep in conversation. Beth carried a coffee cup and a plate from the room-service cart to a sofa placed at the edge of an elaborate oriental rug. She set her cup on the coffee table and bit into a croissant.

Rachel poured a glass of orange juice and joined her. "Any idea what's going on?"

"Not a clue." Beth leaned close. "Except I need four more hours of sleep."

"Late night?"

"Plus one too many cocktails. Did you eat or aren't you hungry?"

"Queasy stomach."

Beth wiped her fingers with a napkin. "My nanny's bringing the kids over this week."

"I'm looking forward to meeting them."

"My thirteen-year-old has a serious crush on Justin. Who can blame her?"

Like her mother. Rachel sipped her juice to avoid responding.

"I promised we'd have dinner with him one night." She nudged Rachel and nodded toward Robert and Justin. "I think we're about to find out why our director interrupted our beauty sleep."

The men approached and settled in armchairs that completed the seating arrangement. Robert, wearing sweats and sneakers, propped his elbows on his knees and laced his fingers. "I don't know who started it, but your social-media feud is drawing a lot of attention."

A knot formed in Rachel's belly.

"Good news is the publicity works in the film's favor." Robert stared at Rachel. "Especially since we're adding an intimate bedroom scene with you and Justin."

What? How could she survive a bedroom scene when she'd barely tolerated the gondola kiss? "The movie is a romantic comedy."

"The scene will add dimension to the love story."

Should she protest? Like she had any clout. How would Charlie react?

Robert unlaced his fingers and leaned back. "About the social-media attention. A magazine reporter is arriving this afternoon to do a story about you three."

Justin crossed his ankle over his knee, revealing a loafer and no sock. "What kind of story?"

"The effect of publicity on your personal lives. Your relationships with each other. Progress on the movie."

Rachel's jaw tensed. No way she'd stay quiet. "I understand the interest, but the last time I posed for publicity shots, I ended up in a bogus photo. How can we guarantee the same thing won't happen again?"

"In this business there are no guarantees. However, this reporter is reputable and the magazine is known for some level of accuracy. In the end, a lot depends on what you tell her."

Beth pressed her palms together. "Interviews are such fun."

"Keep that enthusiasm fired up. I've arranged a six o'clock dinner in my suite to give you and the reporter privacy. To accommodate her schedule, I changed the St. Mark's Square scene to ten this morning." Robert grabbed a ballcap off the coffee table and eyed Rachel. "Do I need to have breakfast delivered to your room?"

Makeup obviously hadn't hidden her dark circles. "Dry toast and ginger tea."

"Done. I need you and Justin on set at nine-thirty."

"We'll be there." Justin winked at Rachel.

She rolled her eyes. The man was incorrigible.

Hours later Robert called a wrap and dismissed the crew. An afternoon breeze ushered in cool air as Rachel melted into the crowds gathered to watch the shoot. She avoided eye contact and made a beeline to the hotel. Emily's ringtone sounded as she escaped into her room. "Hey, sis."

"You sound out of breath."

"Mad dash from the film site. Have you to talked to Charlie?"

"Not since yesterday."

Rachel exhaled, plopped onto the bed, and kicked off her shoes.

"Want to hear the latest scoop?"

"Another body?"

"In a sense." Emily shared the news about Missy and Dennis.

"When they're on stage playing Peaches and Percy, their passion is so palpable the entire audience reacts."

"Speaking of the play, when Missy starts showing, she'll need new costumes."

"And at some point, a well-rehearsed understudy. When's the wedding?"

"Sunday."

Rachel slumped against the headboard as memories swirled. The first time she spotted Dennis begging on the street with his dog. Convincing him and Missy to take roles in *Percy's Legacy*. Directing them to evolve from acting novices to star performers. And now she'd miss the most important day of their lives. How many special occasions would her career steal from her?

"... gown—"

Emily's voice jolted her back to the present. "I'm sorry, what'd you say?"

"Missy won't have time to buy a wedding gown."

"You know they both hold a special place in my heart. Missy's welcome to wear mine."

"I knew you'd offer. By the way they're scheduling the wedding so you can join in remotely."

"With Beth as my plus-one. Who's giving Missy away?"

"They're still working out the details—"

Rachel's phone pinged an incoming call. "Charlie's calling."

"Call me when you have a chance. Love you."

"Love you, too."

Rachel pressed Face Time. "Hey, honey."

"Hi, gorgeous." A muffled bark sounded. "Our four-legged child wants to say hello." He aimed the phone at their golden retriever.

"Hey, Brownie. Are you being good for Charlie, or are you too busy chasing squirrels?" She giggled at the sight of their dog's cocked head and twitching nostrils sniffing the phone.

Charlie's face appeared again. "Have you heard about Missy and Dennis?"

"Emily filled me in. Missy's borrowing my wedding gown. I hope you don't mind."

"Makes sense."

"You're a good man."

"What happened to handsome and sexy?"

"Don't forget easygoing and fun."

"Speaking of fun, what's happening with the movie?"

She had to tell him everything. "Robert added a bedroom scene, and he arranged for a magazine reporter to interview me, Justin, and Beth."

Silence.

"Please say something, Charlie."

"Seems movies require at least one token bedroom scene. And the interview thing ... we'll deal with whatever comes of it."

"Thank you for understanding."

"I'm an understanding kind of guy."

"I promise never again to keep anything from you, honey."

Ten minutes after arriving in the director's suite for the scheduled interview, Rachel regretted not begging off. Although the reporter asked relevant questions and didn't favor one over the other, Beth's interruptions and unabashed self-promotion charged the atmosphere with tension. Justin's expression made it clear he also found her behavior overbearing. By the time they finished the working dinner and posed for dozens of photos, Rachel's body ached from exhaustion.

"I have everything I need." The reporter turned off her recorder and dropped it in her bag. "I'll send you each a review copy before publication. Now I need to catch a couple hours of sleep before I head to the airport for an early morning flight back to New York."

The moment she walked out, Beth headed straight to the fully stocked bar. "We deserve an after-dinner drink to celebrate a successful interview."

"You can count me out." Rachel picked her room key off the end table. "I'm heading straight to bed."

"You won't turn me down, will you, Justin?"

He joined Beth at the bar. "Depends on what you're talking about."

Rachel rolled her eyes. Could he be any more obvious? Something about Beth's vulnerability gave her pause. How could she remain neutral and ignore whatever was going on between two consenting adults?

Chapter 21

Emily parked in Sadie's and Brick's driveway and unbuckled the twins' car seats. They climbed out, spotted Brick standing on the porch, and scrambled up the steps straight into his arms. She followed close behind, smiling. "They obviously love their grandpa."

His face beamed as he straightened and patted their heads. "Grandma has fresh-baked cookies, and I have a surprise for my two favorite little girls."

Clair fingered his goatee. "What surprise, Grandpa?"

He tapped her nose. "You'll see."

"I don't know who spoils them more, you or Mama Sadie."

"We're not spoiling them. Well, maybe a little. Missy and Dennis are waiting for you in the living room." He held the twins' hands. "Now, how about we go into the kitchen with Grandma and tackle those cookies."

Emily followed them inside and walked into the tastefully furnished living room—more twentieth-century antique than Victorian. The scent of vanilla wafted from a candle burning in a cut-glass holder. "Hey, you two lovebirds."

Dennis rose. "Thanks for meeting us here."

"You picked the perfect spot."

He dropped back down beside Missy.

Emily lowered onto a chair diagonal to the couch, slipped her purse off her shoulder, and removed her phone. "Do you mind if I record our conversation? It will help when I write your story."

"I don't." He slipped his arm around Missy's waist. "What about you, Missy?"

"That's okay."

"Good." Emily set the phone to record and laid it on the coffee table. She eyed the original Naomi Jasper oil painting above the fireplace before shifting her focus to the couple. "Why don't you begin by telling me what you'd like the town to know."

"Missy and I plan to be honest, even if some people might think less of us and talk behind our backs."

"We want everyone to understand that our love for each other and the new life God is giving us are what's important." Missy gazed at Dennis. "Which is why we'll raise our baby here, in a town with a big heart surrounded by people we care about."

Emily pressed her palm to her chest. "You two are amazing, and I'm proud to call you friends. Now, let's write a story that will touch hearts and melt away any icy reactions. Question number one. What first attracted you to each other?"

For the following hour, the young couple held hands and answered questions with heartfelt honesty and enthusiasm. By the time she finished questioning and snapping photos, Emily had enough material for a short story. "I have no idea how I'll condense everything into one newspaper article."

"Thank you for doing this for us."

"I should thank you. This promises to become the best feature story I've ever written for our humble little paper."

"I hate to disrupt."

Emily turned at the sound of Brick's voice. "We're finished."

"Good, because there's an issue at the dig site you need to cover."

"The bone drama continues." She dropped her phone in her purse. Emily stood. "Do you two want to read the article before it's published?"

Dennis locked eyes with Missy. "What do you think?"

"We can trust Emily."

"Then the answer's no."

"I promise to make you both proud." Emily slung her purse and camera over her shoulder and followed Brick out to the porch. "Time to switch gears from feature writer to hard-news reporter." She drove behind his car, tapping her fingers on the steering wheel and humming to a country-pop tune.

All seemed right with the world as she navigated the crazy hairpin turns on County Road. Until they drove around the curve leading to the straight section of pavement. "What the heck?" She stared at dozens of cars, pickups, and SUV's parked along both sides of the road. On the right beyond the caravan, multiple pop-up canopy tents created a blue and white sea of canvas rippling in the breeze.

She slowed to a crawl. Between vehicles Emily glimpsed dozens of residents, some standing in small groups, others sitting in chairs under the canopies as if they'd gathered for an outdoor concert. As she inched forward, she spotted a black SUV and paneled van, both marked with GBI identification. Parked yards off the road, they blocked the path leading to the bulldozer.

Emily followed Brick onto the winery driveway across from the vehicles. He parked behind the sheriff's car. She grabbed her camera and climbed out. "Looks like half the town has set up camp."

"I don't know what everyone expects to see. The dig site is blocked by the bulldozer."

Across the street a long table draped with a red and white checkered cloth displayed a *Support Willow Falls High Booster Club* sign, stretched in front of the first canopy. Pitchers and cups covered the top. Teenagers stood behind with an open cash box.

"Are those kids skipping school?"

Emily shook her head. "Teacher's workday. At least a lemonade stand is creative."

Mitch ducked under the crime-scene tape and headed their way. "This is turning into a three-ring circus."

Brick pointed his thumb toward the crowd "Are you gonna shut it down?"

"Not as long people behave and don't try to interfere with the investigation."

Emily snapped a photo of the GBI vehicles before aiming her camera at the canopies. "Based on the number of people who showed up, I'm guessing you have new information?"

"Not even a nugget."

Brick's brow furrowed. "Then why'd they set up a tent city?"

Mitch removed his cap and ran his fingers through his hair. "You've lived here long enough to know a potential crime is too big a deal to ignore."

"Don't those people have jobs?"

Emily chuckled. "You still have a lot to learn about Willow Falls, Mr. Mayor."

Mirabelle dashed to Emily and pulled her aside. "Have you seen the latest?"

"Is today another mail-delivery holiday?"

She dismissed the comment with a hand flick and held up her phone.

Emily stared at a new social-media post of Justin and Rachel on a gondola, kissing. Her jaw clenched as she read the caption. *She says Charlie's her guy. Then why is she on a romantic boat ride with Hollywood's hottest star?* "That's obviously a movie scene."

"Maybe. On the other hand, Justin is handsome as all get-out."

"Knock it off, Mirabelle. You know my sister is crazy in love with her husband."

Brick wandered over. "What's going on, ladies?"

"Your son's not going to like this one little bit." Mirabelle showed him the post.

"Charlie's smart enough to know someone used a movie scene for a stinking publicity stunt."

"Don't you think I know what's going on?" Mirabelle huffed. "Problem is some people around here like to gossip too much to believe that story."

Brick crossed his arms. "I think someone important, like a city council member, should set everyone straight."

"Which is exactly what I intend to do." Mirabelle spun around.

"Well, I'll be." Emily shot a photo of the towns' mail carrier hustling toward the canopies. "Do you suppose serving on your city council has converted our number-one gossip into a purveyor of truth?"

"I have no idea. What I do know is we need someone to take those photos down."

"There's a better chance some teenager will discover a cure for the common cold than anyone will make those pictures disappear."

Brick shook his head. "What is wrong with those Hollywood characters?"

Her sister had definitely set off a publicity firestorm. "Unfortunately, sensationalism sells."

"Rachel and Charlie don't deserve to be embroiled in some Hollywood scandal."

"No kidding."

Mitch's shoulder radio squawked, sending him ducking back under the tape. A hush fell over the crowd as heads turned and fingers pointed to their sheriff racing toward the bulldozer.

Emily and Brick moved to the edge of the cordoned-off area. She zoomed her camera lens on Mitch and two GBI investigators huddled in conversation. Mitch followed the men into the woods and disappeared behind the bulldozer.

"Seems they've discovered something important."

"More details for this week's paper." Her imagination ran wild with speculation. Had they found clues to identify the bones? Or more bodies? Or maybe some sort of murder weapon? "Whatever's going on, there's a fifty-fifty chance it's not good news."

Chapter 22

Rachel gripped her phone in one hand and pounded her fist on Justin's hotel room door with the other.

He pulled it open, his hair wet, a towel wrapped around his waist. "This is a nice surprise. Come on in."

"Not until you put some clothes on."

"Don't go away." He left the door ajar.

Heat spread from Rachel's neck to her cheeks as she nodded at a guest passing in the hall, staring. She tapped her foot. Had they seen Justin? Should she walk away? No, she had to face this head on now.

Justin returned, bare-chested and shoeless, wearing low-cut designer jeans. "To what do I owe this visit?" He pulled the door open and stepped aside.

"This isn't a social call. It's war."

"Uh-oh, you saw the photo."

"What gave you a clue?" She snarled and stormed past him. "Leave the door open."

"You sure?"

She spun and jabbed her finger on his chest. "What are you trying to prove?"

"Not my doing." He held up his hands and stepped back. "Priscilla posted it."

"If you think I'm buying one smidgen of that hogwash—"

"I swear. Look, all I know is she paid a crew member to take pictures."

Was he telling the truth? "What crew member?"

"She didn't say."

"Isn't that convenient. *Your* publicist has an accomplice you can't identify who's determined to make my life miserable."

"I admit the publicity's good for me—"

Rachel opened her mouth to protest.

Justin pressed his index finger to her lips. "I'm not finished. Truth is, I respect you and don't want anything to affect our working relationship."

"Then put a stop to it. Call her."

"I will."

She glared at him. "Now."

"Are you nuts? It's one o'clock in the morning in California."

"I don't care."

"All right, but you'll owe me big time." He picked his phone up off the dresser, punched a number, and pressed the speaker icon.

Priscilla answered after the second ring. "Justin. What's wrong? Are you in trouble?"

"You have to stop this thing with Rachel."

"You woke me in the middle of the night to kid around? Are you drunk?"

"I'm dead serious. No more photos or comments, or you're fired."

"Don't tell me you've lost your competitive spirit. Oh wait. She got to you, didn't she? That little—"

"Careful, Priscilla, Rachel's standing right here."

"All right, Justin, but I want to continue publicizing your fling with Beth."

"Drop that, too. I'll let you know when I need you again."

"You're a fool to think you can ditch publicity without flushing your career down the toilet. Now if you don't mind—" Priscilla's tone oozed with anger. "I want to *try* to go back to sleep." She ended the call.

Rachel uncrossed her arms. "Thank you, Justin."

"Now about a proper thank you—"

"Don't you ever learn?" She crossed her arms tight across her chest.

"What is it with you?" He grabbed a tee shirt off a chair and pulled it over his head. "A thank-you dinner, nothing more. Tonight at six. Strictly as friends." He traced an X on his chest. "Cross my heart."

Should she trust him? What if people saw them together, or snapped a picture and posted it on social media? Was this what fame did to people? Made them fearful and turned them into recluses? She and Justin had as much right as anyone to enjoy dinner in public, as friends. "What about Beth?"

He shrugged. "She's meeting her kids at the airport."

Rachel stared at him. He did make a bold move on her behalf. "All right. But someplace where people won't bother us."

"We have a date."

"No, Justin, we have a business dinner." She walked out, hoping she hadn't made a mistake.

Twenty minutes before time to meet Justin for dinner, Charlie returned Rachel's call. "Sorry I missed you earlier, sweetheart."

"Is everything okay?"

"At the winery, yes."

Rachel glanced out the window. "Did you see the latest so-called publicity photo?"

"What is with that guy?"

"All Priscilla's doing. Good news is he threatened to fire her if she doesn't stop the nonsense. Underneath his inflated ego, I think he's an okay guy."

"All the Hollywood drama makes life interesting, but I trust you."

"Thank you, Charlie. I don't want anything or anyone ever to come between us."

"Impossible. Except Brownie, when she sneaks into our bed in the middle of the night."

"Which doesn't reflect well on our dog-training skills. What's the latest on the bone drama?"

Rachel laughed at his description of residents sitting under the row of canopies waiting for something to happen.

"Email me pictures." She glanced at the bedside clock. "Oh dear, I'm late for a business dinner." No secrets. "With Justin. His way of apologizing."

"In that case, order the most expensive dish on the menu and remind him you're married to a handsome, sexy guy."

"Who stole my heart and still holds it captive."

"Call me tomorrow, gorgeous."

"Until then." She kissed her fingers and pressed them to the phone.

"Not as good as a real kiss." He returned the gesture.

When the call ended, Rachel pulled a jean jacket from the closet and walked out of her room. She met Justin in front of the concierge desk. "Sorry I'm late."

"At least you didn't stand me up."

"Where are we going?"

"You'll see." He escorted her to a reserved table tucked in the corner on the sidewalk in front of a restaurant two buildings from the hotel. "Is this out of the way enough?"

"If we're lucky, we'll remain unnoticed."

When the waiter arrived, Justin ordered a martini. Rachel hesitated. Would a glass of wine send the wrong message? If he overstepped his boundary, she'd walk away. "A glass of Italian red."

Still unsure whether she could trust her dinner partner, she avoided eye contact and reached for the menu, written in English. They remained silent until their waiter returned with drinks. He completed their order then stepped away.

Justin lifted his glass. "Here's to our new friendship, strictly platonic."

"I'm holding you to it." She clinked her glass to his, then sipped. Surprised by the bitter taste, she set the glass on the table. Was it the wine, or were her tastebuds revolting?

They engaged in lighthearted conversation about the movie until their dinner arrived. Halfway through the meal and Justin's second martini, he stared at her, grinning.

"What? Is there spaghetti sauce on my face?"

"You are one fascinating woman."

She held her hand up. "Stop right there. You know this isn't—"

"A date. I know. What I'm trying to say is not only are you married to a great guy, you're willing to undermine your career to protect your relationship. That's unusual in our business."

"Not for professionals like Maggie Warren."

"Like you, she's a rarity." He reached for his drink. "It's easy to get caught up in the madness. All the attention. Everyone wants a piece of you or expects to profit from your success. I've been pitched as a Texas playboy for so long ... it's a tough image to live up to."

"You've achieved enough success to live on your own terms. Maybe you should settle down and raise a family."

"Next month my mom and dad will celebrate fifty years together. They're Texas ranchers. My sister and brother are both happily married with Texas-size families. It'd make my parents happy if I ditched the playboy image, married a good woman, and gave them more grandchildren."

"According to Maggie, normalcy is easier if you marry someone who's not in the entertainment business."

"She lectured me more than once on her theory."

"And?"

He shrugged. "I suppose she makes sense."

"Then you aren't targeting Beth as your third wife?"

His brows arched. "How'd you know ... oh yeah she talks. We had our fun, and I'm not saying I couldn't fall in love with her. Fact is, I plan to stop whatever we have going on."

"Are you serious?"

"Don't look so shocked. Her kids are here. Besides, she's a married woman."

"Wow, you grew a conscience."

"A work in progress."

"I hope one day you'll find a woman who loves you as much as I love Charlie."

"I'm counting on it." Justin picked up his fork and stabbed a piece of fish.

Rachel stared at him for a long moment. Underneath the Hollywood bluster hid a decent guy.

Justin caught her eye and stopped his fork halfway to his mouth. "My turn to ask. What's wrong?"

"Nothing." She smiled. "I'm glad we've become friends."

Chapter 23

Emily grabbed her ringing phone off the kitchen counter. "Hey, what's up?" Her shoulders slumped as she listened to Brick. When the call ended, she released a heavy sigh. "Our mayor called an emergency council meeting. Tonight."

Scott filled a glass with sweet tea. "The town's fire alarm isn't screaming, so nothing's burning."

"Not literally, anyway." She ladled soup into four bowls. "Good thing you're home early."

"Tomorrow's a different story. It's Gertie's day off, and my assistant manager came down with the flu. Which leaves me and two sales staff to run the store."

"At least, you're not posting a '*Closed. Gone to the dig site*' sign in the window, like half the businesses." Emily flipped four grilled cheese sandwiches on the griddle.

Scott placed the bowls on the table. "If GBI doesn't wrap up their investigation soon, Main Street will turn into a short-term ghost town."

"Three years ago, who'd have guessed Willow Falls' residents would achieve enough financial stability to shut down for a few days?"

"Growth and prosperity didn't quash our small-town curiosity."

"One more reason to love Willow Falls."

The twins climbed onto their booster seats as Emily carried sandwiches to the table. She sat beside Scott, across from their girls. "Who's going to say the blessing tonight?"

"Daddy." Jane reached for her sippy cup.

Emily closed her eyes and listened to Scott, filled with gratitude for her family and the town she called home. An hour later she parked in front of Sadie's and Brick's home and joined Patsy Peacock on the sidewalk leading to the front porch. "Any idea what this meeting's about?"

"I suspect it's something to do with the mysterious bones."

"The way things are going, Scott's store and your two will end up the only that remain open."

"Honey, as long as Mirabelle delivers a daily update with the mail, there's no need to go close up shop. By the way, nearly all the copies of your books are sold. We ordered more yesterday."

Emily smiled. "That will impact my royalty checks."

"Not to mention my bottom line. Maybe the Book Nook will turn a profit next year."

"You have the perfect head for business and hats." Emily eyed the royal blue fascinator Patsy had worn at the movie premiere. "The one you're wearing is a real beauty."

"My official after-five-event headwear." Patsy grinned. "Which is why I'm wearing it tonight. It's after five and this is an event of sorts."

Emily slipped her arm around Patsy's shoulders. "When I grow up, I want to be like you."

"Old and eccentric?"

"Fun, fascinating, and full of energy."

They walked inside and headed toward voices and the aroma of freshly brewed coffee.

"Caffeine instead of lemonade." Emily withdrew her arm from Patsy's shoulders as they walked into the den. "A clue we're in for a serious discussion."

"Or a long night."

Mirabelle and attorney, Harold Bishop, occupied the sofa on the left side of the U. Brick motioned Emily and Patsy to the sofa facing the fireplace. "I invited Pepper and Mitch to join us. We'll begin as soon as they arrive."

Mention of the sheriff along with the straight-back kitchen chair positioned in front of the fireplace, piqued Emily's curiosity. She shifted into reporter mode. "What's the scoop, Brick? What can't wait until tomorrow?"

"All I know is Mitch insisted on talking to us tonight."

Sadie set a platter of brownies, dessert plates, and napkins on the coffee table. "Emily, Patsy, decaf or regular?"

Emily crossed her ankles. "Decaf for me."

"Considering our sheriff is showing up, I'll take the leaded version." Patsy held up a finger. "One sugar, please."

Mirabelle reached for a brownie. "Rumor is those investigators found more bones."

Harold gripped his coffee mug in both hands. "Don't you know by now that gossip isn't a reliable source of news?"

Mirabelle glared at him. "If you spent less time cooped up in your office and more time at Pepper's Café, you'd know it's the *best* source." She eyed Emily. "Other than the *Willow Post*, of course. Although it is only a weekly paper."

"Hey." Emily uncrossed her ankles. "Three years ago, we published every other week."

Sadie returned and handed mugs to her and Patsy. "Thanks to the town's new prosperity."

Heads turned toward footsteps striking the foyer floor. Mitch, out of uniform, walked in with Greer. "Evening, folks."

Brick nodded. "Sheriff." He propped his hip on the couch arm beside Mirabelle.

Greer sat across from Mirabelle.

After Sadie delivered two more coffee mugs Mitch turned the kitchen chair's back toward the sofas, straddled the seat, and propped his arms across the top. "I spent the afternoon reviewing the expanded investigation with the GBI guys." He paused, seemingly making eye contact with each council member. "They uncovered more human remains."

Emily set her mug on the end table. "How many more?"

"Hard to tell. Maybe four."

Patsy's eyes widened. "Are they thinking our town is the dumping site for a crime?"

"Looks that way."

Emily's pulse accelerated as images of movie-crew trucks and RV's parked on Falls Street skated across her mind. "When news stations sniff out this story, they'll charge into town like a pack of hungry wolves."

Brick squared his shoulders. "How long before word leaks, Mitch?"

"At the most, a couple of days."

Mirabelle set her half-eaten brownie on the coffee table. "We need to warn folks."

"Talk about unleashing rumors." Patsy scooted to the edge of the sofa. "What's your opinion, Harold?"

"We have a precarious situation on our hands. If we make too big a deal of it, we could shut down the entire town."

Emily shook her head. "And double the size of Canopy City."

Harold squinted. "What are you talking about?"

"Mirabelle's right. You seriously need to leave your office more often." Emily relayed the details.

"Only in Willow Falls." Harold scoffed. "Based on the town's penchant to overreact, I suggest we keep the news low-key until more information surfaces. Maybe reveal the latest details in this week's paper."

Greer nodded. "I agree. A well-written story will help control the situation."

Emily stared at him. "You know we go to print tomorrow morning."

Mirabelle scooted forward. "Emily's right. Besides, do we want to let the whole town think the new council doesn't have a clue? I say we call an emergency town-hall meeting and tell everyone what we know."

Brick fingered his goatee. "What's your opinion, Emily?"

"Both approaches have merit." She hesitated. If they opted for the newspaper announcement, the burden would fall on her shoulders. On the other hand, a public meeting would unleash all sorts of unanswerable questions. "Until we have more details, it makes more sense to treat this as a news event."

Following another half hour of discussion Brick called for a vote. "Then it's settled. We'll go with the newspaper announcement."

Mitch planted his hands on his knees. "Looks like we have a plan. Now I'll have one of those brownies. Just don't tell Pepper."

Sadie grinned. "Your wife knows you have a serious hankering for sweets."

He winked. "Especially your brownies."

"Looks like I'm in for a long night of writing." Emily reached for her mug and pushed off the couch. "Time to fuel up with the leaded version."

Chapter 24

A sudden wave of nausea sent Rachel scurrying to her bathroom. She gripped the sink and gasped at her paler than normal complexion and accentuated freckles until the sensation passed. Her hand pressed against her damp forehead. At least she didn't have a fever. Probably anxiety. She brushed blush on her cheeks, grabbed her purse, and dashed to the elevator. A middle-aged couple smiled at her.

"Good morning."

The woman's head tilted. "Oh my, you're the actress performing with Justin Brooks. We watched you filming a scene yesterday. Goodness gracious, making movies is a long, slow process."

"Yes, it is. I'm Rachel Bricker ... Streetman."

"You sound like a southerner from back home."

"Georgia born and bred."

"Oh my gosh, that makes us neighbors. We're South Carolinians."

A ping announced the elevator's arrival. The woman stepped in. "Where to?"

"Top floor."

"Same as us. Are you going up for breakfast?"

"I am."

"We'd love to have you join us. We being neighbors and all."

"You're sweet to invite me, and I'd love to. Except I'm meeting a friend. Maybe another time?"

The woman's smile evaporated. "We're flying home tonight."

"In that case, if you're ever in Willow Falls, stop by our family business, Willow Oak Vineyard and Winery."

"We will."

The elevator doors opened. As they stepped out, the woman fished a postcard and a pen from her purse. "I'd love to have your autograph."

"I'd be honored." Rachel signed her name with the words *'to my new friend.'* "Have you seen the movie *Joanie's Trial*?"

"No. Are you in it?"

She nodded. "So is Justin."

"We'll look for it. Good luck with your career."

"Thank you." Rachel hugged the woman, a gesture she would never have considered before moving to Willow Falls. "Have a safe trip back home."

Inside the restaurant the hostess greeted her with a smile. "Good morning, Ms. Streetman. Ms. Taylor and her family are waiting for you." The woman escorted her to an outdoor table in the corner away from the railing.

Beth's face lit up as Rachel lowered onto the empty chair at the head of the table. "Everyone's dying to meet you." She pointed across the table. "Chloe's my teenager. Ethan's the eight-year-old."

Rachel eyed the two children, laser-focused on their cell phones and seemingly oblivious to her arrival or their mother's introduction.

As if unphased by their rude behavior, Beth turned toward the woman with salt and pepper hair sitting beside her. "And this little sweetie with Nanny is two-year-old Sophia." She plucked the child from the woman's lap.

The baby giggled, releasing a stream of drool.

"I think she's teething." Beth blotted her chin with a napkin.

The two older siblings' features and skin tones hinted they didn't share the same father. "Your children are gorgeous."

"Please excuse their rude behavior." Nanny rapped her knuckles on the table. "Children, put your phones down." Her tone came across as firm yet gentle. "And say hi to your mother's friend."

Chloe rolled her eyes as she set her phone down. "Hello."

Nanny rapped again. "You too, Ethan. On the table. Now."

He sighed with attitude while complying. "Hi."

It was obvious who took charge in this family. "I'm honored to meet you both. Is this your first trip to Italy?"

A permanent case of boredom clouded Chloe's pretty face. "Last year we visited my stepdad when he played in Rome."

Ethan's chest puffed. "He's a famous rapper."

"So, I've heard. What's it like having two famous parents?"

Chloe wrapped a long strand of dark hair streaked with blue around her finger. "No big deal."

"They buy us lots of gifts." Ethan reached for his phone. Nanny gently smacked his arm. He withdrew his hand.

Baby Sophia sneezed, discharging a bubble of mucus onto her upper lip. Beth scrunched her nose and deposited her back on Nanny's lap. "Chloe, tell Rachel about the part you landed in the school play."

The girl shrugged. "Peggy Sawyer, in *42nd Street*."

"No kidding? I played that role in college. In my teen years, I dreamed of one day performing on a Broadway stage."

Chloe's head tilted. "Is your mother an actress, too?"

"She was a stay-at-home mom. Unfortunately, she passed away before I turned twelve."

"Do you miss her?"

"Yes, but the good news is I met my birth mother a few years ago, and now we live in the same town."

"Too bad all kids don't get to pick their parents," Chloe's voice barely above a whisper.

Rachel's breath caught. Had Beth heard the comment?

Chloe broke eye contact and fingered her leather bracelet, hinting she wasn't in the mood to talk.

Rachel shifted her focus to Beth's son. "What about you, Ethan? Do you also like to act?"

"Nah. I pitch Little League.

Chloe elbowed her brother. "He's pretty good for a goofball."

While the two half siblings launched into a punching contest, Beth plucked her phone off the table and swiped her finger across the surface. When Nanny released an exaggerated throat clearing, Beth looked up, as if suddenly realizing her parental responsibility to role model appropriate behavior. She set her phone on the table and squared her shoulders. "This afternoon Nanny's taking the children to Murano to watch the glassblowers."

"Sounds like fun." Rachel picked her menu off the table as the waiter approached carrying a booster seat for Sophia. He grinned, taking orders in broken English. Rachel noted Chloe's thin frame after she claimed she couldn't possibly break her diet. Her comment drew a sly remark from Ethan and a stern look from Nanny. The girl huffed and opted for an American breakfast of eggs and bacon.

Moments after the waiter collected the menus and departed, Beth nudged Rachel. "Come with me to ladies' room?"

"How'd you know southern women always go to the restroom in pairs?"

Her eyes widened. "They do?"

"That's the rumor." Rachel sensed her friend had more on her mind than powdering her nose. When they arrived at the door identified with a skirted figure, Beth glanced around as if expecting someone. She stepped into the empty space and pulled Rachel aside. "Justin canceled tonight's dinner with me and the kids. He said something about a schedule change. Is he doing a scene with you or is he blowing me off?"

Was that how he ended his flings? Cold turkey without an explanation? "I haven't seen today's schedule."

"I sent him a text an hour ago. No response." Beth stared at her image in the mirror. "Maybe he doesn't like kids." Her eyes narrowed as she faced Rachel. "Or are you—"

"Believe me, Justin and I are friends, nothing more."

"Sorry. The thing is, I promised Chloe she could meet him. I don't want to disappoint her."

Rachel waffled over involving herself with Beth's domestic issues. Except she knew about the breakup, so she was already involved. "Do you want me to talk to Justin? Maybe suggest we all go to dinner together?"

"Please, and find out what's going on."

"Dinner I can accomplish. You need to discuss the other issue with him."

Another woman walked in, forcing Beth to shift to handwashing.

Rachel followed her lead and caught her own image, relieved she didn't face the daunting struggle to juggle a demanding career with the responsibilities of motherhood. Compared to that challenge, acting as Beth and Justin's go-between seemed like a walk in Willow Falls park.

Chapter 25

Rachel entered the hotel meeting room set up as makeup and wardrobe central and settled at her makeup artist's station. Grateful the woman's limited English relieved her of the obligation to chat, she closed her eyes and thought of Chloe. She had sensed a connection to the young girl. Maybe because they both played the role of Peggy Sawyer? Or something deeper, more profound? Only one way to know. Find a way to spend time with the girl.

Beth dashed in, dropped on the chair beside her and initiated frivolous chatter with her American makeup artist. Not a peep about her children. Were they nothing more than fleeting thoughts, or was she transitioning from mother to performer?

Following an hour in makeup, Rachel headed to Doges Palace and entered the great council room where extras congregated in small clusters. She stopped in the center of the massive space, tilted her head back, and marveled at the ceiling covered with intricate paintings, each set apart by ornate gold frames. A dizzy sensation threw her off-balance.

A hand gripped her elbow. "Are you okay?" Justin's voice echoed.

"Momentary case of vertigo. Thanks for the rescue."

"Can't have my new friend fall and break her arm." He released her elbow.

"This is a terrific setting for a movie scene." Overwhelmed by the sheer size of the room, Rachel turned in a slow circle and gazed at huge paintings set amid seven large windows. "How will the cameras capture all the grandeur?"

Justin pointed to the masterpiece covering the entire wall at one end of the room. "That's the longest canvas painting in the world. Tintoretto and his crew created it in the sixteenth century to replace a fresco damaged in a massive fire."

She stared at him. "Are you a history buff?"

"Texas cowboys aren't totally uncultured." He leaned close. "Never heard of the guy. I read the brochure to kill time."

Rachel laughed. "Your secret's safe with me."

Peter approached. "Mr. Nordstrom's ready to shoot your first scene."

They moved into position and into character. Following an hour of takes, Robert announced a break and slid off his director's chair. "Good work, you two."

Justin grinned. "Rachel and I kissed and made up."

She rolled her eyes. "That's Texas talk for we agreed to stop bickering."

"Whatever's going on, it's paying off." Robert dashed to the crew scrambling to set another scene."

Rachel nudged Justin. "We need to talk."

"Are you gonna give me a hard time about my kissing comment?"

"Don't flatter yourself." She motioned him to follow her to the wall-long canvas. "About cancelling dinner with Beth and her kids—"

"I was serious about ending our fling. Which, by the way, she initiated not me."

"How it began isn't important. You need to tell her it's over, face-to-face."

He brushed his fingers through his hair. "It's not that easy."

Rachel propped her hands on her hips. "Don't you have enough experience ditching women?"

"Not in the middle of filming."

"Believe me, things will work out better for all of us if you don't keep her guessing." Rachel caught a glimpse of Beth at the far end of the room. "She's on the way over. This is the perfect time to tell her."

He glanced over his shoulder.

"And one more thing, she promised her daughter she could meet you, so you need to honor her dinner invitation."

A grin crinkled the skin around his eyes. "You are one bossy woman."

"Then dinner's back on?"

"Only if you join us."

"Deal." Rachel shot him her best *I'll be watching* expression. She walked away hoping he would reject Beth with enough grace to preserve her dignity and avoid a scene. At the far end of the room she turned to keep her eye on Justin and Beth. How had she managed to become a director in their soap-opera drama? What if she was wrong about his move making everything better? At least living in Willow Falls had conditioned her to expect the unexpected.

Rachel grabbed a bottle of water, twisted off the cap, and turned her attention to an ancient painting of crowds gathered outside Doges Palace. The exterior looked much like it did today. She imagined wandering among the buildings hundreds of years ago, before tourists, gift shops, and kiosks invaded the tiny swath of roadless land. Somehow she had to convince Charlie to fly over and experience this magical world with her.

"Seems I had Justin figured out all wrong."

Rachel turned and studied Beth's expression. No tears or signs of rage.

"Did you know he has a girlfriend back home? He showed me her picture. She's a gorgeous blonde. He feels guilty about cheating on her. Turns out he's one of the good guys"

Good going, Justin. A little white lie to protect her dignity. "Are you okay?"

"It's for the best, with my kids here and all. And dinner's back on. Justin says you're joining us."

"I am."

"You're a good friend, Rachel. I'm glad we're working together."

"So am I."

Pleased Justin had chosen a restaurant at the base of Ponte di Rialto Bridge, Rachel glanced across the table to Nanny, Sophia, and Ethan. Her eyes shifted to Beth anchoring one end and Justin the other. Odd they had chosen this seating arrangement. For the past hour, everyone had dined on

Italian cuisine while watching passing gondolas and sharing stories about their personal lives. Chloe hung on every word Justin uttered until he and Ethan launched a lengthy discussion about baseball. Rachel mimicked the girl's frown and leaned close. "I can think of a hundred more fun subjects to talk about."

"Baseball is boring, except when Ethan hits a homerun."

"Not my favorite sport either. I like the blue highlight in your hair."

"Last month I added pink streaks." Chloe fingered a curl cascading across Rachel's shoulder. "Your hair is pretty. My best friend has red hair. Her mom's an actress too. Sometimes we go on trips together."

"Family and good friends are among life's richest blessings. Did you enjoy watching the glassblowers this afternoon?"

"Oh my gosh, those guys are so cool." Chloe pulled her phone from her pocket and tapped a photo. "I bought this. Isn't it awesome?"

Rachel eyed the gold and white glass dolphin. "Gorgeous piece of art."

"Don't you think dolphins are the best? You know they talk to each other, and they're almost as smart as people."

"You're a beautiful, bright young lady. You'd make any parent proud."

Chloe stared at her phone for a long moment. "Do you have kids?"

"No. But, I hope to someday."

"You'll make an awesome mom."

The words, underscored by a hint of sadness, grabbed Rachel's heart. She pressed her right hand to her chest and fought back tears. What did Chloe need to hear from her? Maybe a simple thank you. Somehow, that didn't seem adequate. Images of Emily and Mama Sadie danced across her mind. They were both mothers. How would they respond? The connection Rachel sensed with Chloe intensified. She slid her arm around the girl's shoulders and kissed her cheek. "And you, pretty girl, are an amazing daughter."

"You really think so?"

"I do." Rachel caught Justin smiling at her, like a friend who understood. He winked, then clamped his hand on Ethan's shoulder. "You're one good kid, with a ton of potential."

The boy's sheepish grin warmed Rachel's heart while giving her pause. It appeared Beth's first and second born were in desperate need of approval.

Chapter 26

Ten minutes after the *Willow Post*'s scheduled pre-dawn delivery, Emily's phone pinged a text. "And it begins."

"Response to the story?" Scott dropped two pieces of bread in the toaster.

"First one."

"At least no one's bugging you with phone calls."

"Only because I changed my voicemail to *I'm busy with the twins, please text.*"

Scott refreshed his coffee. "Smart move."

"Comes from experience." Another ping. Emily stared at her phone. "Seriously?"

"What now?"

"One of our neighbors suggests Greer planted the bones to create publicity for his new project. Where do people come up with their crazy theories?"

"Small-town folks have big imaginations."

"If you ask me, they watch way too many investigative television shows."

"Or spend too much time trading war stories at Pepper's Café." He set his toast on a plate and slathered on Gertie's homemade jam.

"What do you want to bet the news will send more residents scrambling to set up camp in Canopy City."

"Including you?" Scott carried his plate to the table and sat across from Emily.

"Not until Mitch comes up with additional information, which could be any day now." Emily set her phone on the table and booted her computer. "Until then, I need to finish writing the article about Missy and Dennis."

"Talk about a news flash."

"One that doesn't involve a pile of dead bodies." Emily pulled up her email and scrolled through messages, deleting those she considered irrelevant. She paused her mouse at a subject line that caught her attention. "Invitation to Interview."

"Some kind of hoax?"

"Hard to tell." She opened the email. "It's from a country-music radio station in another North Georgia town. Every Monday they do a public-service program. They want to interview me about my books and my experience as a writer."

"When?"

"Next week. The host wants me to call him today."

"Sounds like a good opportunity." Scott bit into his toast.

"The program's live." Emily pushed up from the table and refilled her coffee mug. "What if my mind goes blank in the middle of a sentence?" She stirred in vanilla creamer. "If I said something dumb or controversial, I couldn't delete and start over."

"You have plenty of experience—"

"Not talking to hundreds, maybe thousands."

"The station's in a small town."

"Okay. So maybe, dozens." Emily carried her mug to the table. "A radio gig would add pizazz to my bio." She took a sip. "If the host hears about the bone investigation, the interview could go in a whole different direction with questions I can't possibly answer. What do you think I should do?"

Scott swallowed the last bite of toast. "Talk to the host, then decide."

"When you think about it, what do I have to lose?" Emily set her mug down and scrolled to an email from her sister. "Rachel sent a picture of her with Beth's daughter, a thirteen-year-old named Chloe. Looks like they're in a restaurant. Do you suppose she wants me to include this photo in *Rachel's Venice Adventure*?"

"What does she say?"

"That Chloe is her new friend."

Scott's cell phone buzzed. "Gertie's calling." He wiped his fingers with a napkin before activating the speaker. "Good morning."

"Is Emily listening?"

"She's right here."

"Good, because I want her to know that Patricia Cornwell's latest crime mystery got me to thinking. You're a good writer, Emily, and if you ask me, you should write a book about Willow Falls' big crime. Who knows, a good mystery could end up a best seller."

"Thanks for the compliment. At this point we don't know if we're dealing with a crime."

"Honey, I've read enough mysteries to know all those bodies didn't end up in the same place by accident. And one more thing. Scott, we need to fill a bunch of little bottles with clay from the dig site and sell them in the store. Call them crime-scene evidence and package them with a picture of the bulldozer or those GBI investigators."

Scott chuckled. "How many cups of coffee have you downed this morning, Gertie?"

"Don't knock the idea until you try it. You know my suggestion to add a soda fountain and homemade fudge ended up making lots of money for Hayes General Store."

"Good point. Tell you what, I'll think about it."

"If you wait too long, someone else will jump on the idea. I'll see you at ten."

"Bye, Gertie." Scott clipped his phone to his belt. "She comes up with the craziest ideas."

Emily pictured a display prominently placed near the store's entrance. "Actually, it's an interesting concept, and Hayes General Store is known for unique merchandise."

"Bottles of dirt?"

"If this investigation turns into something big, they could fly off the shelf."

"Or land me in jail for tampering with a potential crime scene." Scott carried his plate to the dishwasher.

"You told Gertie you'd consider her idea."

"I told her I'd think about it."

"And?"

"Two women ganging up on me before dawn." He leaned down and kissed Emily's cheek. "I'll run it by Mitch. Right now, I'm heading to the shower before you or my soda-fountain, marketing expert bombard me with more whacky suggestions."

Emily laughed. "Sometimes whacky works." Eager to ignore the growing number of text messages from residents, she closed her email, opened her editor file, and scrolled to the Missy and Dennis wedding story.

At nine, after feeding the twins breakfast, she called the radio station.

A man answered. "Clarence here."

"Emily Hayes, the author."

"We have the same last name, except I don't think we're kinfolk. Are you up for a friendly on-air chat?"

He sounded more like a favorite uncle than a radio personality. "I am."

"Our listeners like getting the inside scoop from local celebrities."

What did he mean by inside scoop? "You want to talk about my writing journey, right?"

"Of course."

After ending the call, Emily joined Clair and Jane at their play table. "Mommy's going to talk to a nice man on the radio."

"Daddy's milkshake lady says you're famous like Aunt Rachel." Jane looked up. "What's famous, Mommy?"

"It means lots of people know who you are."

"Lots of people know me and Clair. Are we famous?"

"There's something way better than being famous."

"What's that, Mommy?"

Emily wrapped her arms around her twins and kissed their cheeks. "Being loved."

Chapter 27

Grateful for a schedule-free morning, Rachel ordered room service, leaned on the pillow propped against the headboard, and opened her laptop. She posted a photo on social media of a police boat patrolling Grand Canal and another of her eating a scoop of pistachio gelato. A close second to lemon, her favorite flavor.

Responding to a knock, she slipped on her robe and opened the door, expecting a waiter. "Chloe?"

"Are you busy?"

"Not really." She stepped aside. "Come on in."

Dressed in sneakers, designer jeans, and a pink *Italia Venezia* sweatshirt, Chloe strolled to the window. She laid a small white bag on the desk and plopped on a chair. "Nice room."

"Does your mom know you're here?"

She shrugged. "Dunno. Haven't talked to her. I'm thinking maybe we could explore Venice together. You know, before I go back home tomorrow."

"Does Nanny approve?"

"Ask her." Chloe pressed a number and handed her phone.

Rachel brought the phone to her ear while keeping an eye on Chloe. "Good morning."

"I hope Chloe's not disturbing you."

"Not at all."

"Good, because she's taken a real liking to you. Would you mind showing her around the city?"

Rachel studied the girl's profile. How difficult could it be to traipse through Venice with a teenager? "Sounds like fun."

"Thank you, Rachel. That girl can talk your ear off, so feel free to call me if you need rescuing."

"We'll be fine." She returned the phone and cancelled room service. "Give me ten minutes to get dressed."

"Yay." Chloe's face beamed as she plucked the gift bag off the desk. "I bought us matching hats, except for the color." She pulled two ballcaps with Hotel Danieli spelled out in sequins. "The pink one's mine. The lady said green is a good color for a redhead."

"What a sweet gesture, and the lady knows her stuff."

After changing into jeans, a Willow Falls sweatshirt, and tennis shoes, Rachel pulled her ponytail through the back of her new ballcap. "Have you eaten breakfast?"

"Nope."

"Well then, our first stop is Café Florian."

"Do they have donuts? My favorite's with icing and sprinkles."

Chloe carried on about her favorite donuts while they made their way to the lobby and out the front door. Sunshine glistened off the canal as a water bus pulled up to the dock. Chloe snapped a selfie with the bus in the background. "Don't you love all these boats? My best friend's stepdad owns a fancy yacht. Sometimes he lets us ride on it. But he uses it mostly to entertain important people."

Lifestyles of the rich and famous. "Before coming to Venice, I'd never ridden on a boat." They turned right.

"Not even a little one?"

"Nope."

"We absolutely have to take a ride on one of those adorable little gondolas. Aren't those gondoliers the cutest in their striped shirts? I don't know how they stand up to steer. You'd think they'd lose their balance and fall right in the canal. I water-skied for the first time last summer. I thought it'd be easy, but it turned out way harder than snow skiing. Except I could let go of the rope and never run into a tree."

Did all teenagers talk in circles? "Sounds like you've had a lot of fun experiences."

"I suppose."

They crossed the Bridge of Sighs, passed Doges Palace, and continued to St. Mark's Square .

"Nanny lets me order coffee when we go to Starbucks."

"In Italy they call it espresso, and it's a lot stronger than American coffee." Rachel selected a table in front of Café Florian. "The cappuccino here is delicious."

During a breakfast of biscotti and croissants—in Chloe's opinion, the closest item to a donut—they chatted about her favorite school subjects and summertime activities. After downing second cups of cappuccino, they left the square and meandered along a narrow path between buildings to begin an endless quest for selfies.

Chloe stopped talking mid-sentence and peered into a specialty-shop window. "Aren't those masks the best? We have to go in."

Inside, a middle-aged saleswoman initiated a tour of the tiny shop while inundating Chloe with the history of Venetian masks and the local artists who created the new versions. Five minutes into the sales pitch, the woman's victim pointed to an intricate gold-and-white, life-sized beauty. "That's the prettiest one."

"You have excellent taste, young lady. This masterpiece is from one of our best artisans." She removed it from the display and nodded toward Rachel. "Perhaps your mother would like to buy this for you."

"No need. I'll take it."

Rachel touched Chloe's arm. "How are you planning to pay for it?"

She removed plastic from her pocket and held it up for Rachel. "With this."

"You have your own credit card?"

"Doesn't every kid?"

She obviously lived in a different world. "I didn't have my first card until I left for college."

"Why?" Her brows raised. "Is your family poor?"

"Hardly. Look, you should ask how much the mask costs before deciding."

The clerk turned the back of the mask toward them. "As you can see, this is an original. Signed by the artist. It's a steal at four-hundred U.S. dollars."

Rachel's eyes widened. "That's a lot of money. Would your mom approve?"

"She won't care if it makes me happy. Besides, she never complains about all the stuff I buy." Chloe turned toward the saleswoman. "Can you ship it to California?"

"Of course."

Rachel watched the thirteen-year-old conduct business like a pro. Was that what today's trek was all about? A scheme to load up her credit card without adult supervision? How much did she pay for the hand-blown dolphin? Should she call Beth or Nanny and clue them in? She couldn't tattle and violate Chloe's trust. At least not yet.

When they left the store, Chloe held Rachel's hand. "Know what I want to do now?"

"Buy more masks?"

"No, silly. See how many bridges we can find."

"Sounds like fun."

At the first bridge, Chloe snapped a selfie with the narrow canal in the background. "Oh look." She squatted to pet a dog and looked up at the woman holding the leash. "I have a goldendoodle back home." The woman responded in Italian before moving on. Chloe straightened. "Do you have a dog?"

"A golden retriever. Her name's Brownie."

"Ethan has a labradoodle. Doodles don't shed. That's why Mom let us keep them."

They continued along the path that opened to a small piazza and their second bridge. Chloe climbed the steps and stopped to stare at a man and woman with two young children crossing from the other side. "Do they look like a regular family?"

"What do you mean by regular?"

"You know, two kids with their original mom and dad?"

"Do you consider your family irregular?"

"Not for kids like me. Come on." Chloe skipped down the steps.

Rachel followed, waiting for the right moment to probe further. After giggling, gazing at old buildings, and imagining the Venetian lifestyle two hundred years earlier, they found their third bridge.

Chloe stood at the top and gazed down as a gondola passed underneath. "Sometimes I wish my mom had stayed married to my dad."

"Like a regular family?"

She turned and leaned back against the railing. "If you had kids, would you want a girl or a boy?"

"Maybe one of each."

"When I grow up, I don't think I'll ever get married or have kids. That way I won't have to leave them when I go on location." Chloe dashed ahead.

Rachel caught up with her and looped her arm around her elbow. "I should nickname you Bunny Chloe."

"Because I'm adorable?"

"That, plus you shift from a standstill to a sprint in a heartbeat."

Chloe slowed her pace. They walked in silence until she stopped beside a men's shop. "Did your dad get married again after your mom died?"

"No. After all these years, he's still single."

"My dad and his wife have two kids. He loves them more than he loves me."

Rachel slid her arm around the girl's shoulder. Should she tell Chloe she's wrong? Except maybe she wasn't. "Parents love their children in different ways."

"Does your dad love you?"

Memories emerged of her father walking down the Willow Falls Playhouse aisle two years earlier following *Percy's Legacy*'s public premiere. He carried two rose sprays. One for her. The other for Emily. "In the best way he knows how."

Chloe turned and pointed to a gelato shop. "Oh goodie. Can we get some? Chocolate's my favorite. But I want to try something new."

Reeling from another abrupt subject change, Rachel succumbed to a grin. "Does your brain always move lightning fast?"

"Nanny says I can go in six directions at once."

"Maybe more." After selecting two cones with scoops of cherry-flavored gelato, they continued their journey amid chatter about clothes, little brothers, and the latest movies. They strolled through another narrow path and discovered bridge number four beside a gondola stand with two idle gondoliers leaning on a railing.

Chloe moved close to Rachel. "Isn't the guy with the red and white shirt the cutest? Let's hire him to take us for a ride." She darted toward the young man.

Five minutes later she and Rachel sat side-by-side on a padded red seat, with the cute gondolier standing behind them. Chloe snapped a selfie with Rachel.

"You have to send me some of those pictures."

"So, you won't forget me?"

Rachel touched the girl's arm. "I could never forget you or our time together."

Chloe fell silent as their gondolier navigated under a small bridge with ornate wrought-iron railings. When they emerged from the narrow body of water into the Grand Canal, she transitioned to tourist photographer.

Rachel joined her young friend and snapped dozens of pictures of iconic buildings and rows of gondolas until they turned into another narrow canal. Their gondolier steered to the right, allowing a gondola to squeeze by from the opposite direction. He continued navigating under bridges and past piazzas, some lined with shops and crowded with tourists. Others functioning as small concrete parks featuring benches and potted plants, populated by locals walking dogs, or pushing strollers.

Mental images of Charlie, the winery, and their home played in Rachel's mind until Chloe sniffled. "Are you okay, sweetie?"

"I wish Mom wouldn't go away so often. Sometimes I think she loves her job more than she loves me."

Rachel's heart ached for her young friend. She reached for Chloe's hand and stroked her fingers, praying her next words would bear some semblance of reality. "No matter how far away your mother travels, she'll always love you with all her heart."

Chloe rested her head on Rachel's shoulder. "I hope we can stay friends."

"For as long as you want." Rachel closed her eyes, fearing Chloe's comment about her mother rang true.

Chapter 28

Rachel sat across the table from Beth at the outdoor Gritti Terrace Restaurant and listened to Robert's direction for their scene. As her costar began reciting her lines, Rachel gazed across Grand Canal at the sun gleaming on Basilica Santa Maria's white stone façade. Her mind drifted to Chloe, and her promise to remain friends. If she told Beth how much her daughter missed her, would she violate the girl's trust? A tap on her shin startled her. She blinked and stared at her costar. "What?"

Beth's brows pinched. "You missed your cue. Again."

"Sorry."

Robert approached, removed his sunglasses, and wiped the lenses with his shirttail. "Do you ladies need a break?"

"Not unless Rachel needs one."

"I'm good to go."

"Okay, then." He donned his sunglasses and returned to his chair. The slate clapper clicked with a loud snap. Determined to stay focused, Rachel slipped into character and completed the scene. Following another hour and a half of filming, Robert announced a two-hour break.

Rachel stood and rolled her shoulders, working the kinks out of her tight muscles.

Beth removed a cell phone-size purse from the flowerbed bordering the terrace and slung it over her shoulder. "Want to take a walk with me?"

If they spent time alone, she'd find the right moment to talk about Chloe. "I'd love to."

They left the restaurant and made their way through the Gritti Palace to the hotel exit. Across the wide stone walkway, a cat stretched out on a bench hugging a gondolier shed's lattice-enveloped wall. Flower boxes hung two feet from the top, adding splashes of red to the dark green structure.

Rachel eyed an arched wooden entrance marking another gondola dock jutting into Grand Canal. Did her friend even know she'd spent the better part of yesterday with her daughter?

Beth glanced skyward as they walked toward the piazza where they'd shared scenes days earlier. "By now my children are flying somewhere high above Italy."

She glanced at Beth's profile. "Did you see them this morning before they left?"

"Long enough to give them hugs and tell them goodbye. Are you hungry?"

"A little."

They found seats at a Ristorante's outdoor table under a white umbrella. Beth hung her purse on the back of her chair and glanced across the table at Rachel, her expression hinting of questions.

The perfect time to broach the subject. "Yesterday Chloe and I went on a bridge-finding adventure."

"So I heard."

"Your daughter is a delightful young lady, full of energy. At times I had a hard time keeping up with her."

"Lots of times she talks in circles." Beth looked away, seemingly laser focused on the tiny one-story, brick gift shop wrapped with autumn-colored vines. She remained silent until the waiter arrived to recite the lunch special. Without making eye contact, she ordered and added a Bellini.

Rachel declined Beth's invitation to join her for a Champagne cocktail and opted for a salad and mineral water. Sensing her friend's hesitancy to chat, she focused her attention on the kiosk holding center stage in the piazza. Loaded with masks, scarves, jewelry, and all sorts of inexpensive merchandise, it functioned as an enticing lure for tourists. "How many items at that kiosk do you suppose have an Italian label?"

Beth shrugged.

The waiter returned with the Bellini and mineral water, prompting Beth to tip her flute toward Rachel. "Cheers." She took a long sip, set the glass down, and ran her finger around the rim. "When I was seven, my family lived in Brooklyn, in a three-room apartment on the fourth floor of a run-down building. Rent free because my dad worked as the janitor. When the building caught fire, my mother, little brother, and I climbed down the fire escape. Dad never made it out of the basement. We lost everything. Mom tried her best to provide for us, working long hours in low-paying jobs." Her voice faltered. "Most days we barely had enough to eat."

Rachel moved her chair close to her friend and touched her arm.

"Eventually, my brother took to the streets and ended up in a gang of thugs. Hooked on drugs. He broke my mother's heart. She died a few years later. Lung cancer. During her funeral I vowed never to be poor again." Beth drew in a deep breath. "A week after my sixteenth birthday, I landed my first acting job. A bit part in a little off-Broadway theater. The show ran for six months. On closing night a movie producer found me backstage. He invited me to audition for a movie. I got the part. A low-budget film."

Beth took a sip of her Bellini. "We've chosen a fickle business, Rachel. One day we're rich and famous. The next forgotten and dead broke. You might think I'm driven because I love my career, and you'd be right. I love everything about it. But that's not the main reason I do what I do." She faced Rachel, her eyes moist. "Did Chloe tell you that she and Ethan attend an exclusive private school?"

"The best money can buy."

"I'm gone from home a lot because keeping busy with work is the only way I can guarantee my children will never lack for anything. And Nanny is more like a loving grandmother than a well-paid employee." She broke eye contact. "My daughter chose to spend the day with *you*, not me."

"Because you were busy filming."

"She never asked me about my schedule. And I never told her." Beth polished off the Bellini and flagged down the waiter to order another. "We all have difficult choices to make. Someday Chloe will understand."

Beth's pained expression tugged on Rachel's heart. She had trapped herself and her children in a lifestyle driven by a tormented past and the paralyzing fear of failure. Rachel fought back tears. Her friend needed understanding and compassion not an emotional outbreak. "Your children are fortunate to have a mother who loves them enough to sacrifice for their future."

"You mean that?"

What else could she say? Her friend had made the only choice that made sense to her. "I do."

Tears spilled from Beth's eyes. "Thank you for understanding."

"You know what we need to do?"

Her eyes widened. "Order more drinks?"

"Even better. Polish off lunch with the richest, most fattening dessert on the menu."

"Chocolate. With a mountain of whipped cream."

"Now you're talking."

They both managed to smile before Rachel transitioned into a discussion about Italian versus American sweets and the psychological benefits of chocolate. While eating lunch their conversation continued between bites. During the quiet moments, Beth's expression made it painfully clear to Rachel that she carried the heavy weight of guilt for not spending more time with her children.

Chapter 29

Emily crouched in Mama Sadie's foyer and wrapped her arms around Jane and Clair. "You girls be good for Grandma while Mommy goes to do some newspaper work."

"Does Grandma have cookies?"

"Even better." Sadie patted Jane's head. "We're going to walk to Patsy's and pick out the yummiest dessert. Then we'll visit your daddy at his store."

Emily straightened. "Thank you for the last-minute babysitting chore."

"Honey, every minute I spend with these precious babies makes up for all those years I missed watching you and your sister grow up."

"You're a gem and I love you." She kissed her cheek. "Their stroller is parked on the front walk."

"Perfect." She held her granddaughters' hands while escorting them outside and down the porch steps. Emily's heart warmed at the sight of the mother she and Rachel hadn't known existed for thirty years fussing over her daughters.

She strolled to the driveway, climbed into her car, backed onto Main Street, and drove out of town. As she rounded the final curve on County Road, the long row of cars and pickups parked on the shoulders suggested yesterday's news story had expanded the tent city. She pulled onto the winery driveway, already lined with vehicles. How long before Charlie would be forced to stand guard and keep the entrance clear for paying guests?

Emily pocketed her keys, grabbed her cellphone, and rushed across County Road. She approached the Atlanta newspaper reporter standing beside Brick.

"Mr. Weston?"

He turned. "Ms. Hayes."

"What brings you back to North Georgia?"

"The updated body count. Six smells like a big story."

Emily gasped. "Where did that number come from?"

"A confidential source. Your mayor confirmed it."

Brick nodded. "Mitch and I met with the GBI guys an hour ago." He nodded toward a van parked beside the bulldozer. "They're moving the remains today."

Emily eyed the throng of residents sitting in chairs under the row of canopies. "Are all those squatters clued in to the latest number?"

"We're keeping everything under wraps until we have more information. Weston wants to interview a local but only to uncover facts."

"Which means staying clear of all the squatters." A gust of cool wind forced Emily to zip her jacket.

"Seems you're the chosen one." The reporter removed his cell phone from his jacket pocket and glanced at the screen. "We've been cleared to move to the site."

"The landowner is down there. He might be willing to talk to you." Brick answered his ringing phone and listened before clipping it to his belt. "Mitch is on the way up to help control the crowd. When he arrives, you two can head on down."

Emily caught sight of the sheriff rounding the GBI van and moving up the cleared path. "When does the Atlanta paper plan to print your story?"

Weston aimed his phone at the crowd and snapped a series of photos. "The weekend edition."

"That doesn't give us much time to prepare for a potential news-crew ambush."

Brick fingered his goatee. "With all this bad luck, I suspect a black cat slunk under a ladder somewhere in Willow Falls."

The reporter chuckled. "Are you the superstitious type?"

"Old habit. In case you're taking notes, my comment is strictly off the record."

"An elected official with a sense of humor." The reporter pointed to the sheriff. "Looks like we're up."

Emily moved close to Mitch. "Instructions?"

"Stay this side of the restricted area." He lifted the crime-scene tape to allow her to step under without leaning forward.

The reporter followed and fell in step beside her. "I researched your town. Other than the Canadian your sheriff arrested a couple of years back, it appears Willow Falls is crime free."

"Enough to keep residents from breaking their unlocked door habits."

"How will everyone around here react to the latest news?"

She glanced at him from the corner of her eye. "Have you ever lived in a small town, Mr. Weston?"

"Name's Clark. Not unless you consider Decatur small."

"An Atlanta suburb? Hardly. You can call me Emily, except in your story."

"Done. About the town's reaction?"

"Folks will predict all sorts of interesting theories. Maybe even solve the case, if what they've uncovered is in fact a crime."

"No doubt, it is. What do you think happened?"

"I'll leave speculation to the amateurs." Emily swatted a gnat away from her face. "How long have you been a reporter?"

"Twenty-three years."

"Then you've covered a lot of crimes."

He nodded. "More than I can count."

"Assuming this is a crime, how does it stack up?"

"Depends on what investigators discover about the bodies."

"Makes sense."

When they arrived at the scene, Greer appeared from behind the GBI van and extended his hand. "Greer Streetman, owner of this property."

"Clark Weston. Are you willing to answer some questions?" He held up his phone. "On the record?"

"About the building project, yes." Greer responded to half a dozen questions with concise, no-nonsense answers.

"What do you think happened here?"

"Someone buried bodies. If you want more information, talk to the GBI guys."

"Mind if I take pictures?"

"Are you a fair-minded reporter?"

"If you mean do I stick to the facts, yes."

"Then be my guest."

While Clark walked along the perimeter taking photos, Emily pulled Greer aside. "How bad is it?"

"GBI guys aren't saying much, except they expect to identify the bodies."

She stared at an investigator bagging what appeared to be an arm bone. "Any idea how long the remains have been here?"

"Years, maybe decades."

Emily picked a twig off the ground. The Y-shape conjured mental images of ancient men aiming divining rods at the ground to find water on arid land. Her mind shifted to the unlikely series of events during the past three years that had led Greer to invest in Willow Falls. How many mysteries lurked beneath this clay? "Are they expecting to find more bodies?"

"The search has switched from bodies to potential evidence."

"I hope they discover something significant before rumors go bananas."

Greer raised one brow. "You are talking about Willow Falls?"

Emily glanced over her shoulder at the expanded tent city. "What was I thinking." She turned back to Greer. "How is this affecting your long-term plans?"

"It slowed us down in this section. Which is why I'm moving the land-clearing north a half mile. No matter what happens with the investigation, I'm going forward with this project."

"Some residents are still grumbling about northerners moving in and taking over."

"Streetman Enterprise wouldn't be one of the most successful real estate investment firms in the country if I let grumblers influence my decisions. Enough about crimes and land development. Have I mentioned how you, your sister, and this crazy little town opened my eyes to the importance of family and friends?"

"One day you'll make a wonderful grandpa."

"I'll keep practicing on Clair and Jane until Rachel's ready for motherhood. Knowing her ambition and commitment to her career, I'll have to exercise a lot of patience."

Chapter 30

Rachel stroked the deep-red velvet fabric covering Café Florian's corner seat. The paintings, ornate panels, and gold frames covering every square inch of wall and ceiling space provided an elegant backdrop for a scene featuring a lovers' quarrel, but did little to boost her mood. After she botched her lines for the fifth straight take, Robert announced a ten-minute break.

"You're way off your game today." Justin's tone and pinched expression hinted concern.

"I know and I'm sorry, it's …"

Robert pulled a chair over, propped his arms on the small, white-marble pedestal table, and eyed Rachel. "What's going on?"

How could she explain the depth of her despair? The fact that in fewer than three hours the veteran she had rescued from Atlanta's streets and his beautiful young fiancée—wearing *her* wedding gown—would unite in Holy matrimony. Rachel glanced up. If she didn't get her act together, she'd risk missing the entire ceremony. "Sorry, I'm distracted."

Beth, who'd showed up to watch, wandered over. "You've got this, girl, because we have a wedding to attend."

Robert's focus shifted from Beth back to Rachel. "What's she talking about?"

Rachel swiped a stray curl away from her cheek. "Back home, at seven Italy time. I invited Beth to watch with me."

"In that case we need to nail this scene."

Rachel filled her lungs and slowly released the air. "Okay, I'm ready."

After she and Justin finally delivered a perfect scene, Robert called cut and dismissed the crew.

Beth looped her arm around Rachel's elbow. "Come on, girlfriend, it's time to dress for a wedding."

"You're on." Her friend's infectious smile and upbeat tone helped lift Rachel's spirits as they made their way from St. Mark Square to the hotel.

Back in her room, they changed into dresses and heels. While Beth pushed her hair away from her ears and secured the emerald earrings she had purchased in St. Mark Square, Rachel unrolled her travel jewelry bag. "Which should I wear?"

Beth eyed the assortment. "My goodness. You don't have much to choose from."

"I didn't think I'd need more than a few pairs."

"Not to worry." Beth opened the small bag she'd placed on the bed, removed a black-velvet box, and handed it over. "You can wear these."

Rachel opened the box and stared at elegant diamond earrings. "Are they real?"

"Insured for twenty grand. A wedding gift from my husband."

"Which one?"

"The one I have now. Who knows, maybe he'll be the last. Anyway, they'll look gorgeous with your red hair."

"How can I refuse such a generous offer?" Rachel donned the earrings and moved to the desk. "I could swear I left my computer here."

"You did. I have a surprise for you."

"What are you talking about? And where's my laptop?"

"In a safe place." Beth grasped Rachel's hand. "Come with me."

Rachel eyed the bedside clock. "The wedding begins in twenty minutes."

"Trust me. I promise you won't miss a second."

She followed Beth. "Where are we going?"

"You'll see."

"You're obviously not planning to tell me."

"I like surprises."

Five minutes later they stood outside a door down the hall from makeup and wardrobe. "Attending a wedding in a hotel room doesn't seem right." Beth swept the door open with dramatic flair. "Welcome to our home-away-from-home chapel."

Rachel stepped into the small meeting room smelling of roses. Two vases filled with pink blooms stood on pedestals flanking a lattice arch framing a wide-screen television monitor. Her laptop sat on a small table positioned in front of two chairs covered in white satin. "You did all this?"

"My way of thanking you for making Chloe's last day in Venice special."

"This is beautiful." Rachel eyed the hotel employee standing beside a satin-covered table set for a reception. "Complete with Champagne and a cake?"

"Of course." Beth nodded to the employee. "That good-looking young man is a techie. He's connecting us to the big event in two minutes." She held her arm out. "So, Ms. Streetman Bricker, may I escort you to a front-row seat?"

"Indeed you may, Ms. Taylor."

Rachel's heart pounded as Charlie's face appeared on the monitor. "Hey, gorgeous."

"Hey, handsome."

"I'm here with the man of the hour."

"Are you the best man?"

"That honor belongs to J.T. Jack and I are groomsmen." Charlie aimed his computer toward his friends.

Dennis waved. "I owe this day to you, Rachel. If you hadn't invited me to Willow Falls, I wouldn't be here."

Jack and J.T. appeared beside Dennis. "All three of us would likely still be living in a homeless shelter."

"And now look at you. All looking awesome in your tuxedoes."

J.T. grinned. "Good thing your husband bought these monkey suits for your wedding. Otherwise, we'd be wearing jeans and sweatshirts."

Charlie's face appeared. "There's one more guy up here with us, Missy's stand-in father of the bride." He swiveled the screen until it focused on her dad.

Rachel pressed her hand to her chest as memories surfaced of him walking her down the aisle weeks after his near-fatal heart attack. Now seeing him act as Missy's dad filled her heart with joy. "The bride couldn't ask for a better father figure."

"When Missy asked me, she shocked the dickens out of me." Greer adjusted his bow tie.

Charlie elbowed him. "Your dad's starting to sound like a proper country boy."

Scott's face appeared. "Hi, Rachel."

"Where's your monkey suit?"

"Camera operators don't need fancy getups. Say hi to our distinguished guests."

The den came into view.

Beth's mouth fell open. "Is that Maggie Warren, the movie star?"

"None other. And that pretty lady in the long tunic is a famous southern artist."

"Didn't you say you live in a small town?"

"So small you could ride a bike from one end to the other. If you're surprised by those two wait 'til you see my sister."

"How will I recognize her?"

"Trust me, you will."

Emily stood beside the dresser in Mama Sadie's and Brick's bedroom and gazed at the scene reminiscent of last year's big wedding. For the second time in a year she and Kat wore their bridesmaid dresses while Mama Sadie wore Maggie's—tucked and hemmed to fit her small frame.

Kat placed her hands on the bride's shoulders. "You are an extraordinary young woman glowing with new life, and Dennis is an exceptional young man."

"At first, I thought I'd miss a big, fancy wedding." Missy's face beamed. "But nothing could be more perfect than a simple ceremony with the people I love most in the whole world."

Sadie fastened a pink rhinestone barrette in Missy's hair, securing her silky blond locks behind her left ear. "Even Mirabelle?"

"Is she here?"

"We figured if we excluded her, she'd throw an earthquake-size hissy fit. So, Pepper and Mitch invited her and Frank an hour ago. And don't worry about her blabbing all over town. Kat and I threatened to take her name off the Willow Inn and Redding Arms' suites if she breathes a word before Emily's story is published."

"Will that work?"

"Honey, she'd rather be cornered by a room full of angry skunks than lose one iota of recognition."

"Did you tell her about ..." Missy pressed her hand to her belly. "You know."

"Mirabelle is like a crazy aunt everyone loves despite her whacky idiosyncrasies. But let her in on the family secret? No way. She'll find out with the rest of the town."

Responding to a knock, Emily opened the door and faced Greer looking sharp in his tuxedo. "Are you ladies ready?"

Kat placed a bouquet of six pink roses and a dash of baby's breath tied with a shimmery pink ribbon in the bride's hands. "It's time, honey."

Missy moved across the room to her stand-in father. "Thank you for being my dad today."

"We're all one big family." His smile deepened the lines around his eyes as he escorted her to the top of the stairs.

Kat gathered Missy's train in her arms while Emily and Sadie followed. At the bottom of the stairs, the bridal party joined the groomsmen gathered in the foyer.

Charlie held his arm out for Emily. "Escorting my gorgeous wife's twin is almost like having her here with us."

"In a sense, she is."

Pepper handed each attendant two white roses secured with a shimmery white ribbon. "It's time to get our town's darlings married." She moved the wedding party into position.

An instrumental version of "Endless Love" began to play, signaling Emily and Charlie to move to the end of the foyer. They turned and strolled toward the fireplace. He stopped on Dennis's left. She moved beyond Pastor Nathan and eyed the space serving as a temporary wedding chapel.

An arrangement of pink and white roses graced the coffee table. Naomi, Patsy, and Brick—with Jane on one knee and Clair on the other—sat on the couch facing forward. Behind them, Scott stood beside Charlie's laptop balanced atop a stack of books. Mitch, Mary, and Maggie sat on the left couch. Gertie had settled across from them with Mirabelle between her and her ever-patient husband.

Emily stifled a giggle at the sight of the town's mail carrier grinning like a child entrusted with a delicious nugget of news—eager to tell yet sworn to secrecy. Her eyes shifted to Jack and Sadie walking in, followed by Kat and J.T.

The instrumental morphed into Lionel Ritchie's and Diana Ross's breath-taking rendition of "Endless Love." The guests rose and turned. Missy stepped into view. Her hand rested on the crook of Greer's elbow, her smile angelic. As she began her stroll with grace and beauty, the heart-warming words of the iconic love song filled the room and transformed the young couple's facial expressions to pure bliss.

Emily's heart danced as the distance between the bride and groom narrowed. She turned her face toward Scott. He smiled as if the song had reached in and touched his heart. She choked back tears while watching Greer deliver the beautiful young bride to her handsome prince. Then—as if perfectly timed by a higher power—the moment he placed Missy's hand in Dennis's, the famous duet sang, "no one can deny, this love I have inside, I'll give it all to you."

Tears spilled down Emily's cheeks. A glance at Kat's and Mama Sadie's glistening cheeks confirmed they too understood the significance of the moment. Two young people who had overcome heartbreaking pasts fell deeply in love and chose life.

The rest of the ceremony seemed but a blur until Dennis swept Missy into his arms and kissed her amid cheers and applause.

Naomi rushed forward and embraced her unofficially adopted son and his new wife. "This is the most spiritual wedding I've ever had the privilege to attend. God has blessed you both."

The space around the newlyweds became a flurry of activity as guests rushed forward to offer their congratulations. Scott moved from the back, slipped his arm around Emily's waist, and kissed her cheek. "Have I told you lately how much I love you?"

"You are my endless love." She gazed deep into his eyes until a tug on her dress shifted her attention to two little eyes peering up at her. "Did Missy and Dennis get married?" Emily lifted Jane into her arms. "Yes."

"Can we have cake now?"

Emily snuggled her daughter's neck. "Soon, sweet girl."

When Pepper resumed her wedding coordinator role and directed guests toward the dining room, Mirabelle held her husband's hand and stepped in front of Missy and Dennis. "A lot of people consider me the town's biggest busybody. The fact is, I know what I know."

Emily held her breath.

A smile formed on Mirabelle's face. "What I know today is you are a precious couple, too much in love to wait for a big wedding. Thank you for inviting us to share your special day."

"Well I'll be," Emily whispered to Scott. "The family's favorite whacky aunt actually has a romantic side."

Rachel swiped her fingers across her cheek as Charlie's face appeared on the screen. "Is there a dry eye in the house?"

"I think your dad even choked up a little. How'd your friend react to seeing your mirror image clinging to my arm."

"If her jaw had dropped any lower, it would've hit the floor."

Beth elbowed Rachel. "You could have warned me. I mean, talk about a shocker."

"And miss the fun watching your response? No way."

Charlie laughed. "If my wife and her sister ever decide to dress alike, I'll likely end up kissing the wrong woman. Hold on a sec." He held up his index finger, disappeared from the screen, then returned. "We're ready to toast the bride and groom."

While Charlie moved the laptop to the dining room, Beth filled two flutes with Champagne and carried them to their front-row seats. "I love weddings. They're so romantic, especially this one, and it's almost like we're there."

Rachel stared at the bride and groom. "Almost." Except tonight while Missy and Dennis slept in a honeymoon suite high above downtown Atlanta, she would crawl under the covers alone, missing Charlie with every fiber of her being.

Chapter 31

Emily spotted the brick building the size of a double-car garage on the neighboring town's side street. She eyed the radio station's foot-high call letters attached to the building's front façade. After parking between a white pickup marked with a hardware store logo and a Chevy with custom flames painted on the hood, she stashed her purse under the passenger seat and climbed out. Gravel crunched under her feet as she made her way to the concrete pad in front of the door. With her hand on the handle she whispered, "I can do this."

She entered a reception area furnished with a metal desk and a worn plaid couch, smelling of apple-scented room freshener. A familiar tune drifted from speakers embedded in the ceiling. Posters featuring country-western stars served as decoration. A glass wall with more than a few smudges separated the space from the heart of the station.

A portly gentleman sitting at a table on the other side of the glass waved. He pushed up and moved to the door. "Afternoon, Ms. Hayes. I'm Clarence."

"Pleasure to meet you in person."

He pointed to a metal chair. "Come on in and have a seat." He returned to his chair and thrust his thumb toward a young man sitting in front of broadcast equipment. "That skinny young feller over there is Jimmy. He's the producer, deejay, and whatever other job the station needs."

Emily waved at Jimmy, then pointed to copies of *Percy's Legacy* and *Saving Willow Falls*. "I see you have my books."

"My wife read the first one. Claimed she couldn't put it down. Your second came in the mail yesterday. She'd have come over to meet you except she's feeling poorly."

"Gosh, I'm sorry. I'll be happy to sign the books for her."

"That'd be mighty neighborly of you. First, put those headphones on and let Jimmy do a mike check."

Following pre-show preparation, Emily signed the books and listened to her host rattle off a list of previous guests until their producer and jack of all trades motioned and counted backwards from three.

Clarence leaned close to the microphone. "Good afternoon, country-music fans, and welcome to *Meet Your Neighbors Monday*. Today our guest is a famous author from over in Willow Falls. Mrs. Emily Hayes. No relation and she's mighty pretty, like her picture on the back of the two novels she's written. One's about her town's past and the other about the present. My wife read the first, and y'all know she's a right good critic. She gave *Percy's Legacy* an A plus. Tell us, Mrs. Hayes, what inspired you to write that story?"

So far so good. "As your listeners may know, three years ago my town stood on the brink of failure, until residents stepped up and transformed Willow Falls into a tourist destination. I wanted to contribute by introducing readers to our colorful history."

"How did you go about learning what happened all those years ago?"

"A lot of research and interviews. I never knew how much history folks had stored in their attics and basements. Plus, I found the details handed down through the generations amazingly consistent from one family to the next."

"Is your newest book also based on facts?"

"The events, yes." How had she phrased it for Mirabelle? "The characters represent composites of real people."

Clarence tapped his finger on her second book. "When folks read *Saving Willow Falls*, they'll learn a lot of interesting facts about your town."

"Yes, but remember I wrote a novel not a history book."

"Like I mentioned before we went on the air, my wife raved on about it. We're wondering when you plan to write a story about the big crime discovery?"

That didn't take long. "Are you talking about all the buried bones?"

His eyes widened. "Did someone uncover another murder?"

Don't come across like a suspect in an interrogation. "As far as I know, GBI hasn't drawn any conclusions."

"According to the article in yesterday's Atlanta paper, the clues hint of a big-time serial killer. We've never had one of those in these parts."

"I'll leave speculation to the reporters."

"Aren't you the *Willow Post* editor?"

Why had she agreed to do this interview? "Yes, and I'm in close contact with our sheriff. However, at this point all we know is a bulldozer dug up some sort of grave. The what, how, and why are still under investigation. I imagine your listeners are curious about my journey as a writer."

Clarence's expression morphed into a grin, as if he recognized and respected her tactic. "That sounds right interesting."

For the remainder of the hour—amid commercials from Lilly's Beauty Salon, the local car dealership, and a public-service announcement touting VFW's Friday Fish Fry—they bantered about writing, her favorite authors, and life in small towns.

When the segment ended, Clarence removed his headphones and led Emily to the reception area. "You're obviously an experienced guest."

"Actually, this was my first broadcast, live or otherwise."

"That makes you a natural. If we had some sort of ranking list, your interview would hit the number-one spot."

"I'm flattered and grateful for your expertise."

"I've been doing this segment for going on ten years. Will you come back for a second go-around when more details come out about those dead bodies? Maybe have lunch with me and my wife? And bring a pen, because I guarantee half the folks in town will have books for you to sign."

"Absolutely and thank you for inviting me."

He escorted her to her car before climbing into his truck and backing out.

Emily buckled her seat belt and called Scott. "Your radio superstar is heading home."

"Didn't I predict you'd knock it out of the park?"

"I wasted a lot of breath hyperventilating. Although he did ask about the crime scene."

Scott laughed. "To celebrate your newfound success and return to normal breathing, tonight I'll treat you to a romantic dinner at Redding Arms."

"After dessert we'll sit by the lake and kiss like we did when we were teenagers. Hold on, another call's coming in." She held her phone away from her ear. "Sorry, honey, my publisher's calling."

"We'll talk more tonight. Drive safe."

Emily's fingers stopped an inch from her phone. Had a problem surfaced or sales declined? Her back stiffened as she swiped the answer bar. "Hello?"

"Glad I caught you. Something has come up."

Chapter 32

A cool breeze wafting across the balcony three stories over Grand Canal brushed Rachel's hair away from her face as the camera repositioned over Justin's shoulder. They repeated their lines three more times before Robert called a final cut. As the crew dashed off to set up the next scene, dread released a bout of nausea and sent her scrambling inside for her thermos of ginger tea.

The wardrobe stylist she'd befriended approached. "Come with me." She led Rachel through the elaborate penthouse apartment in the historic, gothic palace to a small sitting room. "Your purse, costume, and street clothes are on the coffee table. I'll stand guard and knock when the director calls a ten-minute warning."

"Thank you." Rachel closed the door, set the thermos on a desk, and dropped onto a velvet love seat. She stared at the flesh-tone strapless, body-hugging camisole, white running shorts, and the terrycloth robe. Fearing another panic onslaught, she dug her phone from her purse, and pressed her twin's number.

"Wait a sec, sis." Moments passed. "I'm driving and had to pull over."

"On your way home from the interview?"

"Uh huh."

"How'd it go?"

"Way better than I expected. You sound tense. Oh wait, today's the day, isn't it?"

"I never considered myself an uptight prude. Besides nearly every romantic comedy includes some sort of bedroom scene." She aimed her phone at the camisole. "That's what they want me to wear."

"Looks modest enough."

"This movie is a huge plus in my career." Rachel carried the phone to a window overlooking a small courtyard illuminated by a light from the adjacent building. "The mere thought of kissing another man in bed makes me want to throw up." Rachel sighed. "Could you pull it off?"

"I doubt it. But then I'm not an actress."

"Maybe I'm more suited for the stage than film."

"Are you kidding me? You nailed your role in *Joanie's Trial*."

"Fully dressed and on my feet for the one love scene. Maybe I'm overreacting." A pigeon swooped down, landed on the sill, and plucked an insect off the stone. Rachel tapped the window, drawing a cocked-head stare. "Then again, I might dissolve into an emotional puddle and ruin the entire shoot. Do you suppose they'd fire me on the spot?"

"Must be a twin thing?"

"What?"

"Mental roller coasters."

"More like mental instability, fueled by a lingering flu bug or a serious case of homesickness." A tap on the door startled her. "Uh-oh. My ten-minute cue."

"Relax and remember how proud the entire town is of one of their two favorite movie stars."

"Who's a mental basket case when it comes to love scenes?"

"Get over it and go perform like a pro."

Rachel eyed the camisole. "Is this your version of a pep talk?"

"Yeah, how am I doing?"

"Not bad for an amateur."

"Hey, I'm a professional writer and, after today's radio show, an up-and-coming media mogul."

"Thanks, Ms. Cheerleader Extraordinaire."

"Break a leg, kid."

"You know that's a stage term." Rachel slipped her shoes off.

"Today it applies to movies."

"In that case, I'm all better now. Say hi to Scott and kiss my nieces for me."

"You've got it."

Rachel ended the call and stared at the camisole. "You can do this." She changed, donned the robe, and opened the door. "I'm ready."

The stylist led her to a tall, elegant bedroom. A chill raced up her spine at the sight of lights, cameras, sound equipment, and the crew crowded into the space. Justin, wearing running shorts, his chest bare, stood at the end of the bed talking with Robert. She swallowed and focused on dusty-blue drapes framing the floor-to ceiling windows. Her gaze shifted to an elaborately painted cornice surrounding the king-size bed.

"We'll shoot the scene from three different angles." The phobic activity eased as Robert issued instructions. He pulled the pale-blue silk sheet back and motioned to Rachel.

Rachel forced her feet to move.

"Are you ready?"

Not even close. She managed a nod and peeled out of her robe. Goosebumps attacked every square inch of her body. She had to get a grip. Everyone expected her to act like a pro.

Justin slid onto the bed. She followed. Robert directed her to lie on her back with her head on a pillow and Justin on his side with his elbow crooked. His face was so close, the scent of his minty breath filled her nostrils.

The lights dimmed.

A camera invaded their space.

A microphone boom lowered.

"Action."

Justin's fingers traced Rachel's jaw and moved to her throat as he spoke the first line.

An overwhelming sensation of guilt and raw exposure unleashed a rush of bile. She bolted upright. Her head smacked Justin's jaw.

"She's about to hurl," shouted a camera operator.

"Cut."

Rachel swung her feet to the floor. Someone handed her a barf bag.

Justin eased off the end of the bed and spoke to Robert while pulling on a tee shirt. He grabbed Rachel's robe off the floor and slipped it around her shoulders. "Come with me." He escorted her from the bedroom to the grand salon.

She dropped onto an antique sofa and held up the barf bag. "Evidence the crew thinks I'm a pathetic amateur."

Justin sat beside her. "My idea not theirs."

She eyed him. "What made you think I'd lose my cool?"

"First time's always unnerving."

"Like you're the voice of experience."

"A hundred and thirty-two." Justin leaned back. "That's the number of takes the director suffered through to wrap up my first bedroom shoot."

"You? Intimidated? Hard to imagine."

"Performing an intimate scene with a roomful of onlookers is unnatural."

"Especially for a small-town gal days away from celebrating her first wedding anniversary. Alone. With an ocean and half of Europe separating her from the man she loves."

Justin stared straight ahead. "An hour ago I pitched an alternative scene. Less provocative. More romantic comedy. Robert agreed if you couldn't make it through the first, he'd give my suggestion a shot."

She ran her fingers along the sofa's velvet surface while staring at his profile. "Did you do that for me?"

"You're a first-class lady, not to mention an emotional mess. Truth is, you've become more like my sister than a movie star I'm aiming to sleep with."

"I don't know if I should feel flattered or seriously rejected."

"Definitely flattered." He winked. "Believe me, it's a lot tougher to make it on my sister list."

"In that case." She touched his arm. "Thank you."

He placed his hand over hers. "You're welcome. Now, let's go deliver a killer scene to convince our esteemed director that my idea is brilliant."

"You're on."

Following three hours of script changes and filming, Rachel's muscles ached with overwhelming fatigue. Eager to call it a night, she slipped into her robe and headed to the door—

"Hold on, Rachel."

She stopped and turned toward Robert.

"I've arranged a late-night supper for you, Justin, and me at Bar Dandolo. A taxi's picking us up at the dock in ten minutes."

Should she beg off? Like she had enough clout to dis the director, especially after her unprofessional response. She nodded and trudged from the bedroom. After changing into jeans and a sweatshirt, Rachel joined Justin on the dock extending from the ground floor main hall. "Any suggestions on how to get out of this?"

"Fake a heart attack or throw up on Robert?"

"I'm not that desperate."

"Good." Justin nodded toward the building. "He's heading our way."

Rachel tucked her purse under her arm, climbed onto the water taxi, and ducked into the cabin. Justin followed and sat beside her. Their director stood on the deck, engaged in a phone conversation which continued until they settled on gold brocade chairs around a glass-top coffee table covered with an assortment of appetizers. He tapped his earbud, motioned to their waiter, and ordered a martini. Justin followed his lead. She opted for ginger ale.

Robert filled his plate and popped a stuffed mushroom into his mouth. "Nothing better than Italian food." He bit into a focaccia slice. "The scene change worked. This time."

Heat rose from Rachel's neck to her cheeks as she fought the urge to flee.

"You're a talented actress with a bright future, Rachel." Robert sipped his martini. "If you expect your agent to cast you in anything other than G-rated films, ditch your reaction to bedroom scenes." He turned to Justin. "Have you ever considered directing?"

"I've thought about it."

Rachel struggled to keep her shoulders from curling into her chest. All the years she worked in her father's company, she'd never experienced a verbal spanking. Should she act like a scolded child and pout or pretend nothing happened while the boys sipped their drinks and discussed the pros and cons of directing? Or swallow her pride and find a reason to escape? She pulled her phone from her purse. "If you gentlemen will excuse me, I need to return a call from a close friend." Before either could respond, she stood, squared her shoulders, and walked out.

By the time she'd reached her room, curiosity had replaced humiliation. She dropped on a chair beside the window and returned the call to Alicia Adams.

"Hey, girlfriend."

"Sorry, I missed your call."

"Are you and Charlie having dinner out on your fabulous deck?"

"I wish." Rachel stared wistfully out the window. "Actually, I'm in Venice—"

"Italy? Oh my gosh, it's past midnight over there and you're still awake?"

"Late-night shoot." Rachel kicked off her shoes. "What's going on?"

"Besides wanting to catch up, I called to talk about what's happening in Willow Falls."

"As a television reporter or friend?"

"A little of both. Since you're not on the scene, I'll reach out to Emily tomorrow. In the meantime, I want to hear all about your newest adventure."

Chapter 33

Emily pushed her menu aside and reached across the table for two beside the wall of windows in Redding Arms' dining room. "Perfect spot for a romantic dinner."

Scott grasped her hand and brought it to his lips. "To celebrate my talented wife's newest accomplishment. I can see a television interview in your future."

"In my dreams." She glanced around the elegant room. "What a shame this beautiful building sat unfinished for thirty years."

He released her hand. "Do you remember that Halloween when a bunch of us teenagers snuck in and turned the lobby into a haunted spectacle?"

"Who could forget. Fake blood everywhere. Kids dressed up like ghouls. Wires attached to the skeleton you guys stole from the biology lab—"

"Borrowed."

"Our shenanigans added fuel to the rumor about ghosts roaming the halls. Can you imagine the stories about to emerge about those dead bodies? J.T. will have to add an hour to his tour to answer questions."

"He could add a nighttime ghost tour to the schedule."

"Like Charleston. Or Savannah, the last place Mom and Dad visited." Emily swallowed, grateful she could finally name the city without tearing up.

Connie, their waitress and friend from high-school days, approached. "I haven't seen y'all here in a while. Are you celebrating something special?"

"Our resident author's debut as a radio star." Scott winked at Emily.

"My sweet husband is exaggerating a bit. Rachel is the real star in our family. I had one interview in a little country station."

"Talking into a microphone would scare me right out of my shoes." Connie poised her pen over her order pad. "If you ask me, your bravery deserves Pepper's special. A prime cut of filet mignon marinated in balsamic vinegar and red-wine reduction, topped with herbed butter, complemented by a side of garlic mashed potatoes. Accompanied by a robust cabernet sauvignon."

Scott chuckled. "Fancy dinner for the hotel where we created a Halloween masterpiece."

"That was one crazy night. Never been anything like it since." Connie tapped her pen to her chin. "Do you remember our quarterback slipping in the fake blood and breaking his arm? Everyone claimed his injury kept us from making it to the state playoffs. Like our team ever had a chance. Last week his sister told me he finally earned his law license and is planning to return before his dad retires. I never thought I'd see folks coming back to Willow Falls. Good things are happening around here, except for those dug-up bones. Anyway, what would you like for dinner?"

Emily leaned back. "The special works for me, medium rare."

"Make it two, with house salads to start and the wine Pepper recommends."

"Excellent choice." Connie walked away.

"She's right about friends returning to our hometown." Emily spread her napkin across her lap. "We can't let anything destroy the progress we've made."

"Are you still worried about your publisher's phone call?"

"I understand her request to write a book about a serious crime, if that's what we're dealing with. But in our town? We want tourists to know us for our good things—our fascinating history, an original play, a first-class winery, the new museums." She swept her arm in a wide arc. "Not to mention this unique hotel and Willow Inn." She sighed. "I don't know, maybe I'm over-estimating the impact of a story written by a mostly unknown author."

"You're looking at two years before the book's release. By then you'll have a lot more fans."

"—who like reading uplifting, feel-good stories."

Connie returned. "Pepper said this is perfect for steaks." She uncorked the wine bottle and poured two glasses. "Enjoy."

Scott clinked his glass to Emily's. "To my talented and conflicted wife."

"You know murder stories aren't my genre."

"Not a problem. All you have to do is think like a reporter."

"Easy for you to say." She swirled the dark red liquid. "What if the mystery is never solved?"

"You can make up your own ending."

"Or what if they discover the bones are all members of a poor family of squatters who died from a mysterious plague?"

"Or succumbed to an attack of aliens who landed the mother ship without anyone in town noticing?"

She snapped her fingers. "Now that would make a good story."

A woman Emily didn't know stepped over to their table. "Excuse me for interrupting. I recognized you from the photo on the back of your book. I loved your story."

"Thank you. I'm honored."

"I won't keep you, but I want you to know that your book is the reason my husband and I drove down from Kentucky. You made the town's history so fascinating."

"How sweet of you to tell me."

"My husband and I have been wondering about all those people camped out across from the winery. Any idea what's going on?"

Emily hesitated. No reason not to tell her. "A bulldozer operator uncovered some skeletons."

"You mean like dead bodies? How exciting. I hope you include that story in your next book. You are planning to write more about Willow Falls, right?"

"Actually, my second book released a few weeks ago." Emily removed a bookmark from her purse and handed it over.

"*Saving Willow Falls*. Intriguing title. Where can I buy a copy?"

"At the Book Nook around the corner on Main Street. If you'd like me to sign it, come to the *Willow Post* headquarters tomorrow around noon."

"I'll be there. Enjoy your dinner." She returned to her table.

"Do you realize this is the first time someone from another town recognized me? Maybe Rachel isn't our family's only celebrity."

"Even better, your fan's comment confirms that your publisher is on to something."

"She did sound enthusiastic. Tell you what. If either a crime or aliens are involved, I'll write that story." Emily lifted her wine glass. "Now, how about a romantic walk in the park after dinner."

"In addition to, or in place of dessert?"

"Since our babies are spending the night with their grandma and grandpa, I'm thinking a prelude to a magical night."

Scott clinked his glass to hers. "To the girl I first kissed behind a barrel of kitchen gadgets in my dad's store who became the mother of our beautiful babies."

"And whose sixth-grade crush on that cute boy still holds her heart captive."

Connie approached carrying two salad plates. "You two look like a couple of teenagers on a hot date." She set the plates on the table.

Scott winked at Emily. "Way better."

"In so many ways."

Chapter 34

Emily read the draft one more time, then pressed save. "I finally finished the article."

Mary looked up from her work. "How did it turn out?"

"You tell me." She pushed her laptop across the *Willow Post* worktable. "Read it out loud."

"Glad to. *Willow Falls' Royal Love Story.* Catchy headline."

"I thought so. Read the rest."

Mary continued reading. "Three years ago, during our lakeside July Fourth celebration, a handsome veteran and a pretty young woman sat on a blanket, eyeing each other for the first time. He struggled from the ravages of war while she yearned to escape her troubled past. They found in each other the love and companionship they each needed to move beyond their circumstances to find peace and joy.

"A year later, Rachel Streetman cast Missy Gibson and Dennis Locke as Peaches and Percy in our town's signature play. The young couple captured residents' imaginations, became our celebrity darlings, and discovered they had found their place in the world. Now they contribute to our community's economic engine. Missy as one of Willow Inn's beloved innkeepers and Dennis as a skilled builder.

"As their relationship deepened, the couple came to believe that God had set their feet on the same path and intended for them to spend the rest of their lives together. A simple marriage ceremony appealed, until we in our collective zeal symbolically crowned them as our very own prince and princess. Missy and Dennis didn't want to disappoint the townsfolk, which meant nothing would do, short of a royal-style wedding with all the pomp and circumstance. The young couple planned to postpone marriage and save enough money for an elaborate event, until their passion and deep love for one another turned two lives into three and placed them at a critical crossroad.

"In today's world, where men and women have numerous options, Missy and Dennis made two important decisions. Honor the life they had created and continue to call Willow Falls their home. Because waiting to marry no longer held them captive, last Saturday in a small, private ceremony, Pastor Nathan united them in holy matrimony. Tomorrow they will return from their honeymoon as Mr. and Mrs. Dennis Locke to begin their new life among people they love and who in return love and respect them.

"Having lived in this town my entire life, I trust we will all find it in our hearts to forgive our newlyweds for denying us another grandiose wedding and welcome them home with open arms."

Mary looked up and pressed her hand to her chest. "Oh my gosh, Emily. It's beautiful."

"How do you think residents will react?"

She returned the laptop to Emily. "A few will fall victim to self-righteous condemnation. Most will understand the magnitude of their decision."

"That's the response I'm looking for."

"Have you selected a photo?"

"The one of them gazing into each other's eyes while they recited their vows." Emily scrolled to the photo and turned her laptop toward Mary.

"I love that picture. It speaks volumes about their love for one another." Mary's phone buzzed. "I need to take this call."

Emily read the article again checking for punctuation, until the front door swung open, followed by a blast of cool air. She stood and greeted her fan from the restaurant and a man she assumed was her husband. "Nice to see you again, Samantha. Welcome to the home of our humble little newspaper."

"I bought two copies of *Saving Willow Falls*. According to the manager, your books are their biggest sellers."

"The big sign they keep in the front window helps. Would you like me to sign both?"

"Please. One for me, the other for our daughter."

Emily obliged. "If you haven't already done so, I suggest you go across the street and sign up for one of J.T.'s tours. He's the tall man with an artificial leg I write about in this book."

"I can't wait to meet him. This is the most delightful town." Samantha placed the books back in the bag. "I posted pictures on social media and recommended all my friends add Willow Falls to their destination bucket lists."

"You'd make an amazing travel agent."

She grinned. "Thank you for signing my books and for being so approachable."

"Thank you for buying my books."

Mary returned to the worktable and nodded toward the exiting visitors. "More fans?"

"My first novel motivated them to visit. Best news is the town's living up to their expectations." Her attention shifted to her ringing phone. "Alicia Adams." She pressed the speaker icon. "Hey, stranger."

"Hey, girl. I talked to your sister yesterday. Her career is rocking along. How's yours going?"

"Better than I expected." Was this a social call? "What's going on in your life?"

"Family's doing well. I'm still working with the improv group. Your sister's success is an inspiration to all of us. And I'm still a television reporter. The weekend's Atlanta Journal and Constitution's article caught my station manager's eye."

And there it was, the real reason for the call.

"How many news crews have swooped into Willow Falls?"

"None so far."

"Good, because our producer wants to feature the town's latest adventure in a third *Around Georgia* segment."

"When?"

"Next weekend. If another station shows up, let me know so we can change our schedule. Until then, tell everyone hello."

"Will do." Angst bubbled up like fizz from freshly poured Champagne. She set her phone on the table. "I've watched nearly every *Around Georgia* story since Alicia first reached out to us."

Mary sat across from her. "So have I."

"Then you understand why I'm concerned."

"Because half their segments are negative?"

"Exactly. The first two *Around Georgia* stories helped launch Willow Falls as a tourist destination. The third could end up undermining everything we've accomplished."

"Depends on how they spin it."

Emily walked to the window and watched a mother pushing a baby stroller past the church across the street. "Even though their program is a human-interest feature, sensationalism sells."

"We can always appeal to Alicia's friendship. She did serve as one of Rachel's bridesmaids."

"Except she doesn't have control over the program's final content."

"She might have more influence than we realize." Mary moved beside Emily. "One thing I've learned as a pastor's wife is that worry too often steals our peace and joy. Willow Falls' folks have proven they're strong enough to weather any storm."

Emily eyed an elderly couple sitting on a bench across the street in front of Florentines, the authentic Italian restaurant owned by Chef Billy Bob. "You have a way of putting situations in perspective."

"Comes with the territory." Mary looped her arm around Emily's. "What do you say we put this week's edition to bed?"

"You're on."

Chapter 35

Following an exhausting day of filming, Rachel yearned to return to the hotel, order room service, and call Charlie. Before she could escape, Beth cornered her. "I'm starving for a yummy dinner and lots of girl talk."

"Not tonight, Beth. I'm tired down to my bones."

"What you need is stimulating conversation and delicious food. I reserved a table beside the window in the cutest little café. I simply can't walk over there by myself."

"You won't take no for an answer, will you?"

"Or miss the opportunity to perk you right up." She linked arms with Rachel. "The owner claims their tiramisu is the best in Italy."

"Well then, how can I possibly resist."

"Excellent, now about that darling store we passed on the way to the set this morning..." While winding their way through alleys and across bridges, Beth carried on about her latest purchases—all authentic, Italian-made goods. During dinner she talked about the movie and their director's choice of settings.

Despite her friend's hour-long, nonstop chatter, Rachel sensed a deeper motive for the invitation lurked below the surface. She set her glass of ginger ale on the red and white checkered tablecloth and pushed her plate aside.

Beth pointed her fork at Rachel's half-eaten pasta. "Hard to imagine you're not starving after we missed lunch."

"I think I ate one too many slices of focaccia."

"The bread is yummy. And this Chianti is delish. Are you sure you don't want a glass?"

"The last thing my jumpy stomach needs is alcohol."

"Maybe we should order you a case of ginger ale."

"Or ginger tea."

Beth wrapped her fingers around her wineglass. "Thank you for coming with me. I wanted us to be alone so we could talk about something important." She fell silent and stared at the dark red liquid as if it held some mysterious power.

Rachel studied her pensive expression, searching for a clue.

"When Chloe turned two, my first husband, her father, abandoned us for another woman. His secretary. They're still together with three children of their own. My daughter is an inconvenient obligation he manages to see twice a year."

Rachel's body tensed at the memory of Chloe's comment about the man. How could any father dismiss their child like an out-of-date suit or last-year's fad?

"My second husband ended up addicted to booze, cocaine, and who knows what else. He'll likely die on the street with a needle dangling from his arm." Beth swirled her wine. "Number three is a decent father to Sophia. When he's not on tour, which isn't often. With women throwing themselves at him after every performance, I can't count on our marriage lasting."

Beth turned toward the window. "Earlier today you left your phone beside your purse. I saw the pictures Chloe texted you. She looked happier than I've seen her in a long time."

A massive dose of guilt pricked Rachel's conscience.

"I could tell from watching your friends' wedding that you live a good life--a happy marriage, a supportive family, a town full of close friends—which makes you the most well-grounded woman I know." Beth's eyes met Rachel's. "Your comment about my children being fortunate to have a mom who sacrifices for them made me think. They deserve better than absent fathers and a part-time mother. I could accept fewer roles and spend more time with them. Except I'd end up jeopardizing my career when it's going strong." She paused. "What do you think I should do?"

How could she possibly answer the question or even contemplate giving advice? Their backgrounds, lifestyles, and circumstances weren't remotely similar. Yet, the anxiety etched on Beth's face demanded an answer. "When I was a little girl our family of three spent every Sunday engaged in fun activities. Picnics. Movies. Educational outings. Dinners in fancy restaurants. Those memories helped sustain me after my mom passed on." Rachel paused. "Perhaps the question you should consider asking is what memories do you want Chloe, Ethan, and Sophia to hold in their hearts?"

Beth held Rachel's gaze for a long moment, then looked away. "I remember Mom reading bedtime stories to me and my brother before she had to leave for her night jobs. Every Saturday when she made us smiley-face pancakes, our apartment smelled of maple syrup and bacon. Those scents still remind me how much I miss her." She took a sip of wine. "Women have managed to balance careers and families for decades. All my friends rely on live-in nannies. Although I admit I spend more time away from home than most of them." She paused. "Those photos of you and Chloe ... you looked more like mother and daughter than friends."

"Chole considered me a convenient friend available to show her around Venice." Rachel reached across the table and touched Beth's hand. "You know she only has one mother."

Beth's head tilted. "Do you think I'm being too melodramatic?"

"You're a compassionate woman who loves her children with all her heart and struggles to find the right balance."

She stared at Rachel, her eyes filled with anguish, until a smile blossomed and extinguished her heartbreaking expression. "Know what I think? We deserve a decadent slice of tiramisu."

Reeling from Beth's mood shift, Rachel blinked. "How can I possibly refuse."

Beth motioned to their waiter and ordered the dessert and another glass of wine. While devouring Italy's best tiramisu, her monologue shifted to Italian food and the type of men who made the best husbands. During their stroll from the café to their hotel, Beth fell silent.

Rachel focused on the scenery and passersby. Had her friend talked herself out or was she still struggling with internal turmoil? Back at the hotel, they headed straight to the elevators. When the door opened on their floor, Beth stepped out and faced her. "You're the only friend I'm comfortable confiding in. Thank you for helping me face the fact that I have some important decisions to make."

Rachel embraced her. "If you let your heart take the lead, you'll land in the best place for you and your children."

"I know."

As they parted and turned in opposite directions, Rachel had the overwhelming desire to talk to Charlie. She pulled her phone from her purse. With her finger an inch from his number she realized it was three in the morning back home. Disappointed, she glanced over her shoulder and watched Beth disappear into her room before sending Charlie a text. *Tonight I may have rescued a desperate family from a heartbreaking future.*

Chapter 36

Sadie placed a tray of cookies, canapes, and fruit on the antique sideboard between two floor-to-ceiling, etched-glassed windows in Willow Inn's parlor. After arranging vintage cups and saucers beside the tray, she eyed the painting over the fireplace. A silver-footed compote bowl filled with pears, apples, and grapes sat on a marble table with a rose, a white lace napkin, and a fancy paring knife. "After all these years, it still reminds me of Mama."

Brick placed a coffee-filled urn on the sideboard. "The painting or the settee?"

"The painting reminded her of God's bounty in our lives. Sometimes when we'd sit on the settee, she'd tell me stories about her childhood and her crazy brother."

"You've haven't talked about him much."

"Last time I saw him was the day he showed up for my fifth birthday party. Mama said he ended up in a heap of trouble." Sadie moved to the bay window and spotted Mittens, the neighbor's black cat stretched out on the sill, its two white paws posed under its chin. "Missy and Dennis are due back any time now, and our feline greeter is asleep on the job."

"She'll wake up when their car turns onto the driveway. Any scuttlebutt about Emily's newlywed article?"

"One of the guests decided to buy tickets to tomorrow night's play so she could meet them in person. Then there's Mirabelle."

"What's she up to?"

"Rumor is she has something up her sleeve. Patsy and Pepper aim to find out and put a stop to any nonsense she might be cooking up."

"They'd have more luck stopping a speeding train with a sheet stretched across the track." He nodded toward an elderly couple strolling up the sidewalk. "Looks like your first afternoon tea customers."

"Thank you for your help, honey."

"Anytime." He escorted her to the foyer, opened the door, and greeted the guests before heading out.

Sadie stood beside the antique desk that once belonged to Emily's grandfather. "Welcome back, Mr. and Mrs. Edmond. Are you enjoying your day?"

"We just finished J.T.'s tour. What a delightful young man. He told us all about last year's movie-crew invasion." They ambled under the elaborate crystal chandelier spilling splinters of light on the marble floor and stopped at the plaque reading *Willow Inn Guests*. Mrs. Edmond pointed to a picture of one of the celebrities. "Where did she stay?"

Sadie nodded toward the Carlie suite at the end of the foyer. "Same one you're in."

Mrs. Edmond nudged her husband. "Just think, darling, you can tell your golfing buddies that you slept in Carrie Fleming's bed."

He laughed. "I doubt half of them even know who that young whipper snapper is." He tapped Maggie Warren's photograph. "Now here's a lady who's almost as beautiful and classy as you are, sweetheart."

"Fifty-seven years of marriage, and he still knows how to float my boat." She patted her husband's cheek. "Are you ready for a glass of sherry?"

"Have been for the past hour." He placed his hand on his wife's back and led her to the parlor.

Sadie greeted another couple breezing in from the porch. "Did you folks buy tickets for the play?"

Mr. Smith held up a four-bottle Willow Oak wine carrier. "Before we visited the winery. Charlie Bricker explained about all those tents. He said residents were bound to show up when investigators return."

His wife clung to his arm. "My husband loves reading suspense novels. Coming to town smack-dab in the middle of a murder investigation is a bonus he didn't expect. He thinks someone should write a book about the case."

"I'll pass your suggestion on to my daughter Emily. She's a talented author. Her novels about Willow Falls are on sale at the Book Nook."

"I must buy one." Mrs. Smith turned toward footsteps striking the dining room floor. She pressed her palms together the moment Missy and Dennis walked in from the dining room and stopped at the foot of the curved grand staircase. "I read about you in yesterday's newspaper. You are the most darling couple."

Missy's cheeks pinkened as the woman rushed toward them.

Dennis slipped his arm around her shoulders and drew her close.

Mr. Smith grasped his wife's arm. "You'll have to excuse her exuberance. She's a hopeless romantic."

"I'm afraid my husband's right. You two are welcome to join us in the parlor for tea."

Sadie stepped beside Missy. "They're most likely tired from the long drive. Besides, I need to update my assistant on a few details."

Mr. Smith aimed his wife toward the parlor. "Come along, dear, and let these young folks settle in."

Dennis leaned close to Sadie. "Thanks for the rescue."

"You're off the hook with our guests but not with me. "I'm dying to hear all about your trip."

Missy's face beamed as they walked through the dining room to the kitchen. "I loved every second. Can you believe the window in our room covered the entire wall and looked right down on a giant Ferris wheel? We rode it three times."

Dennis nodded. "All those years I lived on the street, I'd never taken a ride."

"He showed me spots on the sidewalk where he and his dog Sarge panhandled. We gave two meals to a homeless guy who took over the spot closest to the hotel." Missy touched Dennis's cheek. "My sweet husband talked to him for a long time and tried to encourage him."

"Another vet down on his luck who needed someone who understood."

"After the guy thanked him, we walked over to the Georgia Aquarium and spent the rest of the day there. I could have watched the beluga whales for hours. They're so graceful. And all those colorful fish in the tropical diver gallery. Sitting close to the glass seemed like we'd dived right in with them."

Dennis stroked Missy's hair. "Of all our activities, I think my bride most enjoyed our after-dark carriage rides."

She gazed into his eyes. "People stared at us like we were a prince and princess. Just like the Willow Post article called us."

"Emily texted us a copy." Dennis faced Sadie. "We're curious about residents' reactions."

"Innkeeping has kept me too busy to tune into the rumor mill."

"I suppose we'll find out for ourselves when we show our faces tomorrow. For now, I want to carry my wife up the stairs and across the threshold into *our* apartment."

"I hung a *do not disturb* sign on your door, so no one will bother you. Plus, you'll find two complete dinners in the fridge, compliments of Pepper. And Missy, you're on vacation until Monday."

"You're the best boss in the whole wide world."

"You mean partner. Now you two go on and scoot before more guests discover you're home and corner you."

After they slipped out the back door, Sadie made her way to the parlor and found the two men sitting on wingback chairs talking about football. Across the vintage neoclassical coffee table with a smoke-glass top, their wives sat on the chocolate-colored settee. "Our town's newlyweds send their apologies for not coming in. They need to rest up for tomorrow night's performance."

"We're still young enough to remember what it's like to be newlyweds." Mrs. Smith set her coffee cup on the table. "Besides, we'll talk to them after the show."

A ringing phone sent Sadie scurrying to the foyer. She lifted her cell off the desk. "Hey, Patsy."

"Pepper and I left Mirabelle a few minutes ago. You're not going to believe this."

"Try me." As her friend described the encounter, Sadie stepped out to the porch and dropped onto one of two white rocking chairs. The more she listened, the higher her brows raised. By the time Patsy finished explaining, Mittens had sprung onto the railing to stand watch.

"You're right. I don't believe it."

Chapter 37

Rachel responded to the knock and opened her hotel room door. "I—" She dashed to bathroom, dropped to her knees, and hung her head over the toilet.

Beth followed, swept Rachel's hair away from her face, and pressed a wet washcloth to her forehead until the dry heaves passed.

"Second time this morning." Rachel leaned back against the wall. "Thanks for the cold cloth."

Beth sat on the edge of the tub and stared wide-eyed at her friend. "Are you pregnant?"

"What?" Rachel fought off another attack of nausea. "No. Impossible. I'm on the pill." She pushed off the floor, leaned over the sink, and splashed cold water on her face.

"I'm just saying, it's strange this keeps happening."

Rachel patted her face dry. "I'm dealing with some kind of bug."

"Do you have a fever or chills or feel achy all over?" Beth ran her fingers over Rachel's forehead.

"Are you playing the role of my doctor or a visiting nurse?" Rachel moved to the bedroom and dropped onto a chair by the window.

Beth sat across from her. "I have three children, and believe it or not, I've spent enough time with them to recognize flu symptoms."

"The answer to your question, Dr. Beth, no fever, chills, or aches. I'm nauseous, nothing more."

"Okay then, if you're not pregnant, and if you don't have the flu, you're likely suffering from a serious case of nerves."

"You think?" Rachel held up an index finger. "First, our esteemed director reprimanded me for blowing his PG 13-bedroom scene." She lifted a second finger. "Second, I threatened Justin over a ridiculous publicity stunt." Finger number three. "And third I'll spend my first wedding anniversary thousands of miles away from my husband." She dropped her hand to her lap. "So yeah, I'm a one-hundred-percent certified basket case."

"You want me to call Robert and tell him you need to take the day off?"

"And have him think I'm wimping out again? No way."

"At least let me order us room service to give you time to calm your jitters."

"Thanks. Toast and ginger tea for me." Rachel leaned her head back. "Now that I think about it, I often succumbed to nausea before walking out on stage. Ginger tea saved my cookies, so to speak."

"There you go." After ordering, Beth kicked her shoes off and tucked her foot under her thigh. "When I returned to my room last night, I called my daughter. She didn't answer. So, I called Nanny. She gave her phone to Chloe. We talked for a long time. Did you know she has a boyfriend?"

Rachel shook her head.

"A boy in her school. She called him the older man in her life. Hilarious, considering he's fourteen. His dad's some sort of tech genius. He arranged for a stretch limousine to drive them and three other couples to a school dance next weekend."

Rachel brushed her fingers through her hair. "A lot has changed in the past seventeen years. I didn't ride in a pre-dance limo until my junior prom."

"Kids grow up way too fast these days. In five years, she'll head off to college or out into the world to face all kinds of tough choices. I don't want her to make the same mistakes I made." A crevice formed between Beth's brows. "Or become involved in a relationship with some loser guy in a feeble attempt to compensate for her absent father."

"She can learn a lot from your experiences."

"Up to now, all she's learned is how to spend outrageous amounts of money. Did you know she paid three hundred for that little glass dolphin she bought in Murano and dropped another bundle on a Venetian mask?"

Rachel's cheeks warmed. "She bought the mask during our trek. I debated whether to tell you about it, until Chole insisted you wouldn't mind."

"Why would she think otherwise? I never complained about her out-of-whack purchases. Truth is, deep down I considered them fair compensation for my all-too-often neglect." Beth's shoulders curled forward. "Like I said, she deserves better. So do Ethan and baby Sophia."

Heavy silence enfolded the moment as Rachel struggled to tamp down her emotions and find the right words. "You have plenty of time to make everything right."

"Your comment about what I wanted my children to remember haunted me last night until I fell asleep. A terrible nightmare about my house burning to the ground with my family inside woke me in the wee hours this morning." Beth ran her fingers over her diamond wedding ring. "After this movie is finished, I plan to take two years off, maybe longer, and spend time with my family. I'll ask my agent to schedule a few interviews or maybe a commercial shoot if they're close to home."

"Oh, Beth." Rachel pressed her palms together. "Your decision will bless you and your children beyond anything you can imagine."

Beth sniffed. "Maybe I'm not such a bad mother after all."

Memories of the day she and Emily listened to Mama Sadie reveal the secret she had kept hidden in her heart for thirty years played in Rachel's mind. "In my world the woman who gave me and my twin life tops the list of brave, unselfish mothers." She leaned forward and grasped Beth's hand. "You, my friend, are a close second."

Tears filled Beth's eyes and trickled down her cheeks. "I think both of us landing roles in this movie is way more than a coincidence."

"During the past three years, I've come to believe that a higher power often guides us through what seems like random circumstances to penetrate our souls and reveal truth."

Beth sandwiched Rachel's hand. "When you decide to start a family, you'll top every awesome-mother list anyone ever created."

"We are destined to remain lifelong friends."

Beth grabbed her purse off the desk and removed her phone.

"If you're planning to call Chloe with the news, remember it's the middle of the night back home."

"I'm not calling anyone." Her fingers tapped the screen. "Your number is now on my favorites list. Don't worry, I promise not to abuse our friendship with unnecessary calls."

"I'm honored, and I promise to make your calls a top priority."

Chapter 38

Following the Sunday service, Sadie stood behind the back pew with Kat and Naomi. "The newlyweds aren't here."

Kat shifted her focus from the exiting flock to Sadie. "Missy's still nervous about facing the locals."

"This morning during breakfast, Mrs. Smith couldn't stop talking about their performances last night. Although she was disappointed about them not sticking around to greet the audience."

Naomi shouldered her purse. "Which fits perfectly into our plan."

Charlie approached and stopped beside the women. "An innkeeper, an artist, and a hotel manager. You three lovely ladies are the perfect theme for a big-time Nashville hit. Especially if a dog and a pickup are added."

Sadie patted his arm. "My handsome son-in-law slash stepson is an expert on the subject."

"It took me a year to enlighten Rachel on the finer points of country music. She's still a work in progress. Do Dennis and Missy have a clue about what's happening this afternoon?"

Sadie shook her head. "Mirabelle swore anyone who blabbed would end up with their mail lost for a month."

Naomi laughed. "That woman knows how to wield power."

Kat shook her head. "Lord help her if the wrong out-of-town guest gets wind of one of her crazy threats and takes it seriously. Although, after living in Willow Falls for two years, I'm convinced residents would find a way to rescue her."

"You're right about folks around here not letting anyone mess with their own." Sadie nodded at a friend passing by. "Including newcomers and parolees."

"Good news for you, me, and Missy."

The women followed the last of the worshipers outside and joined Brick on the sidewalk.

Kat swirled her scarf around her neck. "It's almost time for Sadie and me to set Mirabelle's plan in motion."

Naomi's brows arched. "Are you two positive you don't need my help?"

Sadie nudged her. "Two ex-cons are the best people to pull off a sneaky operation."

"Especially two women as smart as my wife and Kat."

Sadie touched Brick's cheek. "That compliment deserves a yummy dessert."

"And a kiss from my favorite ex-con."

Kat eyed Naomi. "Come to think of it, you do have an important assignment. Escort your next-door neighbors to their home and keep them from getting distracted and forgetting about our stealth operation."

"Accepted." Naomi stepped between Brick and Sadie, her eyes darting from one to the other. "First time I've been assigned to chaperone a couple of middle-aged lovebirds."

Brick grinned. "How do you think you'll do?"

"Considering I'm old enough to be Sadie's mother and your big sister, I'll handle my assignment with ease."

"Unless Sadie and I break free and lose you."

"Ha. Not a chance."

The hours seemed to pass at a snail's pace until four o'clock finally arrived. Sadie stepped out of the inn's back door in time to greet Missy and Dennis crossing the driveway from their garage apartment. "You're fixing to make Mrs. Smith happier than a kitten with a ball of twine. She was disappointed you didn't stay after the final curtain."

Dennis held his wife close. "Last night no one, including Mirabelle, said anything about our wedding or Emily's article. It's like everyone was afraid to say what they were thinking."

"Whatever's going on with the town's crazy residents, fans who adore you are waiting inside." Sadie escorted them to the parlor where eight guests stood to greet them.

Mrs. Smith rushed forward. "We all attended *Percy's Legacy* last night and agree the play is the best regional production we've ever seen. And you two—oh, my goodness. Your performance would put Broadway stars to shame."

Missy's cheeks flushed as the exuberant fan opened a floodgate of comments. Following an hour of unabashed praise for the play and positive questions about their wedding and honeymoon, Sadie's phone buzzed. She listened before slipping it in her pocket. "I'm sorry to interrupt y'all. Our hotel manager has a situation and needs Missy's expert advice."

"We understand," Mrs. Smith said with a twinkle in her eye.

Sadie led the newlyweds out to the front porch. "I declare, you two are popular as all get out."

Dennis held his wife's hand. "Thanks for the rescue, Sadie. We'll sneak back to our apartment if you make sure no one follows us."

"Not yet. Kat really does want to talk to Missy."

"Can Dennis go with us?"

"Of course, sweetie."

Sadie chatted about the cooler-than-normal fall weather as they walked beyond the driveway and parking space separating the inn and hotel, and onto the walkway. Dennis held Redding Arms beveled-glass double doors open for the two women.

Inside, they found Kat at the front desk greeting two guests. "Enjoy your stay, folks and please call if you need anything." She directed the guests to the elevator before moving to the threesome. "I apologize for interrupting your afternoon, but one of our guests needs to reserve the ballroom for an event and wants to know which centerpiece to choose."

Missy's head tilted. "I don't understand why you need our help."

"I need Sadie for her decorating expertise and you because the guest is close to your age and was skeptical about an older woman deciding."

Kat led them past the elevator down a long hallway to the ballroom. She pushed the door open. They stepped into the dark room. "Wait here 'til I turn on the lights."

Silence enveloped them.

Sadie's pulse accelerated.

Lights flicked on.

Hundreds of locals erupted in cheers and applause in the room decorated with pink, blue, and white balloons floating above floral center pieces set on round tables.

Sadie leaned close to the newlyweds. "Welcome to Willow Falls' first combination wedding and baby shower."

Missy pressed her palm to her lips as tears pooled and slipped down her cheeks.

"Three times this number of people wanted to come. We couldn't fit them all in. The eight guests who grilled you back at the inn helped set you up. We managed to squeeze them in."

"How, who ..." Dennis's voice cracked.

"Hold your horses." Sadie swept her arm in a wide arc. "This is all Mirabelle's doing, with help from Pepper and Patsy. They swore everyone in town to secrecy, which is why no one dared utter a word last night."

Kat returned, her face beaming. "I love this little town." She led the guests of honor past long tables displaying a mountain of wrapped gifts to a round table set on the edge of a dance floor.

Naomi stood and embraced the couple. "Welcome home, Princess Missy and Prince Dennis."

Charlie clasped Dennis's shoulder. "Glad you're home, buddy."

Emily blew a kiss from across the table.

Brick pulled a chair out for Missy. "You are as beautiful as ever, my dear."

Missy dabbed her cheeks. "Is this all a dream?"

Kat sat beside her. "This is a real party for a very much-loved couple."

Mirabelle moved to the dance floor and tapped the mike set on a stand. The guests quieted and took their seats. "Missy and Dennis, we all want you to know that even though you're not from these parts, and despite what a handful of narrow-minded old codgers think about your situation, you're part of the Willow Falls family, and we are proud of you."

Cheers and applause erupted.

Kat leaned close to Sadie. "Thank you for bringing Missy and me to Willow Falls."

"Now that we have Missy married we need to find *you* a good man," Sadie whispered.

"I don't think a middle-aged, divorced woman with a felony record—"

"Who happens to be innocent—"

"Not according to the jury. Anyway, playing cupid for me would end up a colossal waste of time."

"Maybe...then again—"

"Save your arrows for J.T. or Jack, Ms. Cupid."

"...and so," Mirabelle continued, "tonight is for you. We have one special guest joining us from across the Atlantic." She nodded toward Scott.

He pressed keys on a laptop before turning the screen.

Rachel's face appeared on a large monitor hanging on the wall at the rear of the dance floor. "Hey, everyone."

The crowd responded with waves and greetings.

"Thank you for inviting me to your party. Missy and Dennis, you are far more than stars in our play. Your love is an inspiration to an entire town and motivates us to make choices with eternal value."

As applause erupted again, Brick slipped his arm around Sadie's shoulder. "Just like you, sweetheart."

Sadie's heart overflowed with love as she smiled and squeezed Brick's hand.

Mirabelle tapped the mike again. The applause stopped.

Rachel glanced to her left. "A dear friend is with me."

"Hi, Willow Falls." Beth waved. "Rachel told me all about your town. One of these days I'll come visit and stay at Willow Inn or maybe Redding Arms. Then I'll shop at the general store and Patsy's, and have lunch at Pepper's Café. And of course, attend the best play in Georgia."

Cheers and applause erupted.

Rachel blew a kiss. "I miss you all like crazy. Give Missy, Dennis, and my husband hugs for me."

After Rachel bid the crowd goodbye, Mirabelle pointed to tables laden with casseroles, platters, serving dishes, and a four-layer wedding cake. "It's time to enjoy the delicious food everyone brought." She directed guests to the buffet tables, while the waitstaff poured wine, compliments of Brick and Charlie.

Following dinner, Agnes Peterson, the retired music teacher's wife, settled at a piano to play dance tunes.

Brick stood and held his hand out to Sadie. "Will my wife accept a dance with her husband?"

She rose and kissed his cheek. "What a sweet-as-pie honor to dance with the most charming man in the room."

They crowded into the space with dozens of couples. When Agnes began to play "The First Time Ever I Saw Your Face," Sadie melted into Brick's arms. As they moved to the melody, she peered over his shoulder and glanced at Charlie, chatting with J.T. and Jack. When he turned toward the dance floor, his sullen expression tugged on her heartstrings.

"What are you thinking?" whispered Brick.

"How much Charlie misses his wife."

Rachel closed her laptop and set it on the desk. "The second virtual event you attended as my plus one."

Beth tucked her foot under her knee. "Your little town knows how to throw a party."

"Sometimes to a fault. Like my wedding. A combination elegant, outdoor affair and raucous, country-style hoedown."

"With a big guest list?"

"Big? The entire town showed up."

"And I thought my weddings were extravagant affairs."

"Mama Sadie and Brick are also celebrating their first-year anniversary."

"Are they taking a trip to some romantic location?"

"They're planning an intimate dinner party at their home. Another party I'll attend virtually." Rachel threw her hands up. "What is wrong with me? Here I am in one of the most beautiful cities in the world, living my lifelong dream, and I'm whining like an ungrateful child."

"You're a woman, so irrational, emotional swings come naturally."

"Maybe for some women. I spent seven years as an executive in my father's real estate development firm, working with ambitious, aggressive employees. Mostly men. Believe me, I know how to control my feelings."

"That was then. Now you live in the entertainment world where emotions drive performance."

"I'm perfectly capable of performing without dissolving into a babbling puddle of self-pity."

Beth chuckled. "Tell that to the camera crew that filmed your bedroom scene."

"Touché."

Rachel's phone pinged a text.

"From Charlie?"

"Yeah.'

"That's my cue to exit." Beth popped up and waved over her shoulder as she headed to the door. "See you tomorrow."

Rachel pressed Charlie's number. "Hey."

"I hope my text didn't wake you."

She dropped onto the bed. "More like rescued me from an overload of girl talk. Where are you?"

"In the hall outside the ballroom."

"Wish I could've been there tonight."

"Mirabelle outdid herself."

"Emily's editorial must have done a number on her."

"My sister definitely has a way with words." Rachel yawned.

"I know it's way past midnight in Venice, so I'll let you go. Tonight I'll dream about the day you're back home in my arms."

Back home? She had to come to grips with reality. Charlie wasn't coming to Venice for their anniversary. "I love you."

"I love you, too. Goodnight, sweetheart."

"Sweet dreams." She ended the call and lifted the photo of her and Charlie off the nightstand. An intense longing to lie beside him and feel his arms around her unleashed a stream of tears. She waited for the tears to stop before mentally scolding herself for falling victim to another emotional outburst.

Chapter 39

A ping pulled Emily's focus from her laptop. Should she read the text or ignore another unwelcome interruption? Journalistic curiosity won the debate. She plucked her phone off the worktable. "Just when I thought we'd have one uninterrupted work day."

Mary looked up. "Some kind of emergency?"

"Brick needs me at the dig site. Seems Willow Falls' big mystery is about to hit the fan."

"Any idea what that means?"

"Not a single clue." Emily saved her work, grabbed purse and camera, and headed to her car. As she turned onto Main Street and drove to County Road, her brain switched from newspaper editor to author mode. Had GBI discovered more clues, or had residents ignored the yellow tape and trampled the crime scene? A litany of possibilities raced through her mind, all leading to one undeniable conclusion. It was time to begin writing book three.

She slowed after rounding the last curve on County Road. Other than Brick's car, the sheriff's vehicle, and a red panel van, the shoulders remained clear and the tent city empty. Not at all what she'd expected.

Emily parked, climbed out, and moved beside the van displaying a *Follow the Facts* logo. She craned her neck to look inside. Empty. She peered past the crime-scene tape, down the cleared path. No one in sight. Her phone rang. Brick. "Who does the van belong to, and where are you?"

"A cable TV show. We commandeered the crew to Charlie's office. Back door's unlocked."

"I'm on my way." Emily returned to her car and drove to the winery's lower parking lot. Curiosity mingled with dread as she dashed past the row of planters separating the gazebo from the two-story, old-world winery.

Buster, a yellow Lab, and Merlot, a border collie, bounded from beneath the gazebo to greet her. "Sorry fellas, I can't stop and play today." She continued past the row of tall, arched wooden doorways to the private entrance. Voices drifted from above as she climbed the stairs to the second floor and walked into Charlie's paneled office.

Two men, one with his hair pulled into a ponytail, sat on the tan leather couch beside a blond woman. Mitch stood by the window with his phone pressed to his ear.

Emily moved beside Brick and leaned back against the desk. "Who's Mitch talking to?"

"GBI."

The woman stood and approached. "I assume you're Emily Hayes."

"Yes, ma'am."

"I'm Janet Johnson, *Follow the Facts* producer."

"Pleasure to meet you. What is *Follow the Facts*?"

The woman's laser-focused glare screamed a no-nonsense, take-charge attitude. "I'm surprised you don't know." Her tone hinted of arrogance. "It's a highly rated crime-investigation television program." She nodded toward the couch. "Paul Gross is our research guy. The man with the ponytail is Garrett, our camera operator."

Mitch clipped his phone to his belt. "GBI will meet us at the site tomorrow morning at nine. If you'll excuse me, I need to bring our newspaper editor up to speed." He motioned for Emily to follow him out to the hall. "Have you seen their show?"

"Never heard of it."

"They investigate real crimes. You remember how crazy everyone acted when the movie crew rolled in."

"This is different."

"When cameras are involved, people around here go all-Hollywood. Here's the real issue. Their program competes with law enforcement to solve crimes. They don't care how much damage they inflict."

"That's not good."

"The GBI guys will advise them to coordinate their investigation through my office. I called Greer. He's headed back to town. Sorry to spring this on you, Emily, but you understand reporters, which means I need you to partner with Brick."

"To do what?"

"Stick close to those three and keep them from taking advantage of our residents."

"That's a tall order, Mitch. Did you see the look in that woman's eyes? What makes you think she'll cooperate?"

"We'll lay out our expectations over lunch."

"Where?"

Mitch nodded toward the dining room. "Here."

"The winery's closed today."

"Charlie made arrangements."

"Any idea how long the crew plans to stay in town?"

"They booked hotel rooms for a week."

"In that case, we have a bigger problem. Next weekend Alicia Adams' station plans to film an *Around Georgia* story about the skeletons. I promised to call her if another news team showed up."

Mitch shook his head. "Two media squads stirring up the locals."

"What do you want me to do, Mitch?"

"Call Alicia. We can't afford to alienate the Atlanta station."

Charlie approached from the dining room. "Table's set."

Emily sighed. "Before I jump into the fray, I need to wrap my head around all this."

Mitch touched her arm. "How much time do you need?"

"Five minutes."

"You've got it." He returned to the office.

Charlie escorted Emily to a table set for six beside a row of tall windows in the dining room.

She gazed out at the panoramic view of the vineyard stretching across acres of rolling hills. "Keeping that crew reined in is likely to create all kinds of massive headaches."

"Dad had to deal with a lot of problems and challenging people before he retired. He'll know how to handle the intruders. Do you need anything before I help my chef throw together some kind of lunch?"

"I'm fine. Thanks for stepping up, Charlie." Emily pulled her phone from her purse and left Alicia a voicemail. She eyed the coffered ceiling and partially plastered walls revealing random sections of stone. A space much better suited for a party than a confrontation. The prospect of babysitting a television crew both intrigued and terrified her. On the one hand, she could end up with inside information and valuable insight. On the other she risked crossing professional lines. Emily turned at the sound of voices, summoned her best 'everything's peachy keen' grin, and chose the chair facing the window.

"Impressive winery for a small southern town." Janet's tone hinted of surprise.

"We country folk do our best." Brick pulled a chair away from the table. "Please have a seat." He settled on Janet's left, Mitch on her right.

After Garrett and Paul took their seats, Mitch turned to Janet. "I understand and respect why you're here and what you want to accomplish."

"Then we're good to go?"

"Not yet. My job is to shield Willow Falls from anything threatening to put our citizens or their livelihoods at risk. Which means we need to set some mutual guidelines."

Janet's eyes narrowed. "I assume you understand freedom of the press."

"*Follow the Facts* is a television show."

"You're obviously not familiar with our format, Sheriff. We're investigative reporters."

Emily's body stiffened at Janet's overt attempt to intimidate.

Mitch planted his forearms on the table. "You understand that the site across the street is an active crime scene, which means your team can't cross the barrier without GBI, me, or the property owner granting permission. We also have the right to establish when and where you're allowed to conduct interviews."

"If we decline your outlandish guidelines?"

"You won't."

Janet laced her fingers and glared at Mitch. "What makes you so sure?"

"You want to avoid negative publicity as well as keep me from staking out every move you make."

Janet held Mitch's gaze. "You drive a hard bargain, Sheriff."

"Then we have an agreement?"

"Not yet." She turned toward Brick. "I assume you'll allow us to question residents without interfering."

"As long as your crew doesn't intimidate or bully."

She eyed Emily. "What do you have to say?"

"I agree with our mayor."

Janet unlaced her fingers. "Tomorrow after we interview GBI, I expect to meet with you and the mayor to iron out details."

Emily squared her shoulders. "Noon, at the newspaper office."

"We'll make that work. Now about *our* demands."

As Emily listened to Janet argue then negotiate with Mitch over details, beads of sweat popped out on the back of her neck. Working with that woman would take every ounce of patience she could muster.

Chapter 40

Grateful for an hour alone, Rachel strolled along a wide walkway separating a park from Grande Canal. A smattering of artists' stalls stood on the canal side across from a row of kiosks enticing tourists with an array of souvenirs. Before leaving Italy she'd succumb to the temptation and buy presents for everyone. She stopped to snap a photo of a man wearing a beret, holding a palette in one hand and a brush in the other. The scene partially finished on his easel-mounted canvas summoned images of paintings displayed in Naomi's art gallery. Fighting off an attack of homesickness, she walked to the concrete railing and focused on docked boats. The Venice version of a parking lot. She snapped a picture.

A young woman engaged in a heated phone conversation stopped three feet away. Rachel's melancholy heightened at the sight of her leashed golden retriever's wagging tail. Was Charlie drinking coffee on their deck with Brownie sprawled beside him? Was he thinking of her? She fought to control her emotions and stooped to pet the dog's head.

The woman ended her call and spoke to Rachel in Italian.

Rachel looked up. "Do you speak English?"

"Little. You from US?"

"I am." Rachel straightened. "Your dog is well-behaved."

"She's good dog. Not like *il porco*." The woman stared at her phone while mumbling in Italian.

"She reminds me of Brownie, my dog back home."

"You here on vacation?"

"No, I'm working. Filming a movie."

"Perfect place for another movie." The woman's brows furrowed as she stared at her beeping phone. "*Il porco*. Must go. Enjoy your visit." She pressed her phone to her ear and unleashed a litany of Italian words while pulling her dog away from the railing.

A quick phone search confirmed *il porco* translated to the pig. Had she interrupted a lover's spat or something more serious? Resisting the urge to follow the woman, Rachel adjusted her sunglasses, and spotted a cruise ship drifting away from the city. If Charlie refused to fly over, maybe they'd celebrate their second anniversary on a Mediterranean cruise. If she wasn't on location somewhere far from home.

Her phone vibrated. Charlie on Face Time. "Hi, honey."

"Hey, gorgeous." He held up a mug. "Recognize this?"

"From that cute little Versailles café where we ate breakfast?"

"The second morning of our honeymoon."

"Want me to bring you a Venetian mug so you'll have two from Europe? Better yet, how about a pair of hand-blown wine glasses."

"Now you're talking. Are you finished for the day?"

"In between scenes. What's the latest with Dad's property?"

"He's now officially the owner of a real-life crime scene." Charlie shared the newest developments of the *Follow the Facts* crew. "Mitch assigned your sister and my dad to babysit the crew."

"Last year all over again."

"Except this time the assignment is without pay and for a week instead of two months."

"They'll have to deal with all the over-zealous residents eager to capitalize on their experience appearing on camera. Would you believe I miss all the drama?"

"And I thought you missed my charming personality and Brownie's puppy-dog eyes."

"You two are a close second. Although ..." Rachel tilted her head and tapped her index finger on her cheek. "It wouldn't take much to move up to the number-one spot. Like less predictability and a few fun surprises."

"What qualifies as fun?"

"Definitely not coming home to a yard full of goats and chickens."

"Uh-oh. Back to the drawing board." He snapped his fingers. "How about a couple of cows and a pot-bellied pig?"

"My city-slicker turned country-boy husband is a hoot and a half."

He laughed. "That phrase qualifies you as a full-fledged country girl. Although you're still a work in progress when it comes to country music."

"I'm getting there." Should she mention their anniversary again? Maybe resort to begging? Her phone alarm buzzed. That conversation would have to wait. "Time to go back to work. Keep me updated on the crazy goings-on and email me pictures. Oh, and hug Brownie for me."

"Will do."

"I love you, Charlie."

"Me too. I can't wait to sweep you off your feet."

Rachel ended the call and rushed to an elegant, second-floor restaurant overlooking St. Mark Square. After changing into her costume, she climbed onto a stool to let her makeup artist work her magic.

Justin moseyed over and nodded toward the window. "See that striking brunette?"

"One of the extras?"

He nodded. "She invited the cast to her apartment for drinks after we finish this scene."

"You can count me out. After another long session, all I'll want is a hot bath and a cold glass of ginger ale."

"Is that your cocktail of choice?"

"The stomach wants what the stomach wants. Besides, I'm guessing the brunette has eyes for you."

Justin shoved his hands in his pockets. "No more one-night stands for me, thanks to your influence."

"Are you blaming or thanking me?"

"I'll let you know tomorrow. By the way, any idea what's going on with Beth?"

"What do you mean?"

"Someone called her when we finished this morning's shoot. I couldn't hear her conversation, but believe me I recognize a woman's fury when I see it. Then the waterworks started and she took off. I tried calling, but she didn't answer. I'm worried about her."

"Maybe she and Chloe had a mother-daughter fight."

"Sounded a lot more serious."

"Do you want me to call her?"

"Yeah. Where's your phone?"

Rachel pointed. He brought it to her. She pressed Beth's number. The call went straight to voicemail. "I'll check on her when we finish here." She noted Justin's furrowed brow and tense jaw. "You care about her, don't you?"

"Call me after you talk to her. No matter how late."

Chapter 41

Following hours of filming, Rachel pulled her phone from her purse and pressed Beth's number.

Justin stared at her. "Any luck?"

She shook her head. "Maybe she's out sightseeing or shopping."

"This late? Without her phone? Something's wrong."

Rachel touched his arm. "I'm sure there's a logical explanation."

The gorgeous brunette who served as an extra during three scenes wandered over and slid her hand around Justin's bicep. "You're an amazing actor." Her thick accent oozed with expectation. "My friends are dying to meet American movie stars."

Rachel scoffed. Especially a good-looking Texan known for womanizing.

The brunette eyed Rachel. "Will you come too?"

"Not tonight. You go on and charm our Italian fans, Justin. I promise to call you after I talk to our friend."

"You sure?"

"Positive."

The brunette ogled her captured movie star. "You will love my apartment."

Rachel watched the woman steer her prey toward the exit. What was it with women and celebrities? Bragging rights? Curiosity? She stepped behind a partition. After changing into her own clothes, she pressed Beth's number again. Straight to voicemail. Had her phone's battery died? Except she would have discovered it by now. Wouldn't she? Fearing Justin was right, she dashed downstairs and out to St Mark's Square. Her breathing accelerated as she stepped up her pace. The upbeat atmosphere failed to ease her growing anxiety. By the time she reached the hotel, her heart pounded against her ribs. She headed straight to an open elevator. When it stopped on her floor, she hurried to Beth's room and knocked. No answer. She knocked again. Louder.

The door opened.

Rachel stared at her friend's red swollen eyes and tear-stained cheeks. "What's wrong? Did something happen to Chloe or Ethan?"

Beth shook her head and motioned Rachel inside before trudging to the window facing Grand Canal. She dropped onto a red slipper chair beside a round table. "What's wrong with me?"

Rachel closed the door and sat in the chair opposite her. "What do you mean?"

Beth lifted a bottle of Prosecco off the table and filled a glass. "Why can't I marry a man capable of honoring even one freaking vow?" She swallowed a long drink. "Number three didn't have the decency to wait until we're together to break the news."

"What's going on?"

"My multi-platinum scumbag of a husband called to tell me he's throwing our marriage on the garbage heap so he can move to Paris with some twenty-year-old French supermodel."

No wonder she wasn't answering her phone. "You're right, he is a bum."

"What is it with men and younger women? His new honey isn't old enough to have a fully developed brain. Like that makes a difference."

Rachel's mind drifted to Justin and the brunette clinging to his arm. Why were men such easy prey?

Beth stared at her glass. "He said if I agree to a quick no-contest divorce, he'll give me full custody of Sophia and twenty-five grand a month until she graduates from college."

"That's a lot of alimony."

"It's peanuts compared to the gazillions he makes every year. How could he abandon his own sweet baby daughter?"

"What are you going to do?"

"Short of hiring a hit man?" Beth drained her glass and refilled it. "Why do I always fall for losers? Maybe I don't deserve any better. Goodness knows I've had my share of casual affairs."

"Don't beat yourself up, Beth. You're not the one who walked out on your family."

"I'm beginning to think successful marriages are impossible in our business. Except for a lucky few. Like Maggie Warren." Beth tilted her glass toward Rachel. "Or you and Charlie. Even though you're still newlyweds, it seems you two are headed for an amazing life together."

"There are plenty of good guys out there. Maybe you're looking in all the wrong places."

Beth stared at Rachel for a long moment. "Last time I called home, Ethan carried on about his new buddy." She set her glass on the table." Seems my son and Justin hit it off big time."

"Deep down he has a Texas-size heart."

"And the hots for every costar he ever met."

"People can change."

"Who do you think you're kidding? He's a playboy movie star who spent one dinner making up for ditching me." She sniffled, pulled a tissue from a box, and blew her nose. "No more short-term flings for me. I'm putting my family first."

Rachel's brow furrowed. "Reconciliation?"

"With sleazeball husband number three? Not one chance in a million. Mark my words—from this moment on, before I date any man, he'll need my kids' *and* their dogs' approval."

Was the Prosecco talking, or had she experienced an epiphany?

"Problem is, I don't trust myself. What I need is an accountability partner. You know, like Alcoholics Anonymous."

"What are you suggesting?"

"If there are any decent men left and I meet one I'm attracted to, I want to call you before I go and do something stupid."

"I'm not qualified to give dating advice."

Beth reached across the table and touched Rachel's arm. "Please." Her eyes pleaded. "I trust you, and I want to change the way my life is going...for me and my kids."

How could she say no? "All right, accountability partner."

"Thank you, Rachel. You have no idea how much your friendship means to me." She hiccupped. "Sorry for keeping you up so late."

"I'll rest easy knowing you're okay. So will Justin after I call and tell him you're okay."

Beth stared at her. "He worried about me?"

"More than you can imagine. Sleep well, my friend." Rachel walked out and called Justin.

He answered on the first ring. "Did you find Beth?"

"I just left her room. She's okay."

"Meet me in Bar Dandolo."

"It's past eleven and I'm exhausted."

"Please. We need to talk."

Justin's anxiety-ridden tone set off alarm bells. "I'm on my way." Rachel rode the elevator to the ground floor where she found him sitting at the bar nursing a drink. Alone. She slid onto a stool beside him. The bartender stepped over. "What would you like, Ms. Streetman."

"Ginger ale on the rocks." She turned toward Justin. "What happened to the big fan party and the brunette?"

"Turned out I was the only guest and she was the only fan."

"Why am I not surprised? So what happened?"

"I gave her my autograph, thanked her for the invitation, and left her apartment."

Rachel stared at him. "You turned down a gorgeous Italian who wanted her way with you?"

"Yeah."

"Well, I'll be. Seems Texas-size principles rescued you from a meaningless one-night stand."

"I'm not sure *rescued* is the right word."

"Are you experiencing a smidgen of regret?"

"Maybe I was too worried about Beth. What's going on with her? Why didn't she answer her phone."

The bartender set a glass of ginger ale in front of Rachel and moved to the other end of the bar. "Her husband called to say he was dumping her for a French supermodel. That man's scruples wouldn't put a dent in a thimble."

"How's she taking it?"

"How do you think?"

"She's bummed out."

"Big time."

"Is she swearing off men?"

Rachel sipped her drink. "No, although she claims from now on any man she dates will have to meet her children's approval."

"Not a bad idea." He signaled the bartender for another drink. "Beth wasn't the only reason I walked out on the brunette." He pulled his phone from his belt clip, pressed an icon, and handed it over. "Ethan sent this an hour ago."

Rachel pressed her hand to her chest as she read the last sentences of Ethan's message. *If you're not too busy, will you be my pretend dad? You don't have to marry my mom. She's already got a husband. Even though he's not around much.*

"Oh my gosh, Justin. How are you going to respond?"

"I don't have a clue. Another reason I wanted to talk to you."

How had she become the on-call psychologist for screwed-up actors? Rachel sipped her ginger ale. Should she give him advice or let him figure it out on his own? Maybe a little of both. "What was your first reaction to his text?"

"That life's a lot easier for irresponsible playboys."

"I can imagine." She slid his phone back to him. "You seemed to hit it off with Ethan."

"He's a good kid. Reminds me of my brother's nine-year-old son."

"Ethan needs a father figure."

"Obviously. But why me?"

"It seems children and dogs have an innate intuition about people."

He waited for the bartender to set down his drink and walk away. "What's your point?"

"Ethan picked you because he understands you're a good guy with a big heart."

"Are you suggesting I take on the role?"

"You should do what your heart tells you to do."

Justin fell silent and cradled his drink.

Rachel eyed dozens of bottles lined up on glass shelves behind the bartender. What was he thinking? Would he need more liquid courage to make a decision? The bartender pulling the cork from a bottle of Prosecco brought Beth's comments about poor choices to mind.

"Ethan isn't the only needy member of Beth's family." She touched Justin's arm. "Beth needs a decent male friend. Someone she can trust."

"I slept with her one time and dumped her, so what makes you think she'd trust me or even want me in Ethan's life?"

"Is that what's keeping you from making a decision?"

"She doesn't need more headaches."

Rachel removed her phone from her pocket and pulled up Beth's number. "Call her."

"At this hour?"

"Trust me."

He stared at her for a long moment, then polished off his drink in one long swallow and pressed the number. "Beth, it's Justin." He slid off his barstool and ambled across the room.

The bartender stepped over and removed his empty glass. "Should I bring Mr. Brooks another drink?"

Rachel glanced over her shoulder and noted Justin's expression. "Not yet." She propped her elbow on the bar, rested her chin on her fist, and hoped she hadn't crossed the line. Five minutes passed. Maybe she shouldn't have suggested he call. Ten more minutes. They wouldn't talk so long if everything wasn't okay. Would they?

Justin returned to his stool and set Rachel's phone on the bar.

"Well?"

"She says I'll make a great dad." He lifted his phone off the bar and tapped a text message.

"What'd you tell Ethan?"

"That I'd visit him as soon as we finish filming, and will attend his first baseball game next season."

Rachel patted his arm. "You made the right decision."

"Ironic. I have a seven-year-old kid and no wife. Strange world we live in."

"I'm beginning to think Robert casting you and Beth in the same movie is way more than a random incident."

"Are you playing celebrity matchmaker?"

"Your publicist already played that role. Although it'd be a hoot if her publicity turned out to be accurate."

"Hoot is Texas talk."

"Works for transplanted city gals too."

Justin signaled for another round of drinks. When the bartender delivered them, he lifted his glass. "To my costar who rejected me three times before becoming a life-long friend."

"Cheers." Rachel clinked her glass to his. "If you and Beth become a couple, you have to invite Charlie and me to your wedding."

"You're getting a little ahead of yourself."

"I'm just considering the possibility. Besides, you attended my wedding so I'd expect to attend yours."

Justin sipped his drink. "Now that I think about it, seven is a lucky number."

"What?"

"The total number of our marriages between Beth and me if you playing matchmaker pays off."

"I'd call that a good-luck sign."

Chapter 42

Emily refreshed her coffee, carried the mug to the kitchen table, and dropped onto the chair across from Scott. "Yesterday Janet Johnson's glares sent shivers up my spine."

He stabbed his last bite of scrambled eggs. "Either you've had too much coffee or you've created the opening line for your next book."

"Chances are she flavors her eggs with pulverized nails. That woman could stare down a hungry tiger and send it whimpering back to its pride."

"Are you backing out?"

"And let Mitch and Brick think I'm a wimp? I'll put on my big-girl pants, stand up to her, and gather material for my book. However, if the she-dragon snarls and bares her teeth, I might need you to come rescue me."

"Great name for her. Should I sharpen my sword?" Scott carried his plate to the sink.

"Are you talking about the wooden-handled spatula hanging on our grill?"

"That's the one." He chuckled. "Before wielding my trusty spatula, I have to go earn a living."

"Are you dodging your knight-in-shining-armor duty?"

"Only the one likely to spill blood." Scott leaned down and kissed her cheek. "Keep me posted, fair lady." He patted Cody's head, grabbed his frock coat, and headed to the garage.

Emily sipped her coffee until the twins toddled into the kitchen. "Hey, sweet girls. Are you ready for breakfast?"

After feeding her daughters and taking them to nursery school, Emily found a parking space around the corner from the newspaper office, across from Nathan's Antique and Furniture Emporium. The store where she'd found furniture for Willow Inn. She fingered her mother's engagement ring on her right hand. Her town had come too far to let the she-dragon stir up trouble. Emily grabbed her purse and computer bag and stepped onto the sidewalk.

A neighbor walking his dog smiled. "Morning, Emily. What do you know about the TV crew that checked into the hotel?"

That news spread fast.

"Rumor is they plan to interview everyone in town."

"You know how rumors are."

"Around here, pretty darn accurate." His dog tugged on its leash. "They can count on me to give them an honest opinion."

"I have no doubt." Emily rounded the corner, relieved to find that section of sidewalk empty. She stepped up her pace and walked into the *Willow Post* headquarters.

Mary glanced up from the desk. "They're already driving me crazy."

"What are you talking about?"

"All the calls. How are you handling them?"

"I'm not." Emily fished her phone from her purse, switched it from silent, and stared at the screen. "The sun's barely up and I already have twenty-nine new voicemail messages."

"Welcome to Tuesday in Willow Falls."

"Looks like we're in for another long day." Emily set her bag on the worktable and brought Mary up to speed on yesterday's conversation with the investigative crew. "I can't believe She-Dragon—"

"Who?"

"Janet Johnson, the lead investigator. Anyway, she must have leaked word about the interviews." She grabbed her ringing phone and pressed the speaker icon. "How many phone calls have you logged this morning, Mr. Mayor?"

"More than I can count."

"Where are you?"

"At the hotel."

Emily ignored another incoming call. "Did Janet announce interviews over the PA or hold court in the dining room last night?"

"She's not at fault. Based on the scuttlebutt, a tourist noticed their van's logo. Didn't take long for word to spread."

Mary nodded toward the window. "That explains why half the town isn't lined up outside our door."

"And why I'm standing at the hotel's back stairs waiting to sneak the television crew to my car and escort them out of here."

Emily's eyes widened. "Won't people recognize them?"

"Rumors started after they checked in and ordered room service, so folks don't know what they look like. Anyway, change of plans. I'm driving them to the dig site so they can shoot footage before they meet with us. I'll call you when we're heading your way."

"Thanks, Brick." Emily set her phone on the table and pulled her computer from her bag. "We need to create a plan before Brick and the crew arrives. Here's what I'm thinking—"

Hours later Emily glanced at her watch while drumming her fingers on the table. "Half past noon and no word from Brick."

Mary stopped typing. "You remember how long it took to shoot one movie scene?"

"You're assuming the crew is filming."

"What else would they be doing?"

"I have no idea." Quashing the urge to check her watch, Emily pulled up email and scrolled to a new message. "My sister sent movie scenes for this week's *Rachel's Venice Adventure*. One of Robert Nordstrom directing Justin and Beth, and the other a camera operator filming Rachel standing on a bridge." Emily grabbed her vibrating phone. "Finally." She pressed the speaker icon. "Are you on your way?"

"Another change. Meeting at my house. Forty-five minutes." Brick's tone signaled exasperation.

Emily stuffed her phone in her pocket as a litany of potential scenarios raced through her mind at warp speed. Plotlines for her next book and hard-breaking news items. "I need to clear my head before the meeting."

"I'll hold down the fort here."

"Thanks, Mary." Emily donned her sunglasses, walked out, and breathed in the crisp autumn air. How much trouble had the she-dragon created? She crossed Main, entered the park, and stopped at the new gazebo. Her eyes drifted to the plaque over the entrance. *Dedicated to Mr. and Mrs. Charlie Bricker and Mr. and Mrs. Reginald Bricker, newcomers who made a difference.*

"Did you defeat the dragon, or beat a quick retreat?"

Emily pushed her sunglasses up and turned toward Scott. "Are you trolling, or taking a break?"

"Hunting for beautiful redheads. Seems I captured one."

"Now what are you gonna do?"

"Think I'll marry her." He snapped his fingers. "Oh wait, I already did."

"Lucky me."

"How'd your meeting with the TV crew go?"

"It didn't." They climbed onto the gazebo while Emily relayed Brick's call. "He's not a happy mayor."

"Willow Falls has weathered plenty of storms." Scott wrapped his arm around her shoulders. "We'll survive this one."

She rested her head on his shoulder. "Thank you."

"For what?"

"Being my shining knight."

"Anything for my fair lady. Especially something sweet." He removed a small candy bag from his coat pocket.

"Lemon drops?"

"Your favorite."

Emily popped a sweet in her mouth and savored the sugary sour taste. "Exactly what I need."

Ten minutes before the appointed time, Emily kissed Scott, lowered her sunglasses, and crossed Main Street. She arrived on Brick's front porch as the mail truck pulled up to the curb.

"Wait." Mirabelle raced up the sidewalk. "Are we meeting with the *Follow the Facts* crew?"

Emily pushed her sunglasses up. "I don't see their truck, so I'm guessing no."

"The hotel's a block away. They could've walked."

"Good point." They headed inside and found the council members gathered around the dining room table. Emily sat beside Patsy and eyed the platter of cookies. "You brought comfort food?"

Patsy nodded. "Emergency meetings call for extraordinary measures."

Sadie set a tray of mugs on the table. "Hot chocolate with whipped cream for everyone."

"We're for sure in for one serious discussion," whispered Patsy.

Brick sat at the end of the table. "Thanks for dropping everything, folks. This morning we learned more about the bone discovery. Our sheriff will give you the details."

Mitch planted his forearms on the table. "GBI confirmed they're dealing with a serious crime."

"I knew it." Mirabelle snapped her fingers.

Attorney Harold leaned forward. "How serious?"

"They've identified five of the eight victims."

Pepper's eyes widened. "The body count jumped from six?"

Mitch nodded. "GBI's keeping their identity under wraps for the time being. I suspect by now, you've all heard about the *Follow the Facts* crew conducting a parallel investigation."

Mirabelle reached for a cookie. "Is that legal?"

"As long as they don't interfere with the official probe or step outside the law."

Harold leaned forward. "I'm familiar with their television program. They're vultures when it comes to digging up clues and solving crimes."

"Which explains why they want to interview everyone willing to talk." Brick eyed Emily. "Janet reluctantly agreed to give us twenty-four hours to prepare residents. Mitch, Greer, and I want you to inform the public tomorrow."

"In a newspaper article?"

"Is that possible?"

Emily sighed. "We'll make it happen."

"Good. Now we need to devise a plan to keep the crew in line."

Following two hours around the dining room table and two more at the newspaper office, Emily tapped her fingers on the worktable. "I need you to proof listen."

Mary walked over from her desk. "What's the headline?"

"*New Evidence Confirms Crime.*"

"Blunt."

"No time to quibble. Here's the article."

"GBI forensic analysis identified five of eight bodies discovered during ground clearing for Willow Falls' newest development. Investigators confirmed all are male and those identified are Army veterans. Based on varied levels of deterioration, the discovery hints of a serial murder spanning several decades.

"While GBI continues to search for evidence, the *Follow the Facts* team will conduct an independent investigation. To prevent unnecessary disruption to business and tourist attractions, they agreed to follow the interview schedule posted on page two. If you have information you believe is important, please select the time and place most convenient for you. Like last year's movie scenes, all interviews will be edited for content and relevance. When and where your interviews take place is irrelevant.

"Emily Hayes or Mayor Bricker will accompany the team during all interviews to ensure fair and accurate reporting. Our primary objective remains the same: Show the world we are a caring community, eager to welcome visitors with open arms and delight them with our hospitality and fascinating history."

Emily looked up and eyed Mary. "What do you think?"

"I'm surprised the television crew agreed to a set schedule."

"Mitch told Janet that residents would hound them like star-struck groupies if they didn't. I'm counting on the comment about timing to prevent every television-star wannabe from flocking to the first interview."

"Are you serious?"

"Yeah, I know." Emily released a heavy sigh. "At least we can hope."

The front door opened, emitting a waft of cool air. Mitch strolled in and set two Styrofoam containers on the worktable. "Dinner, compliments of Redding Arms' executive chef."

Emily lifted a lid and sniffed the aroma of tomatoes and garlic. "Are you adding food delivery to your law-enforcement duties?"

"Convenient coincidence." He hiked his hip on the table and handed his phone to Emily. "I wanted you to have a heads-up before chaos breaks out."

She stared at a photograph. "What am I looking at?"

"A piece of evidence the GBI guys uncovered an hour ago. Janet and her crew plan to show a photo to residents during interviews."

Emily held the picture close and stared at the object. "Half the initials are indistinguishable."

Mitch crossed his arms. "Corrosive pitting."

She slid the phone to Mary. "That won't stop folks from conjuring a slew of cockamamie theories."

Mary studied the photo for a long moment. "Does GBI have a theory about who this belonged to?" She handed the phone to Mitch.

"They claim it could have belonged to three of the bodies they identified. They'll release the names in a day or two."

Emily's brain switched from editor to author mode. "Locals finding clues to solve the crime would add exciting plot twists to my next book."

Mitch texted the photo to Emily before pocketing his phone. "A murder scrutinized by a talented writer and an aggressive television crew."

"You mean, two."

"Writers or crews?"

"Alicia texted me twenty minutes ago. The *Around Georgia* team plans to roll into town the day after tomorrow."

Mitch pushed away from the table. "Times like these, I miss the good old days when fender benders were big news. I'll meet you and Brick on location tomorrow morning an hour and a half before the first interview."

Emily brushed her fingers through her hair. "You sound like a director scheduling a movie scene. Too bad you don't have a slate clapper."

"Maybe I'll wear a ballcap and bring a megaphone." Mitch shook his head while lumbering to the door.

Mary reached for a Styrofoam container. "Are you planning to add the photo and details to the article?"

"Not a chance. We'll face enough chaos after Janet reveals the picture to her first victim."

Chapter 43

A gust of wind sent goosebumps popping out on Emily's neck. She turned her jacket collar up and rushed from her car to the tent closest to the crime-scene tape. "Maybe the forecast will keep residents from flocking to the first interview."

"It'll take more than a little rain to scare them off." Mitch adjusted his Atlanta Braves ballcap. "Although lightning might do the trick."

Brick thrust his thumb toward six vehicles following the red panel van. "Our first arrivals." He pushed his sleeve away from his watch. "An hour and twenty minutes early."

"Time to go to work." Mitch strode to the first car and directed residents toward the third tent.

While Paul, the *Follow the Facts* research guy, helped Garrett unload his camera equipment, Janet made a beeline to Emily. "Threatening clouds are perfect for an unfolding drama. Good thing the GBI guys covered the crime scene with a tarp." She turned toward Brick. "I have questions for the landowner. Is he on his way over?"

"Greer left for his Atlanta office an hour ago."

"Too bad."

After securing his camera on a tripod, Garrett donned headphones, signaled a thumbs-up to Paul, and handed a microphone to Janet. "We're good to go, boss."

"Good." She eyed Emily, then Brick. "To make sure we're on the same track, I'll go over plans one more time. One of you will accompany Paul while he screens people willing to talk. The other will stand beside the camera while I conduct the interviews." Her jaw tightened. "I agreed to this arrangement out of respect for law enforcement. Now I expect you to exercise restraint and resist interfering unless you have a legitimate concern."

"Fair enough." Brick pulled Emily aside and turned his back to Janet. "I know she's difficult to deal with. Do you want to take on screening duties?"

Emily spotted a hawk swooping from a high limb to pluck an unsuspecting critter skittering across the cleared path. "I won't let that woman intimidate me. Do you mind if I babysit her and let you stick with Paul?"

"Works for me. Signal me if you decide to switch places."

"I will."

While Brick headed to the staging tent, Emily positioned herself beside Garrett and rubbed her palms together to ease the chill.

Janet stared at her phone. "According to the forecast, we have an hour before the weather turns foul. Which means we need to begin now." She slid her phone in her coat pocket. "Paul's sending the first person over in three minutes."

Emily approached Janet. "I understand your reasoning. However, if you start early I guarantee residents will show up at the next location an hour ahead of schedule."

"In case you haven't noticed—" Janet's tone mocked as she swept her hand toward the growing line of vehicles. "They're doing that now."

Heat traveled from Emily's neck to her cheeks. Brilliant comment if she wanted She-Dragon thinking she's a country bumpkin who couldn't see the obvious. "Point taken."

"We need to keep this session moving. When I lower my microphone and signal you, escort whoever I'm interviewing away from the camera." Janet nodded toward a woman heading their way. "Do you know her?"

"I know everyone in town." Now she sounded like a *sarcastic* country bumpkin. Just answer the question. "She owns the property adjacent to this."

"How far from here?"

"Half a mile."

The elderly woman stepped beside Janet. Upon request she stated her name. "I've lived here all my life, so I know a thing or two about what goes on."

"What insight do you have about the recent discovery?"

"Everyone in town knows about Buster Bishop. He's the nasty old coot who owned this property before Greer Streetman bought it. Even Buster's daughter couldn't stand him. She up and left town after her mom passed on. I don't know why she married that man. Such a sweet lady and a good friend. She grew the best tasting tomatoes in town. All different kinds."

"Do you suspect Mr. Bishop had something to do with the crime?"

"I don't want to speak out of turn, but he did a lot of shooting on this property. Mostly deer and wild turkeys. Have you ever tasted deer meat? Not bad if you marinate it with plenty of vinegar. I have a good recipe."

"Thank you for the tip. About Bishop, did he smoke?"

"Like a chimney."

Janet removed a photograph from her pocket and held it up. "This was found where the bones were discovered. Does it look familiar?"

The woman leaned close and squinted. "Is that a cigarette lighter? The initials are mostly scratched off. It's possible they're both B's. Except that looks a might too fancy for old Buster. Maybe his wife gave it to him."

"Did you ever see him use a lighter?"

"Can't say I did. Is he a suspect?"

"At this point, no one's a suspect. If you remember anything that might help us, contact your newspaper editor or mayor."

Emily rolled her eyes. *Thanks a lot, lady.*

"I'll think back real hard. First, I want to tell your audience to come to Willow Falls for a visit. We have five restaurants now. Pepper's Café is still my favorite, even though Pepper doesn't cook there anymore. She's a fancy chef at the hotel—"

"Thank you for talking to us." Janet lowered her mike and motioned to Emily.

Taking the cue, she slipped her arm around the woman's shoulders and aimed her toward the staging area. She spotted Gertie lifting her floor-length skirt off the ground and walking toward the production tent.

Janet snickered. "How long has that woman been stuck in the nineteenth century?"

"The dress is her work uniform." Emily pressed her lips tight to suppress a grin. *She-Dragon has no idea what she was in for.*

Gertie stepped beside Janet and squared her shoulders. "Last night I watched a *Follow the Facts* episode. The one about the missing twenty-three-year-old waitress. She was so young, and pretty as a spring flower. Such a sad case." Her head tilted. "You look younger on the television."

Janet smirked while lifting her microphone. "State your name."

"Everyone knows me as Gertie, the soda-fountain lady over at Hayes General Store. The business dates back more than a hundred years, which is why I'm wearing this dress. I bought it from the Internet. Can you believe an old lady like me learned how to work a computer?"

"Interesting bit of information. If you don't mind, let's focus on the crime."

"Of course, honey. This is your show. What do you want to know?"

"Do you have a theory?"

"First off, the killer definitely isn't from these parts. Do you know the story about Percy and Peaches? Our town's signature play is all about them. Most everyone around here is kinfolk to one of Willow Falls' early settlers. All decent God-fearing folks. Except for Robert Liles. Turns out he wasn't the town's hero after all."

"Did Mr. Liles smoke?"

"Not that I remember. Of course, no one knew about his secret drinking, either."

Janet revealed the photo. "Does this look familiar?"

Gertie tapped her finger on the picture. "Those initials kind of look like an R and L. Except..." She paused. "Unless some of those killings took place in the past couple of decades, Robert's not the killer."

"Why not?"

"Because Sadie shot him dead thirty-three years ago."

Emily cringed.

Janet's eyes widened. "Sadie?"

"Brick's wife, but no need to go chasing down that gopher hole. She killed him for good reason." Gertie's head tilted. "Come to think of it, a long time ago rumors floated around about a Liles family scandal."

"What kind of scandal?"

She tapped her finger on her temple "The details are buried somewhere up here. I'll try to dig them out for you."

"Any other relevant information?"

"I'm glad you asked." Gertie removed a small, square-shaped bottle from her skirt pocket and held it in front of the camera. "When you folks across America visit Willow Falls, you can buy an authentic piece of history. In addition to unique merchandise, we're selling red clay from the crime scene and a photo of the bones."

Janet lowered her mike as a thunderclap rumbled in the distance and raindrops pelted the canvas roof. "That's a wrap, Garrett. We'll pick back up tomorrow." After Gertie returned to the staging area, Janet approached Emily. "What do you know about Sadie?"

"She's my mother." Emily's pulse pounded in her ears. "Unless you want the entire town's wrath raining down on your crew, I advise you to leave her out of this."

Janet's eyes narrowed. "Are you threatening me?"

Emily met her stare. "From one professional to another, I'm preventing you from going down a path that won't lead to anything other than a colossal waste of your valuable time."

"Point taken."

"Then we have an understanding?"

Janet held her gaze for a long moment. "As long as you're straight with me." She handed the microphone to Garrett and returned to the van.

Emily breathed deeply to slow her pounding pulse, then made her way to Brick to give him a heads-up about Gertie's revelation regarding Mama Sadie

Chapter 44

Dry heaves sent Rachel racing from her bed to the bathroom. She dropped to her knees and hung her head over the toilet. Again. At least no one witnessed this bout. When the sensation subsided she leaned back against the cool tile. If she didn't pull herself together, she'd miss the pre-dawn shoot. Not gonna happen. She pressed a wet washcloth to her forehead and struggled to dismiss growing suspicions.

Rachel pushed off the floor and gripped the towel rack until her head stopped spinning. She stumbled to the bedroom and washed down three saltines with half a bottle of ginger ale. Grateful she'd had the sense to stock an emergency stash, she trudged back to the bathroom, turned on the shower, and caught her image in the mirror. Her makeup artist would have her work cut out for her this morning. When steam fogged the glass, she stepped under the hot water, closed her eyes, and blamed the nausea on exhaustion from too many late nights. Somehow she had to get more sleep.

After forcing her body to abandon the shower, Rachel dressed in sweats and grabbed the half-full bottle of ginger ale. She opened her door, relieved to find the hall empty. On her way to the elevator, she passed 'do not disturb' signs. Guests enjoying a romantic vacation in a magical setting. She fought off envy and mentally rehearsed the morning's lines until she arrived at makeup central and dropped onto her artist's chair. "Good morning, Gina."

"*Buongiorno*, Madame." The woman draped a white bib around Rachel's neck and stepped back. Her brows furrowed. "You sick?"

Did she look that bad? Rachel caught a glimpse of her pale skin in the mirror. Yeah, she did. "Not sick. Sleepy."

While Gina began working magic to transform her pale subject into a camera-ready performer, Rachel tuned out the conversations around her and let her mind wander to her costars. Was it possible they'd become a couple? Logic dictated no. Yet love had prevailed over logic for Mama Sadie and Charlie's dad. So why not Beth and Justin? Texas playboy lassos shopaholic California girl. She suppressed a giggle. Great movie script or a Nashville-inspired song.

Her thoughts shifted to Charlie and their last conversation. She'd come to terms with his decision to stay in Willow Falls during their first harvest. After all Brick had spent a fortune turning his dream into reality, and he counted on his son to come through with quality wine that would position the winery as a serious competitor rather than a mediocre player. Besides she and Charlie had years to celebrate their anniversaries together.

The sudden onset of nausea forced Rachel to push Gina's hand away from her face and swallow mouthfuls of ginger ale.

Gina stared wide-eyed. "You okay? Not sick?"

"Not sick." Rachel traced an X across her chest. "Promise."

"Okey dokey."

The woman's attempt to master English phrases tickled Rachel's funny bone. "Si, okey dokey."

After Gina finished working her magic, Rachel headed to wardrobe and changed into her costume. She wrapped a woolen shawl around her shoulders, grabbed a pair of oversized prop glasses, and walked out of the hotel. After donning the glasses to prevent the predawn chill from triggering tears and destroying her makeup, she crossed the Bridge of Sighs and stopped beside cameras set up between Doges Palace and Grand Canal. Gondolas bobbing and swaying in a water taxi's wake forced her to close her eyes and pray the movement wouldn't trigger another round of nausea.

A hand gripping her arm startled her. "Are you okay?"

She blinked and faced Justin, her jaw set. "Do I look like I'm not okay?"

"You were wobbling."

That's just great. People noticed. "The waves make me dizzy."

"Good thing you're not a native Venetian."

Robert joined them and pointed to the sun peeking over Lido di Venezia. "We have a short window to capture this view." He moved them into position and clasped Justin's shoulder. "This scene is your character's attempt to apologize for his indiscretion."

He nodded. "Got it."

Robert removed Rachel's shawl and glasses before stepping away.

The cameras rolled. They spoke their lines. The cameras repositioned. They completed three more takes, each from a different camera angle.

"That's a rap." Robert returned the shawl and glasses. "Well done, you two. We'll reset and resume outside Doges in an hour."

Rachel pulled her shawl tight across her chest and fixed her gaze on the swath of orange transforming the dark sky above the narrow island east of Venice.

Justin stood close. "Quarter for your thoughts?"

"What happened to a penny?"

"Italian inflation."

"I'm wondering what it's like to walk barefoot on a sandy beach."

"Hold on." He stared at her. "Are you saying you've never vacationed at the ocean? Not even as a kid?"

"Until a year ago, my dad was a consummate workaholic. When I was growing up he considered our big house and pool vacation enough."

Justin shook his head. "You have no idea how much you missed."

"Chloe showed me a little bottle she'd filled with sand from Lido di Venezia beach. That's one souvenir that didn't set Beth back hundreds of dollars."

"You, Beth, and I could taxi over to Lido after today's shoot and give you a chance to satisfy your curiosity."

"Great idea for you and Beth."

"Are you playing matchmaker?"

"I'll leave that role to a seven-year-old smart enough to pick out his next daddy. As for me, I plan to spend the afternoon hiding out in my hotel room and catching up on my sleep." Truth was she longed to share her first beach-walking experience with the man she loved. Maybe next summer in a hotel overlooking the Atlantic ocean.

Chapter 45

Emily adjusted her ballcap low on her forehead to shield her eyes from the noonday sun. Her focus shifted from the crowd gathered in the park beside Redding Arms to Janet tapping her foot on the sidewalk, waiting for her next interview.

"Has the she-dragon fried any of her victims yet?"

Emily turned toward Scott's whisper. "Hi, honey. I didn't hear you sneak up."

"How are the interviews going?"

"Eleven down. Who knows how many to go."

He pointed to the street. "At least viewers will see Pepper's Café and Patsy's store in the background."

"If any of the footage ever makes it on their show. Which is unlikely considering everyone has an opinion but not one bit of relevant information. Funny how they all mention the town as a must-see tourist attraction."

"Because your front-page article made promoting Willow Falls a top priority."

"Janet's plenty annoyed." She leaned close to Scott. "Rumor is GBI will release the victims' names tomorrow."

"That could shake some clues loose." He nudged her arm and nodded toward the hotel. "I can't wait to watch this interview."

"No telling what she'll say. And what's with the basket she's carrying?"

Janet's foot stopped tapping as the next resident closed in on her. "State your name for the camera, please."

"Mirabelle Paine." She set the basket on the sidewalk. "I'm the second-in-command town council member. Also, a United States postal delivery person and costar in our town's signature play. Everyone's talking about those initials on the cigarette lighter."

"I see." Janet revealed the photo. "I suppose you have a theory."

"Buster Bishop wasn't stupid enough to shoot people and bury them on his own property. Which rules him out as a suspect." Mirabelle stared at the photo. "If that first initial is a K, E, or P the lighter belonged to one of the dead guys."

"Why have you come to that conclusion?"

"I'd know if anyone from around here with those initials was mean enough to kill eight people."

Janet lowered the mike. "Then there's no need to continue—"

"Not so fast. I have plenty more to say." Mirabelle grabbed the microphone. "First off, if those initials are R and L, Robert Liles could have owned it. I worked as his housekeeper way back before he married Sadie's mama. While it's a fact he didn't smoke cigarettes, it's reasonable to think he owned a fancy lighter for the box of expensive of cigars he kept for his guests."

Janet retrieved the mike. "Didn't he die before the crime spree ended?"

"Which is why he's also not a suspect. However, some criminal-minded person who visited him could have stolen the lighter. You need to chase down that lead."

"We'll look into it. Are there other locals with the initials R and L?"

"A few. All good people." Mirabelle's brow furrowed. "There is one good-for-nothing thief." She shook her head. "Sorry. Not possible."

"That's the first concrete lead I've heard. Tell me the name, and we'll dig further."

"He left town more than forty years ago. Probably dead by now. Forget I mentioned it."

"Thank you, Ms. Paine."

"Before I go." She lifted the basket off the sidewalk and handed it to Janet. "Gifts from some of our businesses and tickets for *Percy's Legacy*. That play will tell you a lot about our town's unique past."

Emily nudged Scott's arm. "Did you contribute to the basket?"

"Gertie's fudge. Sounded like Mirabelle's last comment referred to her old man?"

"If that's the case, she just opened a giant boatload of worms." She caught movement from the corner of her eye. "This is about to heat up."

Janet stalked over. "I insist on talking to anyone who can shed more light on the missing thief."

A confidential conversation with Patsy Peacock three years earlier raced through Emily's mind. Maybe she should tell She-Dragon to buzz off. Except she'd dig around on her own and create havoc. "Possibly one person. But if she agrees to talk to you, it won't happen on camera."

"I'll settle for a private, off-the-record conversation. Will you take me to her, or do I need to waste my time and question everyone in town?"

Emily glimpsed the throng of residents waiting for their moment in the spotlight. She had enough leverage to take charge. "Announce you've finished today's interviews and go back to your hotel room. I'll call you in an hour."

Janet eyes narrowed to slits. "Who do you think you are, giving me orders?"

Scott's jaw clenched. "Wait just a minute—"

"It's okay, honey. I've got this." Emily moved close to Janet. "Here's the thing. You're in my town, on my turf. Which means if you want my cooperation, you'll take my advice."

Janet held Emily's gaze, while turning her chin toward her right shoulder. "Garrett, tell Paul we've finished today's interviews." She fished a business card and pen from her jacket pocket, jotted a note, and handed the card to her. "My private number."

Before Emily could utter a response, Janet whipped around and headed straight to the hotel.

Scott slid his arm around her shoulders. "Way to go, fair lady. What's your next move?"

"Contact my source and find out if I made a commitment I can't deliver." She pulled her vibrating phone from her pocket and read an incoming text. "Here's one bit of good news. Alicia's *Around Georgia* crew's arrival has changed back to Saturday. If we're lucky Janet and company will leave town before then."

"I wouldn't count on it."

Emily stood in the fourth-floor elevator bank and studied Naomi Jasper's mural depicting Willow Falls' early twentieth-century Main Street. The elevator pinged. She turned as the door slid open.

Patsy stepped out carrying a small white box featuring a *Patsy's Pastries and Pretties* logo. She nodded toward the mural. "How many guests do you suppose have a clue what Naomi's signature makes that wall worth?"

"Anyone familiar with her art. Thank you for agreeing to talk to Janet."

"She promised no cameras, right?"

"Yes, but I have to warn you, she's more than a little overbearing."

"Honey, I've managed a business long enough to know how to deal with pushy women. Besides, there's two of us and one of her."

"Hopefully those odds will give us an advantage." They turned right, walked to the end of the hall, and knocked.

Janet opened the door to the mini-suite and pointed to the small brass plaque on the wall. "Why does every hotel room have a name? And who are all those people?

"I'm glad you asked." Patsy smiled. "Local families adopted and decorated all sixty rooms in themes important to them. This lovely suite is dedicated to one of our dentists and his wife."

"They're obviously into flowers."

"They have the second prettiest yard in town." She stepped inside. "I'm Patsy Peacock, owner of the gift shop and bakery across from the park."

"Let me guess, your hotel room is peacock-themed." Janet motioned toward a royal-blue sofa decorated with floral throw pillows. "Do you always wear hats?"

"I do, but that's another story." Patsy set the pastry box on her lap. "Let's get straight to the point. You want to know who Mirabelle Paine referred to earlier today."

Janet pulled a chair away from the antique desk. "I'm listening."

"She was most likely talking about her father, Roland Lambert, the black sheep in his family. He worked as a part-time handyman when he wasn't too drunk to function."

Janet's brow furrowed. "Why did Mirabelle call him a thief?"

"He hightailed it out of town after a neighbor accused him of stealing money. The bum left his daughter and her older brother alone with their unemployed alcoholic mother. If their grandmother hadn't come to their rescue, they'd have starved."

"Where's the brother now?"

"Buried in the town's cemetery. He joined the army when he turned eighteen. Six years later he was killed while on deployment. Rumors about friendly fire ran rampant."

Emily's eyes widened. "First time I've heard that story."

"After the army returned his body to the family, Mirabelle suffered from deep depression. When she recovered, everyone agreed never to mention him again. No one wanted to send her reeling back into despair."

Janet leaned forward. "Did her father ever return to Willow Falls?"

"He wouldn't dare show his face around here." Patsy paused. "I don't want you to misinterpret what I've shared with you. Did everyone consider Roland Lambert a bum? Big time. A petty thief? Absolutely. But a serial killer? I doubt he had the courage."

"I appreciate the information, Ms. Peacock."

"You're welcome. I brought you a gift." She handed over the box.

Janet lifted the lid releasing brown-sugar and vanilla scents.

"Oatmeal raisin cookies. Emily's mother's secret recipe."

"Sadie?"

Patsy shook her head. "The mother who raised Emily." She stood.

"Sit back down, I have more questions."

Emily froze. Was Janet seconds from transforming into an honest-to-goodness fire-breathing dragon?

"Please."

Patsy eyed Emily.

"Might as well, we're off the record."

She sat back down.

"Despite your doubts about Roland, I consider him a suspect." Janet crossed her leg over her knee. "The man has a jaded past. Suspicion surrounds his military son's death. The identified bodies are all Army veterans. That smells of motive." She eyed Emily. "I need you to introduce me to people who might know more and are willing to talk on camera."

Emily hesitated. If she declined, Janet would delve into faded memories and release all sorts of ugly rumors. If she agreed, she'd maintain some semblance of control. "On two conditions. Promise you won't spread any information beyond the interviews, and if they don't lead anywhere, you won't air the footage."

No response.

Emily crossed her arms. "Willow Falls is a tight-knit community. We protect our own."

"Fair enough."

"Then we have a deal?"

"From one professional to another." Janet extended her hand. "We have a deal."

Emily accepted, counting on the woman to possess enough integrity to honor her commitment.

Chapter 46

Emily spotted a couple emerging from their hotel room and held her breath, hoping they wouldn't notice her lurking at the end of the hall. They clasped hands and turned toward the elevators without glancing in her direction. She released the air feeling more akin to a covert CIA agent than a small town newspaper editor.

The door leading to the stairs swung open. Emily pressed her finger to her lips and led the *Follow the Facts* crew outside. The pre-dawn air nipped her cheeks as they rushed to her car parked across from Pepper's Café. Paul and Garrett climbed into the back.

Janet slid in the front seat beside Emily. "Sneaking out the back door is a bit overdramatic, don't you think?" Janet's tone smacked of sarcasm.

"Trust me. You don't want half the town following your van." Emily pulled away from the curb. "And I don't want rumors running rampant about you suspecting Mirabelle's father."

"Unless you or your Patsy talk, no one will know."

"You're underestimating Willow Falls' nose for news." She turned onto Falls Street. "Especially since you cancelled today's scheduled interviews."

"Engaging in pointless conversations when we have a solid lead is a waste of time."

No need trying to explain. Emily clamped her lips tight, drove the short distance, and turned onto a driveway beside a cottage.

"Let me guess." Janet nodded toward the front yard enclosed by a white-picket-fence. "This is Willow Falls' prettiest yard."

"Agnes Peterson's pride and joy. By the way, I suggest you acknowledge her southern hospitality, accept whatever food she offers, and compliment her culinary skills." She pulled close to the free-standing garage adjacent to the backyard.

The porch light switched on. A short, white-haired woman opened the screen door and motioned them inside. The wide-plank wood floors creaked as she led her guests through the kitchen to the front parlor. "Our company's here, dear."

Wayne eased off his recliner and pointed gnarled fingers toward the red and gray velvet damask sofa. "Have a seat."

Janet and Paul obliged. Garrett remained standing with his camera propped on his shoulder. Emily sat on the piano bench and breathed in the rich scent of cinnamon and vanilla.

Agnes poured coffee into five cups and plated the rolls. "Fresh from the oven."

Janet reached for a plate and a fork. "Thank you, Ms. Peterson—"

"Mrs., but you can call me Agnes."

"Certainly." She took a bite. "Delicious."

Agnes pressed her palms together. "Why thank you, honey. Now what do you want to ask us?"

"We need to capture our conversation on camera."

Wayne brushed his fingers through his thick white hair. "I don't know if that's such a good idea."

"We can trust these nice folks." Agnes pulled a straight-back chair beside her husband's recliner. "Did you know that our house starred in the movie *Joanie's Trial*? Everyone recognized the kitchen and my front yard."

"How nice." Janet set her plate down and signaled Paul to place a multidirectional microphone on the coffee table.

He complied.

She leaned forward. "Are you aware that we're investigating the crime?"

Wayne nodded. "Emily told us you suspect Roland Lambert."

"Possibly."

"What do you want my wife and me to tell you?"

"Whether or not the rumors are accurate."

"Which rumors?"

"To begin, was Roland a thief?"

"Yes."

"Did any evidence ever surface?"

"No."

"Then potential crimes he committed aren't proven." Janet's tone hinted of impatience as she kept her eyes focused on Wayne.

"Correct."

Agnes nudged her husband's arm. "My goodness, dear, these folks expect more than one-word responses."

"They're recording us—"

"Which is why they need the real scoop. Starting with the fact that old Roland was a real scallywag."

Janet turned toward Agnes. "Can you be more specific?"

"The school's principal fired him from his custodial job after money went missing."

Wayne shook his head. "Unproven rumors."

Agnes scoffed. "Afterwards folks felt bad for his family. Roland and his wife—God rest her soul—were what you'd call heavy drinkers. She wasn't from around these parts. He met her while protecting our country—"

"Hold on." Janet held up her hand. "Roland Lambert served in the military?"

Agnes nodded. "Until the army socked him with a dishonorable discharge."

Wayne tapped his fingers on his recliner's arm. "Another rumor."

"No one bothered to confirm?"

Wayne shrugged. "Back then, the sheriff's department didn't have the resources to dig up that kind of information."

Janet's brows raised. "So, everyone let the story fester?"

"The rumor ran its course and died."

"Anyway," Agnes continued. "They settled down and had two children. Mirabelle was such a sweet young girl, except for the rumors about her and Robert Liles."

Wayne touched her arm. "No need to bring that up."

"You're right, dear." Agnes smiled at Janet. "What else can we tell you nice folks?"

"Did Roland smoke?"

"Hmm." Agnes pinched her chin between her thumb and forefinger. "I believe maybe he did."

"You've been a big help, Mr. and Mrs. Peterson." Janet stood. "I think we have all the information we need."

Wayne eyed Emily. "Since you snuck these folks over here in the dark, I assume you want us to keep this interview confidential."

"I think it's best. No need to let rumors about an unfounded theory stir up the natives."

"We agree. Right, Agnes?"

"Of course, dear. We don't want to cause any trouble." She stood. "Did Emily tell you nice folks that my handsome husband is a retired high-school music teacher and composer for our town's signature play? I'll play one of his songs while you finish your cinnamon rolls."

"Thank you, but—"

"They'd be delighted." Emily shot Janet a stern look as Agnes moved to the piano bench and uncovered the keyboard. Following a twenty-minute concert, she thanked the Petersons and escorted the crew to her car as dawn crept over the horizon.

Janet settled in the passenger seat. "What's the deal about Mirabelle and Robert Liles?"

Three years ago, Emily promised Patsy not to share that story with anyone other than Scott. No way she'd break her word. "Most likely another unfounded small-town rumor." She backed onto the street and turned toward town. "I've arranged for you to talk to Gertie next."

"We already interviewed her."

"Not about Lambert." The crew remained silent until Emily parked behind Hayes General Store.

They found Gertie sitting at the worktable in Scott's office. "When I was a little girl, I read every Nancy Drew mystery I could find." She closed the book in front of her and tapped the cover. "This is still my favorite." Gertie pointed to Garrett setting up his equipment. "I won't talk if your camera's rolling."

Janet pulled Emily aside. "We agreed I could capture these interviews on film."

"I know, but Gertie is one of the few people who befriended Mirabelle's mother. If you want to hear what she has to say, you need to back off."

"This had better be worth my time." Janet ordered Garret to stash the camera and leave the room before she pulled a chair away from the table and sat facing Gertie. "Tell us what you know about the Lamberts."

"If you promise to keep my comments ... what they call on those TV shows ... off the record."

"You have my word."

"Okay then." Gertie laced her fingers in her lap. "First off the entire town knew Roland was the Lambert clan's one and only troublemaker. After he enlisted, everyone, including his family, believed he'd left town for good. Couple of years later, he showed up with a giant chip on his shoulder and a wife—a pretty girl named Sarah. When rumors floated around about him getting kicked out of the army, folks kept their distance." Gertie paused and leaned closer to Janet. "I think the town's rejection drove them both to drink."

Janet's brows raised. "How is that relevant—"

"Hold onto your chickens, I'm getting there." Gertie unlaced her fingers. "My family's property backed up to theirs. Mirabelle's brother was born six months after they moved back. Which led folks to believe they'd been forced into a shotgun wedding, if you know what I mean. Three years later, Mirabelle came along."

Gertie paused. "The first time my parents heard screams coming from their house, they rushed out and found Sarah in the back yard with her eye all swollen and bruised. She claimed she'd run into a door."

Emily stared at Gertie. Why hadn't any of these details surfaced when she researched the town's history?

"You said the first time." Janet's brow pinched. "Was she beaten often?"

Gertie nodded. "At some point, Sarah stopped leaving their house. Roland's parents disowned him and eventually moved out of town. Sarah's mother did what she could to help her daughter, but she never admitted she had a drinking problem or suffered from abuse. Pride, I suppose."

"Did anyone else in town suspect Roland's brutality?"

"Bless your heart, honey, but you don't know much about small towns."

"I'll take your answer as a yes. Bottom line, do you believe he was capable of murder?"

"Maybe. Although I suppose no one really knows what's in a man's heart."

"Thank you for agreeing to talk to us, Gertie. You've provided valuable information."

She scooted to the edge of her chair until her knees touched Janet's. "There's something you need to know about Willow Falls folks. We don't cotton to anyone who sets out to hurt one of our own, whether intentional or accidental-like. That's all I have to say." She stood, smoothed her long skirt, and flounced out.

Janet glared at Emily. "Did that five-foot, soda-fountain lady just threaten me?"

"I'd say you've been politely warned."

She-Dragon huffed, popped off her chair, and stomped from the office.

Scott walked in. "Based on Janet's expression, Gertie must have done a number on her."

"Our soda fountain heroine went toe-to-toe with She-Dragon and won."

Chapter 47

Emily walked into Pepper's Café and eyed the white vinyl sign hanging on the wall opposite the door. *Welcome to Willow Falls*, printed in gold and sandwiched between detailed drawings of wine bottles, still released memories of the night she first met Rachel.

"We're over here, sweetie."

Emily blinked and moved to the second of four booths hugging the partially exposed brick wall and slid in beside Pepper across from Patsy. "Sorry I'm late." She nodded toward three locals sitting on counter stools chatting with the chef. "It still seems strange to see someone other than you serving customers."

Pepper smiled. "Some days I miss spending time here listening to friends carry on about all sorts of goings-on."

"Like today." Patsy pushed her menu aside and eyed Emily. "Have you heard about the Petersons' nosey next-door neighbor?"

Dread sent a chill racing to the back of Emily's. "What happened?"

"She watched you and the investigative crew sneak into their house this morning."

"Are you serious?"

"Afraid so."

Emily released a heavy sigh. "I'd make one lousy CIA agent. Did Wayne and Agnes talk?"

"When she called, they didn't answer. They also didn't respond when she knocked on their back door. Although she claimed seeing Agnes peek through the kitchen window. Seems their lack of response intensified the old lady's curiosity. She called around and learned that yesterday's interview ended after Janet talked to Mirabelle."

Pepper placed her arm on the table. "We're guessing she put two and two together and came up with the notion that Roland Lambert is the killer."

Emily's shoulders slumped. "Does Mirabelle know?"

"Her mail truck's still parked at the post office, and no one's seen hide nor hair of her all morning." Pepper tapped her phone. "Neither she nor her husband answered my calls."

"She knows." Emily drummed her fingers on the table. "Is Mitch clued in?"

"He is." Pepper's voice lowered. "When Janet called him to cancel the interviews, he suspected she'd discovered something important. He's conducting his own investigation under the radar, hoping to solve the crime before too much damage is done. In the meantime, Patsy and I are planning to drop in on Mirabelle and make sure she's okay. We want you to go with us."

"Hold that request." Emily removed her ringing phone from her purse. "Speaking of the she-devil. I need to take this." She slid from the booth and stepped outside. "Hi, Janet."

"What are people around here trying to hide?"

This wasn't good. "What are you talking about?"

"Read my text."

Emily lowered her phone and stared at a photo of a typewritten note. *We understand you're after ratings, and maybe you've uncovered a clue. What you need to know is it isn't okay for anyone, not even an important TV show producer, to spread rumors. In our opinion you'd best go chasing down a different snake hole. Every X that follows represents one person's signature. As you can see, we stand united.* "Where did you get this?"

"Someone slid it under my door. I counted ninety-seven X's. All different types of handwriting."

"Please tell me you're not planning to share this on your program."

"That depends."

"On what?"

"Whether the Roland Lambert lead pans out. I changed my mind about today's interview. It's back on schedule. At one. In front of Willow Inn."

Emily nodded at a neighbor passing by the café. "I wouldn't be surprised if no one bothered to show up."

"I don't believe for a New York minute that people around here care more about their town than showing their faces on television. Be there. Today at twelve-thirty." Janet ended the call.

Emily squared her shoulders and returned to the booth. "You're not going to believe this." She read the text.

"Well, I'll be." Patsy grinned. "Someone took a page right out of Mirabelle's playbook. Not the Petersons' nosey neighbor. She's too old and arthritic to go chasing after signatures."

"I have an idea who's behind this, but I want to confirm before saying anything." Emily spread her napkin on her lap. "Now, about our visit to Mirabelle's ..."

Emily stood on Mirabelle's front porch with Pepper and Patsy and rang the doorbell. The curtains parted. Frank peered out. The curtains closed. Moments passed.

Patsy touched her hat. "Do you think he'll let us in?"

"If we're persistent." Emily pressed the bell a second time, then a third.

The door inched open. Frank craned his neck to look over their heads, as if scanning the front yard for more intruders. He stepped back and motioned them inside.

The women followed him through the dining room to the kitchen where they found Mirabelle, dressed in a bathrobe, sitting at the table clutching a coffee mug. Their cocker spaniel lay on the floor next to her chair.

Patsy moved a chair beside her. "You heard the rumor about Roland?"

She nodded, her eyes downcast. "When my poor excuse of a father left town, I wanted to forget he ever existed. Over time the painful memories—what he did to my mother ... to me— faded." Tears spilled down her cheeks. "Today the memories came crashing back. How he stormed out after beating us. The way he waved his hunting knife when ordering us to keep our mouths shut. Now the whole town will see me as the daughter of a mass murderer."

"That's not true." Pepper placed her hand on Mirabelle's arm. "Nothing can change the fact that you're a respected member of our community. The town's residents came within a few votes of electing you mayor, for goodness sake."

Emily nodded. "She's right. The truth about Robert Liles didn't affect how people treat Sadie or me and my sister."

"That's different. He was Sadie's stepfather, not a blood relative." Mirabelle wiped her cheeks and stared at Emily. "You and Rachel never knew him, so you're blameless." She looked away. "Truth is, I didn't do anything to protect my mother."

Frank knelt beside his wife. "You were an innocent child caught up in domestic violence, sweetheart. There was nothing you could have done to stop it."

"My brother tried to stop him until our father beat him half to death. Wasn't long after that he left town." She sniffled. "When he enlisted in the army, folks called him a coward for abandoning Mom and me. Truth is, he believed if he stayed, the guilt would eat away at him until he ended up like our father." Mirabelle clutched her husband's hand. "We need to sell our house and move to another town, far away from here."

"You can't let your emotions get the best of you," Frank said just above a whisper.

"I don't want to live where everyone talks about us behind our backs. Besides, you're a top-notch mechanic so you can open a new business anywhere, and I can always find a job at another post office."

"This is our home. Instead of running away, we need to stay and deal with this together."

"Not only is Frank right, the town's on your side." Emily pulled up the text from Janet and handed her phone to Mirabelle. "Read this."

Mirabelle's brows raised as she scrolled through the message. She looked up and stared at Emily. "Is this real?"

"A hundred percent."

She leaned closer to the phone. "How many X's?"

"Ninety-seven."

"That's a lot."

"Proof everyone cares about you."

Mirabelle dabbed her cheeks with a tissue. "When's the next *Follow the Facts* interview?"

Emily glanced at her watch. "Three hours from now, on the sidewalk in front of Willow Inn."

"I'll meet you there a half hour early." Mirabelle pushed off her chair. "Now, if y'all will excuse me, I have to get dressed. The nice people in our town expect me to deliver their mail." She dashed to the back stairs and climbed to the second floor.

Frank shook his head. "Finally, my wife has returned to normal."

"Indeed she has." Patsy chuckled. "You're a patient man, Frank Paine."

"One reason Mirabelle and I stayed together all these years." He patted his ample belly while pointing to a half-eaten chocolate cake. "Plus, my wife's sensational cooking skills."

Emily stood. "Now that we know she's okay, we'll be on our way."

"Thanks for coming by."

"Like the note said, 'we take care of our own.'"

Chapter 48

Emily climbed the stairs to Hayes General Store's arts and craft consignment shop and wandered among the displays. She stopped and brushed her fingers over a row of hand-stitching on an intricately crafted quilt while reading the note pinned to the edge. A work of art created by the granddaughter of a man whose hands helped build Willow Falls.

"Mirabelle brought it in yesterday." Scott stepped beside her. "Even at that price, I don't expect it to sit here long."

"Her grandmother was definitely a master quilter. Too bad she couldn't protect her daughter and granddaughter from Roland's abuse."

"If Mitch had been sheriff back then, he'd have tossed the man in jail and thrown away the key."

"The guy still might end up behind bars. Enough about him. Is Gertie free to talk?"

"A couple of stools just opened up at the soda fountain."

"Good because I need to find out if my suspicion is valid." Emily slipped her hand around Scott's arm as they descended to the main floor and passed a cabinet displaying bottles of crime-scene clay. "Are customers actually buying those?"

"Sold half a dozen this morning, thanks to Gertie's brazen marketing campaign."

"You've gotta love her spirit." Emily edged onto one of three empty stools at the end of the counter while Scott tended to a customer.

Gertie ended a conversation with a young couple sipping milkshakes and wandered over. "I hear the TV interviews are back on. Don't be surprised if no one shows up."

"I'm curious." Emily crossed her arms on the counter. "How did you manage to pull off such a big project in a few hours?"

"What makes you think I wrote that note?"

"Why else would you assume that's what I'm talking about?"

Gertie leaned on the counter. "Tourists are buying those little bottles of clay I suggested."

"Clever change of subject. Were the X's your idea?"

"Why would anyone sign their name on a note that could end up on a television show?"

"So, you did write it?"

Gertie glanced around before leaning close. "That depends."

"On what?"

"The outcome."

Emily cocked her head. "Janet acted plenty ticked."

"She should be ashamed. Even if Mitch finds out old Roland's guilty, it's our duty to protect the town's most reliable news source. Except for the *Willow Post*, which only comes out once a week, Mirabelle's all over town every day. She's like one of those town criers from way back in Colonial times."

"Was the note caper meant to keep the rumor mill going or shut it down?"

Gertie rounded the end of the counter and stood close to Emily. "Things were different way back when Mirabelle was a little girl. No one talked about people drinking too much or the bad things that happened behind closed doors. But truth be told, everyone knew something wasn't right in the Lambert house. Maybe Mirabelle gossips to keep whatever happened to her from happening to anyone else."

Gertie paused. "Nearly everyone who signed the note is old enough to remember how we all had a hand in letting that family down. The caper, as you called it, is our way of letting Mirabelle know we love her."

Emily swallowed the lump forming in her throat. "You're an amazing woman, Gertie."

"No, honey. I'm simply an old lady who after all these years found a way to make things right with my friend." She pointed her index finger toward the ceiling. "And Him."

The bell above the front door jangled. Gertie glanced over her shoulder. "I need to scoot back behind the counter in case those nice folks are hankering for a soda or one of my famous milkshakes." She touched Emily's arm. "Promise you'll come back later and tell me what happens over at Willow Inn?"

"Of course."

"Thank you, sweetie."

While Gertie returned to her station and struck up a conversation with two tourists settling on stools, Emily moved to the front window and gazed past the display of antiques to the park and the first hint of autumn color.

Scott joined her. "What'd you learn from Gertie?"

"I'm rethinking the plotline for my new novel, no matter what anyone discovers about the crime. I'll fill you in after I learn how much power our soda-fountain heroine wields." She kissed his cheek, walked out, and headed straight to Willow Inn.

Mirabelle stood at the front porch railing and pointed to the empty sidewalk. "Yesterday half the town showed up an hour early. The *Follow the Facts* crew is due in twenty minutes and no one's here. Know what that means?"

"People care more about you than a television show."

Mittens sprang onto the railing, inviting a back stroke from Mirabelle. "Growing up I never had a pet. My father hated cats. He didn't much care for dogs either. Maybe because we barely had enough money to feed ourselves, much less an animal." She paused for a long moment. "After you left my house this morning, I remembered he smoked like a crazy man. Somehow he always had enough cash to buy cigarettes. Anyway it got me to thinking. Maybe he stole Robert's lighter—you know, the one he had for his cigar-smoking friends."

"Did you ever see a lighter in Robert's house?"

"No, but I bet he had one engraved with his initials. I should tell Janet."

"There's no need to muddy the water with unfounded suspicions." From the corner of her eye, Emily caught sight of Janet and her crew walking over from Redding Arms. "Besides, if you grant an interview when everyone else stayed away, you'll disrespect the entire town."

Mirabelle pursed her lips. "You're right."

The crew arrived in front of the inn as Pepper and Patsy crossed the street and climbed onto the porch.

Garrett set up the camera beside the inn's sign. Paul sat on the bottom rung. Janet stood facing away from him with her hands clasped behind her back.

"From here I can't tell if she's angry or confused." Patsy nudged Emily. "Should one of us go talk to her?"

"She'll come up before much longer."

At one, the front yard remained empty. Janet spoke to Paul and Garrett before climbing the stairs and eyeing Pepper. "I've talked to everyone else up here. Are you dissing me like the rest of the town, or are you willing to answer a few questions?"

"There's no point, since I don't have any information to add to what you've already heard."

"In that case, our interviews are finished."

"Not yet." Mirabelle pushed away from the railing. "I have something more to say."

Emily cleared her throat and shot her best what-are-you-doing expression at Mirabelle.

"Go ahead," said Janet.

"I think maybe Roland Lambert killed all those people."

"You're basing your comment on what evidence?"

"Robert Liles probably owned a fancy lighter. Roland chain-smoked. He was meaner than a stepped-on rattlesnake, and he stole stuff. That adds up to circumstantial evidence. When you put all the pieces together, I'll let you interview me about how a poor family survived life with one rotten apple."

Janet stared at Mirabelle for a long moment. "My job has taken me to a lot of small towns across this country. Willow Falls is by far the most bizarre. Time to wrap things up and dig into the one solid lead we managed to unearth." She nodded to Emily. "Walk with me."

Relieved Mirabelle had kept her word and didn't request an on-camera interview, she fell in step beside the producer.

When they reached the sidewalk adjacent to the street, Janet turned to face Emily. "We're packing up and leaving town by nightfall."

"Any plans to return?"

"Depends on what we dig up about Roland Lambert." She paused. "I know we haven't seen eye-to-eye on much, but I appreciate your professionalism."

Maybe Janet wasn't a total she-dragon after all. "Glad I could help."

"One more thing."

Uh-oh.

"Our program could do a lot to generate buzz about Willow Falls and your new book—"

"How'd you know I'm writing another novel?"

"I listen and observe. Anyway, if something new surfaces, I'd appreciate a call."

"You should ask our sheriff to keep you informed."

"Local law enforcement is more interested in solving cases than assisting television producers."

Was she setting her up? "I'd have to run any information by Mitch first."

"You people stick together like peanut butter on toast don't you? At least keep an open mind." Janet waved at the three women staring from the porch before motioning her crew to follow her.

As Emily watched them return to the hotel, an idea took root and sprouted. Was it possible? She dashed to the giant willow oak behind the hotel and called her sister.

Rachel toweled her hair, and peeled off her wet costume, thanks to a scene filmed in the rain. She slipped into jeans and her Willow Falls sweatshirt, stuffed her phone in her pocket, and made her way to the food and beverage station in the makeshift lounge set up between the wardrobe and makeup.

A young attendant handed her a cup of perfectly prepared American coffee, a testament to her status as one of the film's stars.

She set her cup on a table, pulled her vibrating phone from her pocket, and pressed Face Time. "Hey, sis."

"Looks like you just showered."

"Hardly." Rachel fingered her wet hair and dropped onto a chair. "Robert took advantage of the foul weather and added a rain scene, without umbrellas. I'm still shivering. At least we're not filming in an insect-infested jungle. What's going on back home?"

Emily reeled off the latest news about the bone caper.

"So Roland Lambert is the culprit?"

"According to Mirabelle, he's as guilty as sin. Can you believe she transitioned from pretending her good-for-nothing father never existed to claiming his crime will turn her into a television star? Gertie claims her X-filled note is responsible for the transformation."

"Your soda-fountain expert is a treasure." Mental images of Willow Falls' lovable, whacky residents triggered a bout of melancholy.

"The drama around here isn't the main reason I called. I need your opinion."

"A twin thing?"

"Sort of. You know my publisher wants me to write about the current events?"

"Yeah."

"I'm thinking a murder mystery with a big dose of southern-style comedy. With the same characters from my second book, plus an investigative crew."

"Sounds like a winner."

"There's more, and this is where you come in. I want us to collaborate and turn the same story into a new play for our theater. Make it a seasonal production."

"Are you serious? Unlike finishing the partially-written *Percy's Legacy*, it means we'd have to start from scratch."

"Combining my writing and your theatrical skills. Again."

"You're talking about a major undertaking."

"We could begin as soon as you come home and have it ready to premiere by the time your dad opens the convention center."

Rachel cradled her coffee cup in both hands. "We did manage to create a boon for our town."

"Does that mean you're onboard?"

"I'll think about it."

"Fair enough."

Chapter 49

Sadie plated two ham sandwiches and placed them on the kitchen island beside glasses of sweet tea. "Any idea why Naomi wants to talk to us?"

Brick placed a napkin on his lap. "All I know is she arranged for Mitch and Emily to meet us here at one." He bit into his sandwich.

"Maybe she found another unfinished play in her attic." Sadie fingered her sandwich. "Pepper's fixing beef Wellington for our anniversary dinner."

"Haven't tasted that in ages."

"I'll miss having Rachel here."

Brick swallowed. "Charlie's not wild about showing up without her."

"I suspect every time he looks at Emily he thinks of Rachel. Do you suppose he'll come?"

"He'll be here." Brick reached for his tea. "Unless you change your mind about us taking a trip."

"Glory be, honey, everything I want is right here in Willow Falls. My friends. My wonderful family. My grandbabies." She sat beside him and touched his knee. "And my prince charming."

"You are a fascinating woman, Sadie Bricker." He squeezed her hand. "I didn't need a rainbow to know meeting you was the luckiest day of my life."

"That makes two of us."

While enjoying lunch, they reminisced about the months after they met. "The way you waited forever to kiss me kept me confused as a cat chasing a flashlight beam."

"It'd been years since I'd last kissed a woman. I didn't want to get it wrong."

"You got it so right you set off the town's fire alarm. Or was that the fire on the hotel's back porch."

He leaned close and kissed her cheek. "If we weren't expecting guests, I'd do my best to set off a three-alarm blaze upstairs."

"My, my." Sadie giggled as she fanned her face with her hand. "How you set my heart all aflutter."

"Not bad for an old guy." The doorbell rang. "What do you think, should we answer?"

"We could pretend we're not home. Except we'd have to wait for Mirabelle to give us the scoop."

"I'll get the door." Brick slid off the chair. "You're in charge of hospitality." He escorted Naomi and Mitch in. Sadie eyed the weathered leather satchel tucked under Naomi's arm, then led her guests to the den where she'd set a plate of cookies on the coffee table.

Mitch settled on the sofa facing the fireplace. "What gives with the secret meeting, Naomi?"

She laid the satchel across her lap. "I found something interesting, perhaps even relevant to the dead bodies. Before I open that pandora's box, if you don't mind, would you share what you know about Roland Lambert?"

Mitch hesitated. "Only reason I'm willing to divulge any details is because I trust everyone in this room to keep what I'm about to tell you confidential." He leaned forward and planted his arms on his knees. "A couple of months after Roland left town, he tried to hold up a Baltimore liquor store with a hunting knife."

Brick reached for a cookie. "How'd that turn out?"

"The owner out-weaponed him. Shot him in the shoulder. Roland spent the next three years locked up. While in jail he contacted someone in Willow Falls and learned his son had enlisted. When the parole board released him, Roland skipped town, and showed up in Fayetteville, North Carolina. Home of Fort Bragg. The army had already shipped his boy overseas. Roland stayed in that town and kept his nose clean."

Mitch paused. "However, when he learned of his son's death, he launched another crime spree and ended up back in jail. Two years later, following another parole, he disappeared. In my opinion it's a giant leap from robbery to mass murder. But not impossible. Which is why I'm following up on a lead that came in this morning."

"I see." Naomi broke eye contact with Mitch and stared straight ahead. "My parents, each in their own way, found history fascinating. As you know, Mom amassed the collection of antiques on display in my art museum. More live upstairs in my private quarters. Dad, on the other hand, collected what he considered newsworthy information. He had trunks filled with documents and articles. My dad also served as the town's mayor for a couple of years after I moved to Charleston."

Her fingers tapped the satchel. "I discovered this in a trunk marked 'Willow Falls.'" Her bracelets jangled as she unbuckled the strap. "Among the items inside is this." She removed a yellowed sheet of paper. "Given the fact that Roland Lambert is a possible suspect, I doubt it means anything. But then I'm not in a position to determine if it holds any relevance. It's a letter to my parents from Robert Liles' mother." She handed it to Mitch. "Read it out loud."

Mitch unfolded the letter and began reading.

"My dear friends Richard and Irene. I am writing to you not requiring an answer or even an acknowledgement, but rather to unburden my soul and perhaps find a way to live with myself.

"You have always treated our youngest son, Philip, with decency, even though other neighbors didn't look upon him kindly. Although he is but nine-years-old, his proclivity to engage in destructive behavior has frequently brought his father's wrath crashing down upon his youthful shoulders. While I do not believe in corporal punishment, my husband rules with an iron hand, like he did when serving as an army officer during the war, thus rendering my opinions inconsequential.

"For the past few years, I have struggled to find a way to calm the urges which drive my son, and for a while I believed I had made progress. That is, until we learned he had committed an act so heinous, even I had to admit he desperately needed more help than I could provide. His father is convinced he is at the core an evil child. I am not. However, there is one fact upon which we do agree. We cannot let his behavior put our family and our neighbors in jeopardy.

"We will tell our friends and neighbors that Philip is attending a prestigious military school. The truth is, yesterday Philip's father drove him to South Carolina and had him committed to a private mental hospital. He will bear the financial cost. I will bear the burden knowing I have failed my own child. I do not know if we will ever see him again or what will become of him. I pray that with professional help, he will find the answers to whatever haunts him and discover his proper place in the world.

"Please forgive me for burdening you with these words. I implore you to place this letter where no one other than you will find it and unfairly judge the three of us who remain behind."

As Sadie listened to the words, her mind drifted to the days after Robert Liles married her mama and moved them into his house. Was Philip the reason he never spoke of his family? A knot formed in the pit of her stomach. Had he been afraid people would discover the monster also lived inside him?

Mitch read the writer's signature, then stroked his beard. "I don't know if this means anything, but it's worth looking into. Do you mind if I keep this for the time being?"

"The paper is old and fragile." Naomie handed Mitch the satchel. "Protect it in this."

He slid the letter inside and pushed up. "Unless this letter leads to something, there's no reason to let anyone else know it exists."

"I agree." Naomi stood. "I'll walk out with you."

Sadie moved to the window overlooking the backyard and gazed at a spiderweb stretched between two posts supporting the deck roof.

Brick encircled her waist and pulled her close.

"It's fascinating how some spiders spin a web one day and make it disappear the next." She paused. "I want to know more about Robert's family."

"Why dredge up the past?"

"Maybe the truth will help me understand how he ended up so different in private than in public." She turned away from the window. "There is one person who might shed some light."

"Want me to go with you?"

"I need to do this alone." She pressed her hand to his cheek, walked out the back door, and made her way to the front sidewalk. Her pace quickened as she crossed Falls Street and passed tourists strolling in and out of shops. When she reached Patsy's Pastries and Pretties she hesitated for a moment before walking inside.

Patsy moved from behind the glass case displaying an array of decadent sweets. "Hey..." She touched Sadie's arm. "You're not here to buy dessert are you?"

"Can we talk somewhere in private?"

Patsy stepped away and spoke to her salesclerk before escorting Sadie through the back and upstairs to her apartment's all-purpose room. "What's on your mind?"

Sadie dropped onto the floral-patterned couch and eyed the array of photos of young Patsy and her husband Tommy—the love of her life who had died years earlier. "I need you to tell me everything you know about Robert Liles' family."

"I see." Patsy poured two glasses of lemonade and placed them on the coffee table. "Everyone who knew Robert's parents is dead and buried, so what I'm about to share comes from stories my mother told me."

"I understand."

She sat beside Sadie. "To begin with, Robert was named after his father. His mother's name was Hannah. She was fifteen when Robert's father enlisted in the army, ten years younger than he. Although Robert Senior had never been the friendly sort, when he returned four years later, he'd become bitter and angry. Lots of folks were surprised when Hannah agreed to marry him. Probably because she was plain and painfully shy, which left her few prospects in a small town. It's also why she didn't leave him, even when everyone knew he drank heavily and beat his boys." Patsy took a sip of lemonade. "Back then people didn't question men who ruled their households with absolute authority or women who succumbed to their control."

Sadie leaned forward. "Maybe if someone had stopped the abuse...what do you know about their youngest son, Phillip?"

"That boy got into more trouble than a whole gang of modern-day juvenile delinquents, no matter how often his father beat him or his mother defended him. After they sent him away, Hannah became a recluse, a prisoner of sorts in her own home."

"Shame is a powerful emotion, right up there with guilt."

"Maybe that's the reason both parents died from illnesses in their fifties. When Robert inherited their house and money, everyone thought he was the stable family member. Until we learned he'd squandered his family's wealth—" Patsy touched Sadie's hand. "And the truth about why you shot him."

Sadie breathed deeply and released a long, cathartic sigh. "Thank you for sharing."

Patsy patted her hand. "Whatever the reason you wanted to know, I hope it helped. Now how about we go downstairs and indulge in a slice of cake."

"Make that lemon with buttercream frosting?"

"Your daughters' favorite." Pasty stood and looped her arm around Sadie's. "Everyone misses Rachel. It's sad she won't be here to celebrate the anniversary of the biggest wedding this town has ever experienced."

Chapter 50

Emily drummed her fingers on the newspaper worktable as memories of *Around Georgia's* two previous features about Willow Falls raced through her mind. Both positive stories. Although she trusted Alicia Adams, she couldn't say the same for the station manager. Motion outside the newspaper office caught her eye. She rushed to open the door as the Atlanta television station's van pulled into a parking space.

Alicia climbed out and embraced her. "Hey girlfriend. I feel like I'm hugging both you and Rachel."

"We have that effect on people." Emily smiled at the pretty young woman with flawless skin and jet-black hair. "Good to see you again."

"Hard to imagine next weekend will mark one year since your sister's big wedding."

"A lot has happened since then."

Two men stepped from the van onto the sidewalk.

"You remember Al, our equipment guy, and Kevin, our camera operator?"

"Of course. Come on in, guys. The coffee's hot and the Danish fresh."

Alicia and the guys followed her inside. "Every time I come up here, I love this little town more." She pointed to the plate of Danish. "From Patsy's?"

"None other."

"I promised the staff I'd bring back a box of her brownies."

Emily poured four cups of coffee. "About today, what's your station's objective for this new segment?"

"Like a good reporter, you get right to the point." Alicia reached for a Danish. "The show's manager wanted to focus on the dead bodies, all the gory details."

Emily pressed her lips tight to keep from protesting.

"However, the reason we postponed our trip from earlier this week is because the station's owner had a different perspective. A couple of months ago, his sister and her husband spent their anniversary at Redding Arms. They bought one of Naomi's paintings and fell in love with the town."

"Same thing happens to a lot of tourists."

Alicia wiped her fingers with a napkin. "She convinced him a story about the town's growth as a tourist destination, with a glimpse into residents' reactions to the crime, would be far more interesting to our viewers."

"That's a relief. Especially with *Follow the Facts* breathing down our collective necks."

"I know all about Janet Johnson. She's a pit bull when it comes to tracking down evidence and cracking cases. I didn't see their van anywhere."

"They left town after Gertie gave her what for." She top-lined the story.

Alicia snapped her fingers. "That's the kind of human-interest angle we're looking for. This morning we'll begin with a tour of the town so we can highlight what's new. Later we'll interview some key residents."

"You know when folks find out you're here, they'll flock to you."

"I'm counting on it. Now, tell me about those tents out on County Road."

At two o'clock, after capturing hours of video and dozens of down-home comments, Kevin and Al packed up their gear. Alicia stood on the sidewalk fronting the park. "We have plenty of material for another heartwarming story." She faced Emily. "You and Scott need to visit Atlanta and wow your daughters with a trip to the aquarium."

"Maybe in the spring." She hugged Alicia. "Thank you for everything you've done for us."

"Girl, you know Willow Falls is my favorite small town. I'll give you a call when the story's ready to air." She climbed into the van, closed the door, and waved as they pulled away from the curb.

Emily headed straight to her family's store. The bell over the door jangled as she walked inside. She passed customers occupying every soda-fountain stool and caught snippets of Gertie's commentary about the upcoming *Around Georgia* segment.

Scott closed the cash register. "The way she's talking about her latest interview, one would think she's Willow Falls' most enlightened citizen."

"Along with everyone else who voiced their opinion."

"By the way, Mitch wants you to call him."

"Maybe he solved the case." Emily moved to the back and pressed his number. "What's up?"

"Where are you?" His tone hinted of urgency.

"In Scott's office."

"I'm on my way."

Emily laid her phone on the desk and eyed the picture of her snuggling with Jane and Clair in her recliner. Her favorite writing spot. She leaned back against the desk and eyed a faded photograph of Scott's great grandfather, the man who built Hayes General Store. Her focus shifted to the picture hanging beside it. Twelve-year-old Scott posing in front of the store with his dad.

The door swung open. Mitch marched in carrying a leather satchel.

"Have you solved the case?"

"Still working on it." Mitch removed a folded sheet of paper from the satchel and handed it to Emily. "Names of the eight victims."

"Anyone from Willow Falls?"

"No one I'm aware of."

She unfolded the paper and stared at the list. "Are they in any way connected with each other?"

"Don't know. GBI wants you to publish the names and ask if anyone around here recognizes any of them. There's something else you need to know." Mitch reached into the satchel and withdrew a yellowed sheet of paper. "You need to read this."

She traced her finger over the delicate handwriting. "Who's Richard and Irene?"

"Naomi's parents."

As Emily read the letter, her reaction vacillated between intellectual curiosity and empathy for the woman who wrote it. The guilt she must have experienced. The humiliation. As she reached the end of the letter, her eyes landed on the signature. *Fondly, Hannah Liles.* She gasped. "Is she Robert's mother?"

Mitch nodded.

Her paternal grandmother. A woman she had never met or even thought of. Her voice faltered. "Has Mama Sadie seen this?"

"And Brick, but no one else."

"What are you planning to do with the letter?"

"Honor the woman's wishes and keep it private, unless her relatives decide to do otherwise."

Emily carried the letter to the copier before returning it to Mitch. "For now, keep this between us. If at some point it makes sense to go public, Rachel, Mama Sadie, and I will let you know."

"Fair enough." Mitch slipped the letter into the satchel. "I'm obligated to inform GBI about Philip's existence."

"I understand."

After Mitch walked out, Emily closed her eyes and pressed her fingers to her temple. Two more people needed to hear her grandmother's words. Scott and her twin. She plucked her phone off the desk and pressed Rachel's number.

Chapter 51

Sweat invaded Rachel's forehead. "Sorry ..." She swallowed the bile threatening to erupt and dashed from the hotel dining room to the restroom. Hanging her head over a public toilet was a lousy way to spend her anniversary. She wiped her brow with her sleeve and opened the stall door.

Beth stood in front of the sink. "I hope you feel better than you look."

Rachel swept a curl off her cheek. "I doubt it."

"Robert's arranging for a doctor to check you out. He doesn't want you on set until he knows what's going on."

"Just what I need. Our director thinking I'm a liability." Rachel wet a paper towel and pressed it to the back of her neck. "What does he suggest I do?"

"Take a break and wait for the doc to call. I'd stay with you except he moved my afternoon scene to this morning."

"You're a good friend, Beth. I'll be fine." Rachel tossed the paper towel in the trash and made her way to the ground floor. Desperate for fresh air she left the hotel and headed to St. Mark Square. What could a doctor possibly tell her? That spending her anniversary alone had triggered a serious case of anxiety? Or that she'd developed an ulcer? She passed the bell tower and maneuvered around the crowds. Why did everything remind her of Charlie?

"*Scusami*, are you Rachel Streetman?"

She turned toward the woman. "Rachel Streetman Bricker."

"I recognize you from social media." She fished a scrap of paper from her purse. "You mind your name?"

"My pleasure."

"*Grazie.*"

"*Prego.*" Rachel's phone vibrated. "Sorry, important call." She turned away and pressed her phone to her ear. "Hello." An hour later she stood by the window in her hotel room and stared wide-eyed at the doctor. "Are you sure?"

She nodded. "Positive."

Rachel gazed out at a water taxi pulling away from the dock. "Will you do me a favor and tell my director I'm not contagious and am cleared to work?"

"I understand, and yes."

"Thank you." Responding to a knock, she opened the door and accepted an arrangement of red and yellow roses from her favorite bellman. She set the flowers on the desk, rewarded him with a generous tip, and closed the door.

The doctor dropped her stethoscope into her bag. "Special occasion or adoring fan?"

Emily read the card. "Both. From my husband. Today's our one-year wedding anniversary."

"Congratulations. Beautiful color combination."

Rachel breathed in the sweet aroma. "Reminiscent of our first date when we discovered we'd attended rival universities. Red for mine, gold for his."

"Sounds like a great guy."

"He's fun, romantic, smart." Rachel counted three dozen roses. "Generous."

The doctor glanced at her phone. "Emergency. I'll send a prescription for nausea right up, and happy anniversary."

"Thank you." The moment she walked out, Rachel called Charlie. He didn't answer. She left a message and called Emily. The call went to voicemail. She tossed her phone on the bed. With hours to kill before her scheduled online visit to Mama Sadie's and Brick's anniversary celebration, she plopped beside the window, turned on the television, and scrolled through the list of in-house movies. Thirty minutes into a chick flick, her phone vibrated. "Hey, Justin."

"Nordstrom's taking advantage of your clean bill of health. The scene he'd scheduled tomorrow night on Terrazza Danieli is rescheduled for seven tonight."

"What?" She bolted to her feet. "Why?"

"The restaurant needs the space for a big party tomorrow."

"You know I have plans."

"I told him the timing's lousy. Problem is, he doesn't have a choice. Neither do you. I'll meet you outside wardrobe in an hour."

How much more could go wrong? Rachel texted Charlie, pocketed her phone, and raced to the elevators. A door yawned open. She stepped in and nodded at the occupants. If she and Justin performed to perfection, maybe she'd make it back to her room in time.

At ground level she raced to makeup. Gina's pinched expression made it clear she wasn't happy about the last-minute change. "Sorry."

She mumbled in Italian.

Fifty minutes later Rachel stood in front of a wardrobe mirror and stared at her emerald green, off-the-shoulder, body-hugging gown. She dug her fingernails into her palms to keep from tearing and destroying her makeup. The assistant handed her a pair of diamond earrings. They looked familiar. She pressed them into her ears and walked out.

Justin released a long whistle. "Great dress."

"It's way over- the-top for an early evening shot."

He held up his phone. "Smile. I'm taking a picture to show Charlie what he's missing."

"Give it a break, Justin." Rachel rolled her eyes and headed toward the elevator.

He caught up with her. "I think you need an attitude adjustment."

"No kidding." Desperate to transition from abandoned wife to movie star, she mentally rehearsed her lines.

When they arrived at the restaurant, the hostess smiled. "Good evening, Ms. Streetman, Mr. Brooks. They're waiting for you."

They walked through the dining room to open doors at the other end. Rachel peered at the diners sitting on the terrace at tables graced with candles. Confusion rocked her brain. "What's going on, Justin? Where's the crew? Why haven't they set up cameras and lights?"

"Someone's waiting for you." He turned and walked away.

Rachel's pulse accelerated as she stepped out and caught sight of the setting sun kissing the horizon and casting shimmers of golden light on Grand Canal's rippling surface. Was it possible? She scanned the space and spotted a man standing at the railing at the far end of the terrace. Facing the canal. His shoulder's broad. She maneuvered around the tables and stopped beside an empty table. "Charlie?"

He turned. "Happy anniversary, gorgeous."

"You're here." She melted in his arms. "When? How?"

"Do you remember what I said about your dad and Maggie Warren on our wedding day?"

"If she managed to break down his all-work-no-play philosophy, you'd treat me to a trip to Italy for our first anniversary."

His breath warmed her cheek. "Five days ago, I knew I couldn't spend tonight thousands of miles away from you."

"If you asked me to marry you all over again, I'd say yes." She inched from his arms and gazed into his eyes. "Spending our first anniversary in one of the most romantic cities in the world with the man who captured my heart is magical."

Charlie stroked her hair and held her gaze for a long moment. "As much as I want to hold you, I think we should take our seats before someone tells us to get a room." He winked and pulled a chair away from the table. "*Per favore*, Madame."

"You learned some Italian."

"A phrase or two." He kissed the back of her neck, sending a tingle up her spine.

Rachel's heart swelled as she watched Charlie settle across from her. "How did you arrange all this?"

"With help from Justin and your director. I booked a suite for three nights. Robert rearranged your schedule so we can spend time together."

"I owe him big-time."

Charlie reached across the table and held her hand. "Do you like the earrings?"

"Are they from you?"

"Beth picked them out yesterday. The third member of my covert team."

The waiter approached, carrying a bottle of wine. "Good evening, Mr. and Mrs. Bricker, and happy anniversary." He displayed a bottle.

Charlie released Rachel's hand and nodded.

"Very good, sir." He removed the cork and poured a small amount.

Rachel watched the man she loved swirl the dark red liquid and breathe in the aroma before tasting. "Excellent."

The waiter moved the bottle toward Rachel.

She covered her glass with her hand. "Would you mind filling mine with ginger ale?"

"As you wish, madame." He filled Charlie's glass, set the bottle on the table, and walked away.

"I take it you haven't developed a taste for Italian reds."

"Do you remember the day we met?"

"How could I forget?"

"I had a nasty cold."

"You were still the most beautiful woman I'd ever laid eyes on. You blushed when we shook hands. I couldn't tell if you were suffering from fever or overwhelmed by my engaging personality."

"It was the electrifying quiver your touch sent surging through my body." She paused. "I have an important question itching for an answer."

He winked and squeezed her hand. "Should we skip dinner and go straight to our room?"

"Even better." Rachel paused and tilted her head. "When we welcome our firstborn into this world, would you prefer to hold a baby boy or baby girl in your arms?"

"Doesn't matter as long as ..." Charlie's eyes widened. "Are you saying what I think you're saying?"

"Being here with you on this glorious night ..." She covered his hand with hers. "Carrying your child is a blessing beyond anything I ever imagined."

"Are you serious? We're having a baby?"

"In the spring."

His eyes moistened. "Rachel Streetman Bricker, I have never loved you more than I do at this moment."

The waiter returned to pour her ginger ale.

Charlie's eyes remained locked on hers as he lifted his glass. "To the woman who captured my heart the moment we met, and to our amazing little family of three. Justin arranged for a gondolier to take us on a moonlight ride later tonight."

"Perfect."

Following dinner and a romantic trip through a maze of canals they strolled arm in arm into a hotel suite awash in beige and gold.

Rachel turned in a slow circle, gazing at the ornate furniture and exquisite artwork. "This is gorgeous."

"The best suite in the hotel. I have another surprise for you." He led her to a plush couch and booted his laptop. Emily, Scott, and Rachel's closest friends were gathered in Mama Sadie's and Brick's den, waving and offering congratulations. "They filmed this an hour ago."

Rachel pressed her hand to her chest. "All the people I love most."

"Be right back." Charlie dashed from the room. Moments later he returned. "Now it's our turn." He held his phone at arm's length and pressed record. "Tonight, I surprised my beautiful bride by showing up unexpected. Little did I know she had an even bigger surprise for me." He kissed her cheek. "You do the honor, gorgeous."

Rachel smiled at the phone. "Tonight, my handsome husband and I are celebrating our love in a new way. Grandma Sadie, Grandpa Brick, next spring you will have another grandchild to hold in your arms and shower with love."

Tears of joy pooled and trickled down her cheeks. "Mama Sadie, your sacrifice all those years ago to save the babies you carried inside made all this possible. I love you with all my heart."

Rachel returned from the massive, marble-encased bathroom, opened the curtains, and slipped back into bed.

Charlie propped up on his elbow. "You okay?"

"Morning sickness. It'll pass." She lay back and stared at intricate paintings and elaborate molding. "That is one extravagant ceiling."

"Want me to hire an artist to fancy up our bedroom?"

"With clouds, maybe. Cherubs, no. Definitely stars on the nursery ceiling. When the nausea began, I ignored my suspicions, thinking I couldn't possibly be pregnant."

He stroked her cheek. "I'm glad the pills didn't work."

"So am I." Rachel smiled. "For the first time in weeks, I'm actually hungry for breakfast. How about we begin today's festivities with breakfast at Café Florian."

"Great idea." Charlie pulled her close. "After a delicious morning appetizer."

An hour later Rachel donned her sunglasses and held Charlie's hand while they strolled across a bridge and passed moored gondolas bobbing in Grand Canal. "Do you know how many times I wished you were here with me?"

"More than a dozen?"

"Way more."

They rounded the corner of Doges Palace, continued up the wide path to St. Mark's Square, and chose an outdoor table in front of Café Florian. After ordering, Rachel pushed her sunglasses up. "Breakfast here is our second quintessential Venetian experience. Last night's gondola ride was the first. Kissing on a bridge will definitely be number four on my list."

Rachel caught Charlie staring at her, grinning. "What?"

"If we have a girl, she should look exactly like her gorgeous mother."

"What if we have a boy?"

"A miniature Charlie, of course."

"You know, we could have twins." Rachel reached for his hand. "Do you want to know the sex before our baby or babies are born?"

"Heck, yeah ... that is, if you want to."

"Definitely. Enough talk about babies. We have a lot to see before you leave. Beginning with number three on my list."

"Which is?"

"A secret."

After breakfast they walked to the dock in front of Hotel Danieli and boarded a crowded water-bus. Charlie wrapped his arm around Rachel's shoulders and pulled her close. "Where are we headed?"

"You'll see."

The bus moved east across a wide stretch of water and docked at Lido di Venezia. Rachel nudged Charlie as they disembarked. "We need to rent a scooter."

Charlie located the closest stand and selected a scooter for two. Rachel straddled the seat behind him, wrapped her arms around his chest, and breathed in the musky scent of his aftershave. "Head to the east side of the island."

"Your chauffeur is at your service, Mrs. Bricker." He drove onto a tree-lined street and eased past shops, restaurants, and residences. When the road ended, he turned right.

"Stop here."

He parked on a wide walkway and nodded toward a block-long building. "Are we going to the hotel?"

"Nope." She climbed off and held his hand as they walked across the street.

The scent of the sea air and sound of gentle waves nipping at the shore greeted them as they moved through an entrance to a long wooden walkway. At the end, Rachel slipped out of her sneakers and drank in the view. "I've waited all my life to walk barefoot on an honest-to-goodness seaside beach."

"Prepare to be amazed." Charlie kicked off his loafers and rolled up his jeans.

She held his hand and stepped onto the sand. The warmth radiated through her as a gentle breeze tousled her hair.

"Is it everything you expected?"

"Way better than I ever imagined." She squeezed his hand. "Next time we walk on a beach you'll carry an adorable toddler on your shoulders."

Charlie brushed a curl away from her cheek. "There's no one that comes close to you, could ever take your place, 'cause only you can love me this way."

Rachel locked eyes with him. "Are you quoting a Keith Urban song?"

Finally." He grinned. "My sophisticated, city-slicker wife has transitioned to an honest-to-goodness country gal."

"Only one guy on the planet could've made that happen."

Chapter 52

Emily sat beside Mary and played Rachel's and Charlie's baby-reveal video. "Every time I watch their joyful expressions, my heart sings."

Mary grinned. "Rachel's dad is strutting around town like a peacock."

"The moment Greer cradles his grandchild in his arms, he'll melt like butter in the hot summer sun. I suspect he'll be spending a lot more time in his Willow Falls condo than his Atlanta mansion." Emily's phone pinged a text. "So much for celebrating babies."

"Another emergency council meeting?"

"Half an hour in Mitch's office. If he's uncovered details about the crime, at least we have time to write a story for this week's paper."

"The mystery has hounded us for nearly five weeks."

"Some murders take years to unravel." Emily stared at her laptop and struggled to focus on her unfinished editorial. Had Mitch found enough evidence to convict Mirabelle's father or tagged the murder as an unsolved cold case? "Think I'll head on over."

"Good luck."

Emily slipped into her leather jacket and stepped out into the cool autumn air. At the corner she stopped beside the antique mailbox and gazed across the street at the rippling sea of gold willow-oak leaves dancing in the gentle breeze. Three young children played catch, while their mothers chatted in the gazebo. A woman exited Hayes General Store, carrying a large bag. A pleasant afternoon in her hometown.

She walked past Pepper's Café and Patsy's Pastries and Pretties, rounded another corner, and eyed the Willow Falls Playhouse marquee. *Percy's*

Legacy. An Original Play. Rachel still owed her an answer about writing a new play. Emily cut across Falls Street, entered the Municipal Building lobby and climbed the stairs to the sheriff's headquarters. Inside Mitch's office she settled on a metal chair beside Sadie. She peered around Sadie at Brick and Naomi. This obviously wasn't a council meeting. "What's going on, Mitch?"

"Roland Lambert isn't the killer." He pushed a sheet of paper across the desk. "This is a copy of his death certificate dated twenty-four years ago. He crashed his car into a bridge abutment. Drunk."

Emily read the document. "Does Mirabelle know?"

"I'll tell her after she finishes her route." Mitch moved to the front of his desk and hiked his hip on the corner. "After eliminating Roland as a suspect, I chased down another lead. Two days ago the case cracked wide open." He picked the marred cigarette lighter off his desk. "Turns out this belonged to Robert Liles' younger brother."

Emily's muscles jumped under her skin.

"While some of the details remain private, what I can tell you is Philip Liles was a deeply troubled man who spent his entire adulthood in and out of mental hospitals—the last two years in a Virginia institution. Seems he knew his days were numbered when he requested to speak to the police. Three days later the Richmond PD sent two detectives to hear him out."

Mitch fingered the lighter. "He confessed but died before revealing where he buried the bodies. Seems he blamed the army for turning his father into a cruel, heartless man incapable of loving anyone, least of all his sons."

Emily cringed. "Which is why all his victims were soldiers."

Mitch nodded. "Randomly selected. All in the wrong place at the wrong time."

Sadie lifted her hand. "Any idea why he buried his victims so close to home?"

"My theory? He wanted the bodies found—" Mitch flipped the lighter lid open. "And this to implicate his old man. I gave Janet the news an hour ago."

Brick fingered his goatee. "We won't have to deal with the *Follow the Facts* crew again."

"Emily, will you follow up with Clark in case the Atlanta paper wants to run the story?"

"I'll call him today."

"Good." Mitch returned to his chair. "Before I inform the other council members, Naomi needs to tell you about something else she found in her attic."

"That's my cue." Naomi lifted her purse off the floor and removed two sheets of yellowed newsprint. "Remember me telling you about my dad's penchant for collecting documents? I looked through a box of newspaper clippings and found these two letters to the editor. Both dated the same month Hannah wrote to my parents. The first is unsigned. It says in part, *Money and position do not excuse evil behavior. When a child tortures and kills innocent animals, the family bears responsibility and must be shunned.*"

"Oh my gosh." Sadie pressed her hand to her chest. "The heinous act that forced his parents to commit him."

"So it seems. The second article is the response my mom wrote. It says, *Who are we to judge or even claim to understand? Are we a collection of individuals eager to rebuke based on unfounded rumors? Or are we a community of decent people that understands grace and wraps its arms around a family in their hour of need. I pray we are the latter.* Her response is reminiscent of Emily's editorial appeals. It clearly touched hearts and minds."

"What happens to those articles and the letter from Phillip's mother is up to you, Naomi." Mitch removed her satchel from his bottom drawer and pushed it across the desk.

She opened the satchel, slid the articles inside, and secured the strap. "Sadie and her daughters are the Liles' only living relatives, which means the fate of these documents belongs to them, not me." She reached around Brick and placed the satchel on Sadie's lap.

Sadie stroked the satchel's worn leather. "When I prayed for the courage to forgive Robert Liles for what he had done to me, I experienced peace that helped me survive all those years behind bars. Now I'm blessed with a town full of friends, a loving family, and a man I love with all my heart."

She touched Brick's thigh. "If Emily agrees, I suggest we let Naomi return this to her attic."

"Speaking for me and my sister, I agree."

"Good, now how about we all go over to Patsy's and celebrate with big slices of cake and cups of hot chocolate."

"That's the gal who stole my heart." Brick slid his arm around her shoulders.

Emily reached for her mother's hand. "The perfect answer, Mama Sadie."

"Well now." Mitch cleared his throat. "Other than Emily breaking the news in tomorrow's paper, this case is closed."

Chapter 53

Following an eleven-hour flight from Venice to Atlanta, Rachel stood outside customs with her costars. "How long before your flight leaves for LA?"

"Forty-five minutes." Justin pulled his ball cap closer to his sunglasses and slid his arm around Beth's shoulders. "Our kids are meeting us at the airport."

Beth, wearing gigantic sunglasses and no makeup, leaned into him. "Ethan and Chloe are thrilled we're taking them to Disneyland next weekend. Justin hasn't been since he was a boy."

"First time in years I've had a reason to go."

"I'm gonna miss you both."

"You and Charlie have to come visit us."

The excitement in Beth's voice warmed Rachel's heart. "Absolutely. Until then you two take good care of each other."

"We will," they responded in unison.

Beth embraced Rachel. "Thank you for showing me that nothing is more important than family."

"You just needed a little nudge." Rachel struggled to keep tears at bay. "You two need to scoot before I turn into a blubbering mess."

Justin touched Rachel's arm. "Thanks for everything."

She patted his cheek. "I'm glad you turned out to be one of the good guys."

"You and me both." Beth gave her a quick hug. "Tell Charlie hi for us."

"Will do." Rahel turned and waved over her shoulder as she walked away. Five minutes later she stepped onto the escalator rising to ground level. Her pulse raced as she stepped of and spotted Charlie. She rushed into his arms.

"Hello, gorgeous."

"I can't wait to sleep with you in *our* bed."

"Should we let your husband know about us?"

The woman standing beside Charlie gave him a double take.

Rachel giggled. "I think he's already suspicious."

"He must have found the pictures of us, or maybe your hot love letters." He reached for her carry-on and held her hand as they moved toward baggage claim.

"We should be ashamed for shocking that poor woman."

"We did her a big favor. She spent the last half hour gossiping about the irritating relatives she drove thirty-five miles to pick up. I just gave her new material." He leaned close. "Mirabelle's influence."

"Blaming our esteemed council member for your mischief? You deserve a spanking."

"You promise?" He winked.

As they waited for her baggage to arrive, Rachel slipped her hand around Charlie's bicep. "My agent called before I boarded the plane." She paused. "A multi Oscar-winning director wants me to fly to New York next week and audition for the lead in his new movie."

Charlie's silence spoke volumes.

"She called it the offer of a lifetime. Filming begins in Seattle next summer. After our baby arrives."

"At least that's closer than Italy."

"I turned it down for a better offer."

"What offer?"

"Writing a new play with Emily."

He stared at her. "Are you abandoning your career?"

"A major course correction." She kissed his cheek. "In addition to acting and directing in our little hometown theater, my new role is mothering or baby or babies and keeping my mischievous husband happy and out of trouble."

"Are you serious?"

"Beth claims I enlightened her about the importance of family. Truth is, she helped me understand that everything and everyone I need for true happiness is in a crazy little town called Willow Falls."

Charlie wrapped his arms around her, pulled her close, and kissed her. "When their lips parted, he gazed into her eyes. "I'm glad you're home gorgeous."

"So am I, handsome."

Thank you for reading Bridges, Books, and Bones. Want to find out about upcoming
releases, receive free short stories, and become acquainted? Join my VIP reader's
list:

https://www.subscribepage.com/pat-nichols-newsletter

AFTERWORD – Writing *Bridges, Books, and Bones* was especially fun because Venice is my husband's and my favorite European destination. We celebrated our fortieth anniversary there and stayed at Hotel Danieli. Revisiting the city on Goggle Earth brought back so many wonderful memories. Venice is a magical place.

If this is your first Willow Falls book, perhaps you're wondering how Emily's, Rachel's, and Sadie's paths crossed after thirty years. Or why Sadie killed Robert Liles and spent thirty years in prison. Both mysteries are revealed in book one, *The Secret of Willow Inn*.

You might remember a brief mention of Sheriff Mitch arresting Winston Hamilton, Willow Inn's mysterious guest. In book two, *The Trouble in Willow Falls*, you'll discover what leads to his arrest. The story follows residents' struggles to transform Willow Falls into a tourist destination, as well as the challenges Emily and Rachel face while writing, casting, and directing the town's signature play.

In book three, *Star Struck in Willow Falls*, the town is thrown into chaos when famous movie stars and a film crew arrive on the scene. Weeks before Rachel's and Charlie's wedding, Rachel lands a role in *Joanie's Trial*. The story includes a stranger's unexpected visit that threatens Sadie's and Brick's relationship, and a shocking discovery about Rachel's father. And, of course, there's a big wedding.

The Secret of Willow Inn

www.amazon.com/dp/B07JR5CKZB/

I'd be honored if you'd follow me on BookBub.

https://www.bookbub.com/authors/pat-nichols?follow=true

We can also connect on social media.
Facebook https://www.facebook.com/pat.nichols.52459
Twitter https://twitter.com/PatNichols16

275

ACKNOWLEDGEMENTS – Seven years ago, when I made the decision to abandon retirement and become an author, little did I know how many amazing people I would meet. Now one of the most rewarding aspects of my writing journey is interacting with other authors and readers. To the book club members who chose one of my books, you made my heart sing. To readers who wrote reviews, thank you for taking the time to share your impressions.

To Sherri Stewart, my friend, editor and mentor, we had no idea years ago when we were in the same small group that we would one day travel this road together. Thank you for your insight, guidance, and encouragement. You make me a better writer.

To my friends and beta readers Pat Davis and Beverly Feldkamp, who were on this journey with me from the beginning, and Kathy Warner, Kitty Metzger, and Carlene Dunn who joined along the way, thank you for your insightful advice. To Creston Mapes, thank you for inspiring me to take a leap of faith and pursue a new path to publication.

Thanks to all the members of my launch team. You're the best.

To my friends at American Christian Fiction Writers North Georgia Chapter, thank you for engaging excellent speakers and creating a warm and welcoming environment where we can all spread our wings. To my friends in Word Weavers International, Greater Atlanta Chapter, thank you for your support, candor, and positive reinforcement.

A special thanks to my number one fans and cheerleaders—my wonderful family. Your belief in me and encouragement gave me the courage to take the most liberating and exciting step in my writing journey. I love you all.

Above all, I thank God for His grace, unconditional love, His Son our Savior, and gift of eternal life.